A MOUTHFUL OF SAND

M. R. D. Meek is Scottish born and English educated; she has worked variously as short-hand-typist, secretary, general practitioner's wife, civil servant and solicitor. Widowed at forty, she took a Law degree and qualified in 1969.

An avid reader and collector of crime fiction, she has come late into writing it. Now remarried to a retired government scientist, she lives in Cornwall.

A Mouthful of Sand is her sixth novel. *The Split Second* is also available in Collins Crime.

by the same author

A WORM OF DOUBT
IN REMEMBRANCE OF ROSE
THE SPLIT SECOND
HANG THE CONSEQUENCES
THE SITTING DUCKS

M. R. D. MEEK

A Mouthful
of Sand

FONTANA/Collins

First published in Great Britain by
William Collins Sons & Co. Ltd, 1988

First published in Fontana Paperbacks 1989

Printed and bound in Great Britain by
William Collins Sons & Co. Ltd, Glasgow

To the coxswain and crew of the Padstow Lifeboat.
Mine the fiction, theirs the real heroism.

Prologue

It was the hour when there is scarcely a line between the end of the day and the beginning of the night, just as, far out on the estuary only a faint luminosity, vaguely curling over and over and for that reason sinister, marked off the sea's rim from the sky.

'All the way from Lundy Bay to far-off Labrador . . .' he shouted into the rising wind, and he reached for the hand which fluttered at her side like a falling handkerchief. 'Come on, I'll race you to the water.'

She gave an uncertain laugh; she was not yet quite into his mood. She let him take her hand. 'If we're going to run,' she said, catching her breath, 'then I'll need your help, the ground's so very . . .' Her words were lost in the whistle of the wind blowing steadily in through the headlands from the open ocean beyond. It tore at her hair as they began to run down the slate-strewn beach, he swift and sure-footed, she stumbling in white sandals designed for style, not speed. But even in her a sense of exultation rose as they sprinted through the gathering dusk towards that creamy undulation where the edge of the tide lapped the rippled shore.

Before they reached it the flat sands levelled out, and she felt her stride grow heavy as the dampness clung round her ankles. 'Stop,' she cried, 'it's like quicksand.'

'Nonsense,' he said, 'these sands are firm enough. Take off your stupid shoes. We're going for a paddle.'

She caught the echo of a childish glee in his voice, and responded to it as she had responded to him in all ways during these last few weeks. She kicked off her sandals, and sprang over the sucking ground so lightly that the bare imprint of her toes filled up in seconds with tiny pools of foam, leaving no trace.

They came to the water's edge where the long, tired rollers from the Atlantic laid their spent waves one after the other along the shoreline like last feeble breaths of the dying.

The chill of the first steps clutched their feet with an embrace soft as silk yet sharp as splintering glass. 'Ouch!' she yelled, then threw a lace of seaweed at her companion as he waded in, trousers rolled to the knee.

They splashed each other, shrieking with laughter like overwrought children, high on excitement, scooping up handfuls of water which fell around them in arcs of silver spray.

But of course they weren't children.

Quietening, they stood together by the margin of the flowing tide as it came gently, folded over and retreated, eddying at their feet.

'It's sexual,' he said, his arm at her waist, as they watched the small whirlpools chase the fronds of weed backwards and forwards through the sand ridges. She said nothing. She was looking at her own white toes gleaming like shapes of fish under water.

Later, she said: 'I must find my shoes. Where did we leave them?'

She was tired now but she had to find her shoes. She ran up the beach. She thought she was going the way they had come. She could hear his voice above the wind. 'You're going off in the wrong direction. Don't worry about your shoes. I'll get them . . .'

8

But she ran on, searching over the dun-coloured sand and the ridged banks where the brown wrack lay along another tideline.

He found his own canvas sneakers and slipped wet feet into them, glad of the warmth, and pulled his trouser legs down over his ankles, for, with the excitement gone, he had sobered and felt cold. Then he set off to look for her sandals.

He heard her scream.

He stopped, trying to gauge where her voice had come from but it was blown about, fragmented by the wind. She was still screaming, a high-pitched sound, raucous as a sea-bird. He set off again, peering into the darkness as he ran. When he saw her she was a mere glimmer of white ahead, against the rise of the beach, and she was struggling up the soft sand fighting for breath. The screaming had stopped but she was making a horrible half-sobbing whimper as she scrambled to get a foothold on the loose ground.

He reached her as she collapsed at the base of the sandhills.

He knelt beside her and twisted her face round so that he could look into it. Her eyes were wide, staring, and her mouth twitched.

'What on earth's the matter?' he asked, as he stroked her pale cheeks.

'Down there . . .' she gasped, the words hoarse, coming from the back of her throat. 'There's a head . . . a head . . . half-buried in the sand . . .'

She could feel his unbelief in the way he took her roughly by the shoulders and began to shake her.

'What did you see? You were running. It was too dark to see anything.'

She sat up, evading his hands. She tried to brush

9

the hair back from her forehead. 'But I did see it. I saw something . . . a head and a neck. As if it was buried . . .' She shut her eyes, hysteria rising in her like a huge soft lump from her stomach. She put her hand over her mouth, and retched.

He threw his arms round her. 'Ssh . . . hush, I say. You've had some kind of shock. Look, kids build sandcastles, sweetie . . . They leave them for the tide to come in . . . That's all you've seen. Believe me, it could look like a head . . .'

She stared down towards the water. Now there was nothing there but darkness. She shuddered. He tightened his hold on her.

'If you think you saw something, shall I go and have a look?'

Her whole body was shaking, and she was cold.

'I saw it, I tell you. It was a head on the sand . . . sticking out of the sand. There was seaweed on it . . . I can't go back.'

'Then I'll go. Here, put this round you.' He took off his jacket and wrapped it round her shoulders. She gripped his hand. 'Don't leave me . . .'

'If I don't go and take a look at this sandcastle, it'll become one of your nightmares . . . and it'll make you ill again. Let me go and see. And I'll bring you back your shoes.'

He disengaged her clinging fingers and scrambled to his feet.

She watched the faint blur of his white shirt till it was lost in the cloud of darkness which had come down over shore and sea alike, then she huddled herself into the warmth of his coat, and waited.

She had been cut off from all sense of time. She didn't know whether ten minutes or an hour had passed before she heard his voice as he came running towards her.

He threw himself down beside her, and took both her hands, warming them. 'What a little fool it is!' he exclaimed fondly, smiling at her, laughing even. 'Do you know what you mistook for a head? A beach ball! One of these huge things you can buy in Tommy's shop. Caught up in the seaweed behind one of those ridges. Oh, my poor pet, what a fright it must have given you . . . But that's all it was.'

Now it was her turn to disbelieve. But she took it slowly, searching her mind for that instant, that terrible stop in time, when she had seen the thing.

'I'd have known if it was a ball. It wasn't . . . it wasn't that kind of shape . . .'

'It was. Take my word for it. It was half-covered with sand, just like you said. Even I, for one short moment thought . . . But that's all it was – a great big beach ball.'

His eyes were close to hers, willing her to believe him. How very dark it had become, and how near the uncertain beat of the waves; he must have been away longer than she thought.

'Darling,' he said, wheedling, 'you've been through a lot lately with one thing and another. We both know that. You're a bit strung-up. Perhaps I shouldn't have brought you on the beach so late, perhaps it's been all too exciting for you. And now, this . . . Don't you see, in the state you're in it's easy to get carried away by imagination?'

She wanted to believe him, but at the same time she wanted to believe in the evidence of her own eyes. She wanted to know for sure that she was not going mad. So many things had been happening lately . . . He treated her so devotedly, he had made her happier than she had been in a long time . . . What had he meant when he said it might only add to her nightmares? She couldn't remember how much she'd told him . . .

Now he was chafing her hands, grinning down at her, reassuring her.

'Time I took you home,' he said, pulling her to her feet. 'What a chilly little silly you are – imagining a nasty great beach ball was a severed head!'

But she was aware as they walked across the dunes that he too was different. There was no more high-spirited laughter, none of his usual jokes, and less of his loving talk. Perhaps he had caught her mood as earlier she had been affected by his.

They stopped where the path from the beach met the coastal track, and looked back. An ink-black sea covered the sands as it came to the full tide.

'What did you do with that . . . that beach ball?' she asked, aware that her voice trembled.

'Kicked it into the sea, of course. Booted it far out till it sank in the silver sea.' The singing lilt in his voice which always charmed and amused her, did not hide the underlying roughness.

She shivered. That was a brutal thing to say, she thought. Even in the short time she had known him she had grown used to his changes of mood from high to low but never before had she glimpsed anything deliberately cruel. But he was doing it for her, to reassure her that what she had seen had only been a holiday plaything . . .

Against her will it rose up before her again, sad holes for eyes, sanded hair, a neck . . . Cut off at the neck . . .

I have to believe him. For the sake of my own sanity, I have to believe him.

But something deeper in her, something cold and rational persisted; she had seen a head. The thought was more than her weakness could bear.

Chapter One

Vincent Snape liked to give the impression of being a self-made man. He was in fact no such thing, having merely inherited certain characteristics of the breed from his father and grandfather, along with their considerable wealth. But the entrepreneurial air and the blunt Lancashire accent he cultivated sat so comfortably on him that more often than not he was taken to have hoisted himself up by his own bootstraps, and the image thus created did him no harm in the City where he ran the London end of the family stockbroking firm. He also had his speculative thumbs through the crust of many a richly-fruited financial pie, and as a consequence was considered in all his aspects to be a warm man.

Lennox Kemp had had the benefit of a quick sketch of him from old Archie Gillorn before facing Snape across his desk at the Newtown branch of Gillorns, Solicitors, on a Monday morning early in June.

'Young Snape is as sharp as they come,' Archie had said on the telephone, 'like his father before him, so don't be fooled by the common touch . . .'

Although Kemp regarded himself as kindly-disposed towards all prospective clients, he was not easily fooled and certainly never by those anxious to make an impression.

'What's he doing coming out to the backwoods of Newtown?' he had asked, somewhat querulously. 'The

City must be awash with expensive lawyers eager for Snape's business?'

'Now, now, Lennox . . . Spare a little charity for the rich.' There had been a chuckle from the old man. 'Do this as a personal favour to me. I've known Cedric Snape for years. Apparently his son, Vincent, would like to talk to a solicitor from outside London. One not altogether caught up in the rat-race . . . nor concerned with purely monetary considerations . . . and . . . discreet. Naturally I thought of you,' he ended blandly.

'Thanks very much,' said Kemp, 'no irony intended.' Archie Gillorn might have retired but he had obviously not lost his talent for persuasion. 'Of course I'll be glad to see your friend's son. As we can rule out Company and Revenue Law – on which I bet he has plenty of other advisers – and I don't suppose he's thinking of buying a semi-detached in Newtown, it's either matrimonial or probate. I plump for matrimonial.'

But Archie was not to be drawn. 'I know nothing of these matters any more,' the thin voice distanced itself from them. 'Pay us a visit one of these days, Lennox. The roses are just coming into bloom.'

Now Kemp eyed Vincent Snape across his desk. Snape had already, with disarming candour, assured Kemp of his gratitude for the interview, as if laying a splendid carpet at both their feet as a foundation for a caring relationship. Although recognizing it as a purely occupational ploy, Kemp was amused by the easy manner with which it was accomplished. He took clients as he found them – nervously overplaying whatever role they had seen fit to adopt in relation to the problem which had brought them to a solicitor. And Vincent Snape was no exception. He exuded businesslike charm and bonhomie, at the same time conveying by briskness of tone and a no-nonsense attitude to small talk that they were both men to whom time was money and not to be wasted.

'I'm a plain-speaking man, Mr Kemp. I like to put all my cards on the table.' Snape accompanied the words with a surprisingly boyish grin.

He'll shuffle them first, thought Kemp, and keep the joker up his sleeve. He might just as easily have said, I play my cards close to my chest. It would depend on the circumstances. Kemp returned the grin with a small smile of his own, and waited.

The cards, however, were slow in coming. Snape opened the proceedings with the kind of preamble he might have used to bring a board meeting of fellow directors round to his way of thinking.

There was general chit-chat about changes in the City, about fresh winds blowing through the older establishments, about the new climate engendered by the speed-up in communications, about the high pressures of international competition . . .

'Is it raining in Tokyo?' murmured Kemp, appreciating the weather report but wondering when the man was going to get around to the home front.

Snape's laugh had a genuine ring to it. 'Hancock,' he said. 'But, seriously, all these things are putting a strain on everyone who works in the markets. Many of the people I meet in business nowadays, and some of my own colleagues, are under considerable stress. Of course we all cope – it's part of the job. What bothers me is that when there's an additional worry, an added anxiety – say, a bereavement, or an illness, or domestic trouble, it's then that people crack up. I've seen it happen too often. Men who can take complicated financial deals in their stride, sound men in their field, they can go to pieces at such times . . .'

Kemp nodded. Snape was not just a talker; he had a point. The medical profession recognized stress as an important factor in disease. Sometimes it was the straw that broke the camel's back. He said as much to Snape, who took him up eagerly.

'That's just it. And if we've got any sense we go to a doctor who understands the effects, and get a medical report . . . Then at least we're forewarned. We can watch out for the thumping heart, or the indigestion or whatever – but at least we're no longer in ignorance, the remedy's in our own hands . . .'

He seemed to brood for a moment before continuing: 'It's not knowing is the trouble. Having things happen that you don't understand . . . Shouldn't allow that in the business world – at least not in my business. If I want to know something I go to the expert in that line, get a report and digest it down to the last syllable. But, you see, Mr Kemp, there's a whole area in your line of country where the ordinary man in the street's left floundering. Company law – though we might not always agree with it – at least it's there in black and white for us to read. Same with revenue and taxation, it may be a bind but we've got lawyers and accountants to keep us straight, and it does make some sort of sense . . . As for criminal law, about the shortest subject in your student curriculum, eh?'

Kemp agreed. 'Exciting, but in essence uncomplicated. Unless you fall foul of it, of course. But you mentioned my line of country?'

Without naming it, Vincent Snape ventured into that debatable land.

'To the average man in this country – and I'm as

average as anybody,' he said with the complacency of one who set himself well above the mean, 'the whole thing's a mess. The average man is led to believe divorce is easy, painless, just a matter of shuffling papers, and that all can be settled amicably round a table. Then he hears these horrendous stories . . . cases taking years to settle. And he's told that the law is fair, but he finds out that someone he knows has been the victim of dreadful injustice. Nowhere can he get at the truth – even the law reports are full of conflicting information . . .'

Kemp picked up a pencil and turned it in his fingers.

'That's because every case is unique. We're dealing with individual people, not rows of figures, not balance sheets, not stocks and shares. Are you married, Mr Snape?'

The sharp question was rewarded with a beaming smile.

'Yes – and very happily. Mirabel and I have been married for four years. I have a son, young Simon Vincent is almost two. Don't misunderstand me, Mr Kemp, this is not a personal matter. As I've explained, I see the stress caused by domestic troubles in all walks of life and I want to try and understand the implications as it affects my business. To give you a small example: I recently had a clerk, brilliant youngster with a good future in the firm. He got married to what seemed a decent girl, bought a house and furnished it. They had a baby, and blow me if she wasn't off within a year with another fellow . . . My chap lost his home, and his son, and has to make payments for the little lad whom he'll likely never see again if she has her way. We've carried him in the office as long as we could, but he's no good

19

to us any more – his work's all gone to pot . . . A perfectly innocent man ruined . . .'

'So might any investor be who bought duff shares and saw them go down. Like your client, only guilty of an error of judgement.'

Snape snorted. 'An error of judgement?'

'He picked the wrong woman.'

'You can't compare the two cases,' Snape expostulated. 'Sometimes one has to take a calculated risk on the market, but at least one can weigh up the odds beforehand.'

Kemp spread his hands.

'Marriage too can be a lottery . . .'

'You take a cold view, Mr Kemp. But we're moving away from the point.' Snape was not to be diverted by any side wind. 'Perhaps I was wrong to bring up a particular case. My concern is with the way the law operates in a general sense . . . and with the public's ignorance of that law. I don't like areas of ignorance. That's why I've come to you.'

'You want me to explicate for you the laws as they govern the relationship between the sexes? How far back do you want me to go? Anne Boleyn?'

Snape laughed. It was a good, hearty laugh which momentarily lifted his somewhat heavy features, and made him likeable. If it was practised it still came out as fresh as the rosebud in his buttonhole.

'Not that far back. I'm not asking for a history lesson . . . Just a rough outline of the main points, a rundown of the salient features that have emerged in recent years. All we get is gossip at the Club, exaggerated no doubt . . . We've really no idea how the Courts come to their decisions about property, or children, or future financial provisions. What about a man's private pension rights – or a woman's, for that matter? Phrases are thrown at us by the Press – we heard about Casanova's charter, and the one-third rule, now they're talking about the clean break, and telling us the little woman has gone too far . . .'

'Your interest's on the dangerous edge of things,' Kemp murmured, marking up in his mind particular words out of the general.

'Browning – or near enough,' said Snape almost absent-mindedly. 'But you get my point? Take my own business. I deal in prospects both in the market as a broker, and outside it as adviser to various companies. There's a high degree of autonomy allowed to individual directors in some of the big financial concerns. If a man's shaky in his personal life, if he's under even temporary stress, a tricky deal can easily go wrong . . . Am I making myself clear?'

For a plain-speaking man Snape was using some fairly fancy embroidery. Nevertheless, Kemp nodded.

'If I want information in the City,' went on Snape, warming to his theme, 'I go to an expert analyst for a report, then I trust my own experience and judgement. If I misinterpret or misread, the fault is mine, but at least I know where I stand. What I want from you is just such a report – on your special subject. As in the stock market, I like to anticipate the trends . . .'

Kemp was silent for a moment, considering both Snape and his rather unusual request. Finally he said: 'I do understand what you're getting at; one man's field can certainly be another's quagmire. All I could give you is a précis of the relevant statutes, and perhaps a brief résumé of case law since the new Acts came into force . . . Mind, it won't be altogether comprehensive since the Courts treat each particular matter strictly on the issues brought before them. They are not supposed to be influenced by trends . . .'

Vincent Snape knew when to clinch a deal.

'Then you'll do it? I am most grateful. You do understand my motives? To a certain extent they are bound up with a feeling of responsibility – to my firm, to my business colleagues. With a little more understanding of the consequences of . . . er . . . matrimonial difficulties as they affect a man's financial position . . .'

'You can't insure against it,' remarked Kemp drily.

Snape put on shock like a veil.

'When I said understanding, it was the human side I had in mind.' Then, briskly: 'I'm sure it will take some time and you're a busy man. Naturally, your fee would take that into account . . .'

Kemp was conscious of discomfort. 'I shall regard it as a self-improving exercise – as if I was preparing a paper for students,' he found himself saying. Had he really promised to do it? Snape's way was a smooth takeover. 'It'll take a week or so to prepare. I'll be moonlighting on it.'

The stockbroker had already risen, and was reaching for his hat.

'Take all the time you need, Mr Kemp. Give me a ring when you're ready, and come to dinner with us. Mirabel gets back from holiday next week, and I'd like you to meet her. Perhaps happy marriages are a bit out of your line, eh? Didn't someone say they all resemble one another?'

'Tolstoy,' murmured Kemp, not to be outdone in the game of displaying erudition, 'and it was happy families. The bottom line – as I think you call it in your business – was that each unhappy family is unhappy in its own way.'

'And that's where you come in?'

'I'm glad that in your case it's only in a general sense,' said Kemp courteously, showing Snape to the door. 'And I accept your dinner invitation, thank you.'

Returning to the other work on his desk, Kemp had little time that day to think about the stockbroker and his curiously general interest in matters matrimonial, but later he gave a mind to both.

Perhaps it was not such an unusual request after all. There had been a lot of sense in what Vincent Snape had said, especially on the uncertainty caused by ignorance. Kemp was aware that he himself had areas of ignorance, one of which was undoubtedly the square mile of the City and all that went on there; he was not sure whether he could distinguish between insider trading and share support strategy, and would not have cared to have to define either.

If Snape had indeed come, however obliquely, for personal advice he had certainly laid a thick smoke-screen round it, and in any event nothing specific had been mentioned. On the other hand, Kemp found it hard to believe the motive could be pure philanthropy – a moral responsibility to understand the strains and stresses laid on his fellow businessmen by domestic disasters. That particular hare wouldn't run – at least not in Kemp's view. A more down-to-earth explanation was that Vincent Snape had been dallying in the fields of extra-marital amour, and was anxious to compute a possible shortfall in assets if caught out.

Without divulging too much of his client's confidence – though somewhat surprisingly no promise of confidentiality had been required of him – Kemp had a short word on the phone with Archie Gillorn.

'Mirabel Snape? No, I've never met her. Cedric approved the match. Let me see . . . She was a Trevanion, I think. Old Cornish family. There wasn't any money, but breeding, yes . . . How did you find Mr Vincent?'

'Likeable chap – I think,' said Kemp cautiously. 'Quite impressive in his own way. Deeper than he lets on. It's not an office matter. He's only picking my brains – for a fee, of course.'

'H'm. Make sure it's a sizeable one. He can afford it. Out of the office, you say? What do they call it these days – moonshining?'

'Moonlighting, Archie. They call it moonlighting. In my case it'll be more like burning the good old-fashioned midnight oil.'

Chapter Two

When he got down to it Lennox Kemp quite enjoyed the task set for him by Vincent Snape. It recalled his student days, although so much of the matrimonial law he had learned then was now water under the bridge. Still, he could not help but regret what had had to be wiped from the memory; all those lovely velvety old cases, the hushed Victorian scandals, high jinks in demure parlours, and the flamboyant excesses of the Edwardian era, tussore silk, taffeta and tinsel, rubbed out for ever by the modern march towards equality of the sexes while the textbooks which so lovingly chronicled them were consigned to dust along with the volumes of sermons which Sunday after Sunday had striven to stem the tide. He'd not been altogether joking when he'd mentioned Anne Boleyn – though he'd rather have put in a word for Catherine of Aragon, the wife instead of the other woman, when it came to who set the pace in the beginning. Now there was a divorce that had sounded down the centuries . . .

But Vincent Snape was not going to be charmed by historical dissertation, he'd want a neat package as up to date as tomorrow's *Financial Times*. Kemp sighed, and applied himself to modern interpretation, abstracting relevant information from statutes, and assiduously scraping the surface of recent decisions in order to compile a summary of the state of the nation as it concerned itself with the manifold interactions of the sexes, their property, their aspirations, and their off-spring – an account he hoped might even be comprehensible to a newly-arrived Martian who might show an interest in such things. Perhaps marital discord as well as the legendary harmony was part of the music of the spheres.

The intellectual exercise took some two weeks to complete but it had come at a fortunate moment, for he had little else to do to fill his leisure hours. There had just developed a species of lacuna in his personal life. He and Penelope Marsden had reached a state in their relationship which required a breathing space. They had decided not to see each other for a month, then to have a short holiday together during which they would consider their future – whether it was to be shared or whether they would each go their separate way.

It had all sounded so sane and rational when they had made the agreement – the decision-making process in operation between two sensible people. Too damned sane and rational for Kemp's peace of mind; if there was no spark between them, no fire could be lit, and despite being over forty Kemp still grasped at old romantic shreds. It would be touch-and-go whether the tatters would endure into middle age. Dealing with too many marital disharmonies had worn the fabric thin, and to settle down with Penelope, despite his fondness for her, seemed sometimes as if it would be taking unfair refuge.

After he had put the final polish on his draft Kemp gave it to his secretary, Elvira, to type.

'It's very good, Mr Kemp,' she said, laying the typescript almost reverently on his desk. 'You going to take up lecturing?'

'Not likely. Let the students find their own way. Besides, I'm not the academic sort.'

He rang Vincent Snape.

'I have that report ready for you.'

'Very good of you to do it. There's just one snag.' Snape sounded brusque but perhaps that was his normal telephone manner. 'Mirabel's not back from Cornwall. It's a damned nuisance her staying away so long.' His voice was aggrieved.

Kemp glanced out of his window. Even the grey rooftops of Newtown were spreading with a golden haze under a sky of pure azure. '"It serves for the old June weather,"' he murmured, '"Blue above lane and wall . . ."'

'What's that you say?' Either Snape hadn't heard or he disdained poetry in his business hours. 'Anyway, it's spoiled our dinner plans . . .'

'It doesn't matter. I shall be up at Clement's Inn tomorrow. Not far from you. I'll bring the papers over to your office.'

'Would you mind? Jolly good of you. Unfortunately I won't be here. Have to shoot off to Manchester first thing. But you can leave the report with my secretary, Mrs Forbes. I'll tell her to expect you.'

'Right, I'll do that.'

'Sorry about not being there myself. Looks like being a hell of a week. I'll leave an envelope for you to pick up. And I won't forget that dinner. You must come out to us when Mirabel's back.'

'Which part of Cornwall is she in?'

'Oh, some little place on the north coast. Rocksea, they call it. Nobody's ever heard of it. Mira has an aunt there but the old lady's fit and well . . . Can't think

why Mira's staying away so long . . . Damned incon-
venient for everybody . . .'

Kemp conjectured that anyone who caused incon-
venience to Vincent Snape might be in for a thin time.
Well, even in happy marriages there are little cracks.

Vincent Snape sounded sour-tempered on the subject of his wife this morning but not above sharing his
grudge on a man-to-man basis.

'Women can be so thoughtless at times . . . Simon's
already had to miss one appointment with our
doctor . . .'

'Nothing wrong, I hope?' Kemp inquired politely.

'Just a whooping cough injection. One can't be too
careful with the little chap . . . But Mirabel knew
about that appointment . . . Well, mustn't keep you.
Most grateful to you. I'll be in touch.'

Not a particularly interesting name, Mrs Forbes, Kemp
thought the next day as he left his own firm's London
branch, but she might yet turn out to be as chic as a
page in *Vogue* and aflame with passion for her boss.

But no. Once Kemp had passed through the discreet
portals of old stone flanking the short stairway up to
the offices of Snape, Wilson & Snape, been duly
inspected and found credit-worthy, he was ushered
down various corridors edged with glass cells full, it
seemed, of flickering screens and eager, spectacled
dwarfs, to a large cool room inhabited only by Snape's
secretary which was unexpectedly old-fashioned, even
cosy. And so was Mrs Forbes, a grey-haired comfortable lady with a Lancashire accent stronger than her
employer's and more authentic in origin.

She fussed around Kemp like a mother hen. She
took the package from him – he had advisedly marked

it private and confidential – and without a glance at it she locked it in a drawer of the massive desk which dominated the room. 'Mr Snape told me to expect you. You'll not have had your tea.'

She produced a tray set with solid white china. 'He's very sorry not to be here. Mr Cedric has the monthly board meeting home in Manchester today, and Mr Vincent always goes up for that.'

She made a strong pot of tea and left it to infuse while she produced an envelope which she handed to Kemp. He saw it was addressed to him, and tucked it away into his pocket.

Finding a responsive listener, Mrs Forbes was disposed to chat. She had been with the family firm since she left school. 'And I'll not tell you how long ago that was . . .' Her warm chuckle took any coyness out of the words.

Kemp inquired how she liked London. Doris Forbes sniffed.

'One place's much like another when you've got a good job. I'd no children, you see, and when my husband died Mr Vincent gave me the chance to come down here with him. That's ten years ago, and I've no complaints. Of course it's all modern now, and newfangled, but when you've been in stockbroking as long as I have, Mr Kemp, the real business hasn't changed.'

Hearing her talk of the old days, and the transition into new methods with which her shrewd Mancunian brain had coped on a practical level, Kemp guessed her to be a very sheet anchor to the firm. There were few of her sort left. She would be utterly dependable, absolutely devoted to the business, and close as a clam where the confidence of her employers was concerned. As for Mr Vincent, to whom she owed her position, she would certainly lie for him, possibly die for him. It was a new light on the character of Kemp's client.

'I understand there's another young Snape coming up in the family,' he remarked.

'You mean little Simon? Mr Vincent's pride and joy, that one. He's fair daft about the kid. Nice to see, though. Has him in here often . . . with Mrs Snape,' she added, without enthusiasm.

'I have not met Mrs Snape,' observed Kemp, accepting another cup of tea.

'She's from the West Country,' she said, making it sound an outlandish place. 'Delicate. Highly-strung, I think they call it nowadays.' It was implicit from a new acerbity in her tone that she considered robust health to be both a prerequisite in a businessman's spouse, and something only the North could guarantee.

Kemp rose to take his leave.

'You have been most hospitable, Mrs Forbes.' Indeed she had. Here she acted more as hostess than secretary. It was as if this office – at least this particular room – were her home.

'Oh, before you go, Mr Kemp, there's one thing. Your dinner appointment with Mr Snape.' She picked up a large leatherbound diary, rustling the sleeves of her fussy satin blouse as she turned the pages. 'He hoped the nineteenth of next month would suit you? I'll give you the address, it's in Chelsea.'

Kemp considered his own long-term plans. Beyond the next two weeks they stretched into an arid distance so far as his social life was concerned.

'The nineteenth will suit me perfectly. Please tell Mr Snape I shall be glad to dine with him and his wife.'

'He apologized for making it so far ahead but it's to give time for Mrs Snape to return . . .' Mrs Forbes wrote rapidly on the page, then snapped the diary shut. 'He's very worried about her . . .'

It did not seem in Mrs Forbes's official capacity to be so confiding to a comparative stranger. Kemp could only assume she did not regard Mrs Snape as coming under any office file, or it may have been something in his own manner. It had happened before; his innocently chubby face tended to invite, even encourage, confidences.

'Mrs Snape is ill?'

'Not what you or I would call ill.' Mrs Forbes had accepted him as one of her own sort, the sensible, responsible kind. 'But she behaves strangely at times . . . Like this going off to Cornwall and staying away so long . . .'

Kemp laughed. 'With weather such as this, I don't blame her.'

Mrs Forbes did not even glance out of the windows where the great bluff cubes of the City skyline caught and held the brilliance of the sun till all the glass mirrored and magnified it, each pane a blinding light. Weather where she came from meant warm underwear and the need for a raincoat.

'Mrs Snape ought to be with her husband,' she said tartly, 'helping with all the entertaining he has to do. Overseas clients, particularly Americans, they prefer to be dined in private homes, and the Snapes have a lovely house in Chelsea . . . Stockbroking isn't just facts and figures, Mr Kemp, despite what goes on out there . . .'

They listened to the muted whirr of the machines tapping money in and out of computers across the world.

'But you have made this a pleasant haven, Mrs

Forbes.' He smiled at her and gestured vaguely at the panelled walls discreetly hung with rather old-fashioned pictures. He guessed she'd had a hand in the room's furnishings and indeed she took the compliment to herself.

'Mr Vincent always left such matters to me. Most of these have come from the Manchester office. I try to keep them tasteful.'

They were indeed so; good prints and some hazy water-colours of Northern moorland scenes. As he walked to the door Kemp noticed an unframed oil which broke the harmony, a modern abstract painting at odds with its decorous surroundings, formal geometric curves of black, slashes of angry blue and silver, peppered with stark white impasto. He looked closely at it.

'Oh, that one's got nothing to do with me,' said Doris Forbes, hastily disclaiming any responsibility. 'Mr Snape had it some years ago from a struggling young artist. Supposed to be a breaking wave. Can't say I think much of it. I like a sea that looks like a sea. Don't understand this modern stuff myself but I suppose Mr Snape thought he would help the young man. Mr Vincent's always so generous . . .'

Having firmly established her employer not only as a successful businessman but patron also of the indigent young, Mrs Forbes turned away, and opened the door for Kemp.

He went out into the shadowed canyons of the City, and sought coolness in a leafy square. But even there the people were drooping on the benches, unaccustomed to such sudden early heat, while the softly-pecking pigeons at their feet seemed happily dazed by it.

Although not a countryman either by nature or upbringing, Kemp had an unexpected wish to be where there were green fields and a sight of the sea. Only another few days to go and his holiday could begin.

Coincidence. The odd playfulness of fate. It had been Penelope who had suggested Cornwall, and Rocksea. It hadn't mattered to Kemp where they should go – he was more concerned as to the outcome. Was their pleasant steady relationship to founder there, be wrecked upon that wild North Cornwall coast? He knew the place slightly. Some years ago he had worked temporarily in a solicitors' office in Westerbridge, the nearest town to Rocksea. When Penelope had mentioned she had old friends who ran the White House Hotel, six bedrooms, a garden and path to the beach, open May to October, he had taken little interest, leaving her to make the arrangements.

Had Vincent Snape not been so short-tempered on the telephone Kemp might well have exclaimed how strange it was that Mirabel Snape should be staying at the same tiny spot on the Ordnance Survey map chosen for Kemp's own holiday.

As it was, it struck Kemp as interesting; he had no sense of foreboding.

Chapter Three

Penelope Marsden had been at the White House for three days when Kemp arrived that Saturday in the middle of June. She had had time to settle down, meet other guests enjoying the unexpected benison of a heatwave engendered by a ridge of high pressure over the Azores, and she had even taken a plunge into waters unaffected by it and still coldly assertive of their Northern origin.

The first thing Kemp was aware of when he got out of his car in the driveway of the modest Edwardian house, white-painted to give it its name, was the silence. This to him had always been the miracle of Cornwall, this absence of sound. Of course the sea murmured beyond the dunes, and the garden was full of the sharp twittering of birds going about their own business of nest-building, but such noises only deepened the silence.

Kemp took out his bag and went up the steps past stone urns already planted and packed deckchairs still awaiting the hands of holidaymakers yet to come. Penelope came running. That was surely a good sign. That he took it to be such meant that he was becoming dependent on favourable omens.

Later that evening they took the dusty little path through the hedge and on to the beach where the sea stretched like wrinkled satin out towards the great bands of purple, orange and vermilion left in the sky by a sun already set.

'We should have been here to see it go plop into the water,' said Penelope, 'it would have sizzled like a hot coal . . .'

'While we were swilling wine . . . A sunset is just a sunset whereas food and drink is the stuff of life . . .'

'Oh, you're just immune to scenery and all that, Lennox. You've about as much romance in you as a baked potato.' But she giggled to show she didn't mean it, and changed the subject. 'Did you say over dinner that your man Snape's wife is here, in Rocksea?'

'So I believe. She's supposed to be of a Cornish family. Could be local. Name of Trevanion.'

Penelope shook her head.

'I've not met any local people yet. You could ask Bob and Phyl at the Hotel. Do you really want to make inquiries?'

'No. It's got nothing to do with me. Only curiosity.'

Penelope gave him a sidelong glance.

'That'll be the death of you, Lennox. Mirabel Snape – it's a pretty name . . . Looking her up will give you something to do while you're here.'

He pulled her round to face him. There had been a bleakness in her voice which disturbed him.

'Hey, there. This is our holiday. Yours and mine. It's got nothing to do with Vincent Snape or his wife.'

'We shall see,' said Penelope calmly. Perhaps, she thought, I take everything too calmly. But she lacked the temperament to make scenes, to be what she termed emotional, as though that were a symptom of neurosis. She was fond of Lennox, deeply fond, as she had been of her husband, Richard, dead from cancer before either of them had reached thirty-five, and who still lived in her memory more as the childhood sweetheart he had been than as the companion of their brief marriage. Richard was neatly folded away into her past life, the trauma of losing him softened by time, and she was never troubled by his memory. She felt herself fortunate to have it unsullied. Talking with other women, women who had been married and divorced, Penelope sometimes thought hers was the more blessed state, for nothing could spoil the bedrock laid down in the years Richard and she had had together, no bitter aftermath, no recriminations, no resentful might-have-beens.

'Sometimes it's better to be widowed than divorced,' she had once murmured to one such friend, who had looked at her in shocked surprise.

Now her work as Sistor Tutor at a London teaching hospital satisfied Penelope completely, giving her the independence her sturdy personality had always wanted. She was not sure that she was ready to give it up.

She had met Lennox Kemp two years ago at the home of her uncle and aunt, Archie and Florence Gillorn. She was amused by the old man's obvious wish to see his junior partner settled into matrimony, and warmed by her aunt's compassionate interest. They both saw marriage as an end in itself, and she was touched by their innocent matchmaking, but things are rarely so tidy to those upon whom such wishes are thrust, no matter how tactfully and well-intentioned.

Penelope enjoyed Kemp's companionship when he came up to London, the concerts, theatres and dinners – as what single woman would not in a world still based on the pairing-off principle? They invariably slept together afterwards at her flat, and that too was a relationship pleasant, leisurely and undemanding – although Kemp could at times appear distrait, almost as if he were somewhere else without consciously wishing to be so. Certainly he had no hankering for his former wife, that beautiful gambler Muriel for whom he had risked, and lost, his career. To settle her debts he had dipped brazenly into trust funds, been caught, and paid dearly. Struck off by the Law Society, he had spent some six years in the wilderness, eking out a modest living as an inquiry agent in Walthamstow before being reinstated and returning to respectability and a place in Gillorns. Archie Gillorn's faith in him had been justified, and Kemp's future with the firm was now on a solid footing.

Yet Penelope sensed that those years on the underside of the law had left their mark. They had given him an insight into the way people live, an unorthodox perception rare in the legal field, and it tended to make him impatient with the status quo. She guessed he had acquired not simply a sneaking aptitude for the sleazy side of life but even a preference for it. It was an area into which she could not follow him, being naturally unadventurous and conservative in her outlook. It was that unknown quality in him which scared her now when she contemplated their possible marriage.

These thoughts ran like an undercurrent in her mind even as they laughed and talked of other things, strolling back through the dunes where the dry spears of marram grass stirred faintly in the small wind creeping up from the sea.

But as she lay in his arms at night her doubts dissolved in the sensual warmth of his nearness. I'd be a fool to give him up, she thought, there'll never be another like him.

Chapter Four

The Morrises at the White House Hotel, determined that their guests should have access to local social events as well as the scenery, let it be known the next day that tickets were available for a luncheon in aid of the Royal National Lifeboat Institution to be held at the Yacht Club – thus ensuring profit for a good cause on the one hand, and blameless Sabbath diversion on the other. It was no longer expected that churches or chapels would provide holidaymakers with the latter.

'Charity may begin at home,' remarked Kemp on hearing of the project and having had his wallet eviscerated to the extent of ten pounds, 'but she's soon out on the street looking for customers.'

By ten o'clock in the morning (because the tide was in) he had been led like a reluctant lamb into the deceiving blue waters of the Atlantic curling with innocent guile on the shore of Rocksea. That he was accompanied by other hardy idiots similarly hypnotized by the old June weather into the error of supposing the Gulf Stream had any influence on the sea temperature, did nothing to allay shivering anxiety about possible cardiac failure on the first dive. After that, it wasn't so bad.

In fact by midday when he and Penelope were crossing the wooden structure leading somewhat precariously to the Yacht Club building Kemp was experiencing that peculiar feeling, part languid, part life-enhancing, which tends to follow a dip into man's primeval habitat.

Immediately upon entering the premises, however, the life-enhancing part slipped away. He had to admit to himself that he was not a particularly social being, and the sight of the crowded bar, the high inanity of chattering voices, and the array of massed sandwiches, sausage rolls, and parsley bedecked quiches, dampened his spirit. He could not have said why this was so. He recognized the ritual as being as much Britain in the eighties as Chinese takeaways along the Old Kent Road, but he also knew he could never be a part of it.

Penelope was greeted by the Carradines, an elderly couple who were staying at the hotel while they scoured the district for a retirement home. There were plenty on the market, from seaside bungalows to more picturesque relics of grander days, and John and Sophie Carradine were having a delightful time poring over estate agents' brochures and details of desirable properties in local newspapers.

Finding no available seat, Kemp procured drinks, then drifted back to the bar, listening to the broken conversations around him. There was sailing talk, and golf talk, and talk of the weather, but more than anything else there was travel talk; everyone in this gathering seemed to have been somewhere beyond the shores of Britain.

Kemp realized he should not have been surprised by what was a perfectly natural phenomenon. The majority of the company were retired, many from the Services – there was a preponderance of admirals, the sea apparently still in their blood – and most of them had reached that stage in life when memories are more of a comfort than today's news (only fit for lamentation) and to reminisce on the past a shared indulgence. For these veterans, no matter what had brought them here, the way ahead had become an easy path, comfortable and without anxiety for the future: a breathing space before death. So they slipped gratefully into their memories; old soldiers and civil servants alike, engineers who had built bridges (or knocked them down in war), judges from forgotten Colonies, ladies who had taught in dusty corners of the Empire, couples who had endured danger and shrivelled skin in the course of duty abroad, all content now to end their days in this tranquil haven.

'When we were in Quetta . . .'

'Of course things in the Gulf were different then . . .'

'I recall an incident at a Mexican mine . . .'

'Sally and I met in Martinique . . .'

'Did I ever tell you about that time in Cairo . . .?'

Kemp felt quite transported into the past, and an illustrious past at that, and all of it a long way from this Clubhouse so loosely attached like a seaside pier above the beach at Rocksea.

It still being term-time at universities and colleges, and too early in the season for families with schoolchildren, there were few younger people present. Those who were, Kemp guessed to be local. Their womenfolk wore fancier clothing than the others and were smartly coiffured, as if to make the best of what to them was an up-market occasion. The men, one and all, were appropriately rigged out in roll-neck sweaters so that they looked like fishermen even when they weren't. The snatches of conversation from these groups had a more present significance.

''Course he's not missing, he's just away on one of his trips . . .'

'You talking about Steve Donray? Well, what I've heard is . . .'

Kemp lost the rest though he had registered the accents, as he was buttonholed by a large man in a navy blazer bearing what could only be the Yacht Club crest.

'Down on holiday, eh?' He blinked behind his pink gin.

'Yes.'

'Great little place, Rocksea. What's that you're drinking? Have another . . .' He waved an authoritative hand at the bartender.

'Very kind of you.'

'You from London?'

'Yes. Tell me, who is Steve Donray?' Kemp spoke not so much out of idle curiosity as simply to establish contact.

'Fisherman. Has a boat out of Padstow. Unreliable, though . . .' He fell silent as if brooding over some iniquity. Another man jogged his elbow. 'Did you say Donray, Peter? Has he let you down too?'

Peter turned to the new face. 'He certainly did. Promised me faithfully a mackerel trip last Friday. Never turned up . . .'

'It's happened before. You can't rely on them. Just like your average native. I remember when our lot were trying to build a landing-strip in Malaya . . .'

They became engrossed in the anecdote, and Kemp drifted off, reflecting on the theory that an individual's attention span is only thirty seconds long – if that – and also on the corresponding axiom attuned to modern high-speed selling that no point is worth making if it can't be done in thirty seconds flat. Here it seemed that conversationalists had all the time in the world, no matter that the wavelengths between talker and talker rarely met, and as often as not the messages sped past each other and bounced away into outer space like happy neutrons.

Kemp drifted from group to group, greeted here and there, becoming less of a stranger, but most of the time just listening, amused, finding nothing to perk up his ears. Well, next to nothing . . .

'I'll skin that Donray when he turns up. He owes me . . .'

'He's up to something, I can tell you that for sure. If it's money you're after you'd best get it quick . . .' This in a rolling Cornish mutter. The speaker drained his pint mug, and set it back on the table with a thump. 'Your turn, Trev . . .'

In the ensuing movement towards the bar Kemp heard no more.

The heat and noise were becoming oppressive, and he already felt he'd had too much to drink. Through the open door he glimpsed the sea, and wandered out on to the wooden verandah to feel its breath. He leaned on the rail, dazzled by the shimmer from the water where boats bobbed like children's toys, the tinkle of metal on mastheads a tinny dulcimer accompaniment to their game. The harsh sound of a car's tyres screeching to a stop made him turn. People were still arriving at the landing-stage.

The car that had braked so noisily disgorged a young man whose hair shone golden in the sun as he ran round and pulled open the passenger door. He seemed to be gesticulating to someone inside, someone reluctant to emerge. The young man leaned in and took hold of an arm. With much protestation the female passenger was eventually persuaded to alight, and stood for a moment wavering, a hand shading her eyes as if bemused by the brightness of the day.

The small scene interested Kemp. He watched the two figures as they came across the wooden slats. There was no doubt the woman was being propelled forward against her will, although her escort, almost dancing along by her side, was exerting no obvious pressure. Indeed his raised voice was soothing.

'Oh, come on, angel, it's no den of wolves. They're your kind, remember. You know everybody . . .'

'That's not the point, Robin. I just don't feel like company. Sometimes I can't stand all that yammering . . .'

I know exactly how you feel, lady, thought Kemp, turning his eyes away and looking down at the sea. But he caught a whiff of perfume, and realized that instead of making for the doorway she had walked across the tiny pier and was leaning on the rail only a few feet from him.

'Okay, Okay, if you really want simply to look at the sun why didn't we stay home on the patio? But I got these two tickets . . . Bloody hell, they cost me five pounds apiece . . .' From the lightness of his tone the young man's grievance wasn't serious.

The woman's voice changed from petulance to an amused murmur, carrying the unmistakable undertone of love. 'Robin dear, is that all that's worrying you? Poor impecunious artist! But it's for charity, my sweet . . .'

Kemp could clearly see their hands on the rail, the male with bronze hairs on the back, hers overlapping, frail and blue-veined. The young man laughed, a high joyous sound.

'I know. For all these husky types who brave the

dangers of the deep. From Padstow Point to Lundy Light is a watery grave from day to night . . .' he sang.

Her fingers tightened, gripping hard on the wood as if for a hold on reality. Kemp felt the sudden flurried movement of her silk dress as she turned.

'Stop it, Robin. If you don't, I'm going home.'

This time Kemp had to look at her properly. Her face was stormy, huge eyes dark – they could have been any colour in that strong sunlight – but the untidy hair round the thin brown face was blue-black. For the first time she seemed aware of the presence of an onlooker. She stared at him, and he felt like an intruder yet he could not take his eyes from her.

It may have been the effect of the glaring noonday light, a light which destroyed all tonal relationships, flattening colour and form, and into which she had come like a shadow or a cloud. Whatever it was, they were for the moment transfixed in time.

Another voice intervened, a sweet voice but with the carrying force of authority.

'Mirabel, are you coming in or not? My dear, you're in danger of causing a scene . . .'

The figure emerging from the door of the Clubhouse was one Kemp had seen multiplied a dozen times within the luncheon party. Neat grey cauliflower curls above a pink, kindly face, a middle-aged woman, staunch supporter of all charity causes such as this, she came forward and laid a firm hand on Mrs Snape's arm. Mirabel turned in gratitude.

'Aunt Susan! Of course I'll come in if you want me to.'

'Susie to the rescue – as always.' The young man sounded pleased. 'That's all Mirabel needed. And me

44

too. We are your chickens, Aunt Susie, your little chickens.'

Susan Trevanion gave him a look of tolerant indulgence, and indeed it was like a mother hen that she unobtrusively gathered her charges, and shepherded them through the doorway.

Kemp flicked his cigarette out over the water. Well, well. So that was Mirabel Snape, wife to his stockbroker client, descendant of an old Cornish family, and mother of a two-year-old son. She had sounded no more than a sulky child herself.

He followed the trio and found the interior of the building to his sun-blinded eyes dark brown and fuzzy with smoke. He groped his way over to the corner where Penelope and the Carradines were by now at lunch. The crowd around them had thickened but Penelope pulled him down beside her on to an upturned barrel. The table-top gleamed silver and gold as a shaft of sun struck the array of bottles and glasses.

'I got you some food,' she said, 'I knew you'd never think of it on your own. And there's a drink for you. Not beer, I'm afraid. I think they've run out. G and t all right?'

'This ship's sinking in a sea of gin and tonic, but I don't mind going down with it. I haven't had so much to drink since the last Law Society dinner.' Nevertheless he took the proffered glass, and relished its ice-cold tingle.

'Well, none of us has to drive,' put in John Carradine happily, 'that's the joy of it. We're just going to love retirement here, they're such a friendly crowd.'

It was true. By now the party was in full swing, all initial stuffiness departed, social barriers broken. Total strangers were invited into the confidences of bygone exploits and travellers' tales of faraway lands. On the other side of Sophie Carradine a wizened brigadier was reliving for her benefit the battle of El Alamein, setting ashtrays to annihilate beer-mats on the smeared table. She didn't tell him she'd lost a son in that engagement; Sophie was a kind woman and not one to sound a discordant note.

At Penelope's shoulder a weatherbeaten lady was assuring a young girl in vivid pink culottes that fox-hunting was necessary and had nothing to do with cruelty to animals, no matter that the girl's wide eyes were elsewhere and her ears too stunned by other conversations to hear what she was saying.

A gentleman in tweeds caught Kemp's arm – fortunately not the one he was using to raise yet another drink to his lips – and shook it violently. 'You're a lawyer.' It sounded like an accusation. 'You'll know what I'm talking about. I've been telling your fiancée here . . . Ramblers interfering with my land . . . Saying there's a footpath. Damned nonsense. Here, have this one on me . . .' He took off, erratically, for the bar.

'Sorry about that.' Penelope shook her head, but she was laughing, her cheeks flushed, her eyes bright. 'But he did ask what you did for a living, and it set him off. In this crush everyone gets things wrong.'

'It's the atmosphere, ducks.' Kemp squeezed her hand. 'Like the pubs in Walthamstow. Too matey, by half. All these fragmented dialogues. By the way, who's Steve Donray?'

'He's one I haven't met. At least, I don't think so.'

'Steve Donray?' It was the pink young woman, disengaging herself from the diatribe of the fox-hunter. 'Everyone's looking for Steve, me included.'

Kemp turned round to her. 'Who is he?' he asked.

'We all know who he is,' she said curtly. 'It's where he's vanished to we all want to know.'

'Why'd you say he's vanished?'

'Hasn't been seen for a week.' She held her glass upside down to see if there was a drop left, or if the elusive Donray was hiding at the bottom of it.

The tweedy man was back with two brimming drinks which he planted unsteadily on the table. 'Now, I'd like your legal opinion on this matter of my land,' he announced with the careful enunciation of one who knew himself to be fairly intoxicated but felt still capable of making a point which was clearer to him now than it had ever been in cold sobriety.

Kemp closed his eyes, and bit into what turned out to be a delicious pasty. He was prepared to listen politely. He always gave his clients the courtesy of a ready ear, even when they talked drivel. He wasn't sure the acceptance of a drink established any professional relationship, but it would pass an idle moment to hear what was possibly a fascinating tale of land rights in Rocksea.

As it happened the man's story went untold, for there was a diversion at the far side of the room. A woman's voice, high above the clamour of talk, rose to a shriek.

'Stop it, Robin! You mustn't . . . Stop saying that!'

Heads turned towards the group. Kemp recognized the lady called Aunt Susan. Her protective arm was trying in vain to reach Mirabel Snape, who had risen and was standing with her back to the wall, clawing it for support. At their table the golden-haired Robin had spread his arms wide in a theatrical gesture, and although he did not seem to raise his voice the clear singing note in it penetrated to an audience already silenced, and, it seemed, avid for sensation.

Kemp's companion broke off his demand for free legal guidance, and looked across the room. 'My God,' he said, 'it's the Snape woman and her beau. There's going to be another scene.' If there was, he was quite prepared to relish it.

Penelope's rounded eyes met Kemp's. He shrugged. 'It's a small world, my dear. And Cornwall is the smallest.'

Over on the other side, the drama was developing. One of the young men called out: 'It's only a story, Mira, let Robin finish it.'

Robin turned as if on a stage.

'I read about it somewhere,' he sang out, 'these jolly old warriors used to bury their captured enemies in the sand of their compound, up to their necks, then ride their horses down the lines . . . and end up playing polo with the heads.'

There was a subdued murmur from the rest of the room, even the clash of glasses at the bar was stilled, there was a twitching of skirts, a sibilant sound as of indrawn breaths, before the large man in the blazer exclaimed loudly: 'I say, Robin, old chap, that's a bit much for our ladies' stomachs.'

There was uncertain laughter from the younger members of the group at the Snape table. It only seemed to encourage the young man, Robin. He snatched an oar from a set-piece on the wall and leapt into a clear space in the middle of the floor. He had stirred up excitement, and now, like an actor, he was enjoying his power to sustain it.

'Watch them ride up and down the sandy field,' he

cried, swishing the blade to and fro. 'Hear the thunder of the hooves. See the severed heads go rolling . . .'

There was grace and venom in his movements as he imitated first the motion of a raging steed, and then the sudden vicious thwack with his improvised weapon.

It was all an act, of course, over as soon as begun, and once the room had recovered from the shock, there was even a splatter of applause.

'Quite a turn that young man puts on,' remarked Carradine to Penelope, but she had shuddered and now gripped Kemp's hand tightly.

He for his part had never taken his eyes off Mirabel Snape. She had slid from her painful stance against the wall, and had fallen with her head among the debris of plates and glasses on the table. He watched as Susan Trevanion lifted her gently, and then motioned imperiously for the rest of the party to make way. One of the young men, looking abashed at whatever admonition she had addressed to them, helped her carry the limp body from the room.

'That young lady fainted,' said Sophie Carradine, with compassion.

'Drunk more likely,' observed the man in tweeds. 'We all know what's the matter with Mrs Snape.'

'And what is that, exactly?' asked Penelope, who had an innate distaste for gossip.

Disconcerted by her tone, the man was flustered.

'I only know it's the talk of the place. She and that young man, Mr Adair. Carrying on . . . Well, I don't know . . . But they're talked about.'

'She might at least put a comb through her hair before coming to an event like this.' It was the girl in pink. ''Spose she thinks she can get away with anything, being who she is . . .'

The retired brigadier put in his word.

'Terrible shame. Actually, Miss Trevanion's a good friend of mine, and that niece of hers is becoming a real problem. Don't like all the talk myself . . . Never listen to it. But it's a worry to Susan since the girl came . . . No harm in young Adair that I know of. Excess of high spirits, perhaps . . . Local artist. Lots of our memsahibs go to his classes . . . Mrs Snape's too flighty for her own good. Ought to be in London with her husband, not sky-larkin' about down here . . .'

Penelope glanced up at Kemp. He had neither moved, nor spoken. She relaxed her hold on his arm. Something in his immobility warned her.

'I think we should be getting back to the hotel,' she said, and made the little prattle of farewells for both of them since Kemp's mind seemed to be elsewhere.

When they passed the group with whom Mirabel Snape had been sitting there was no sign of Robin Adair, and when they emerged from the building the car had also gone.

'"What's this dull town to me? Robin's not here . . ."' Penelope hummed the tune. 'That surely can't be his real name, or whatever was his mother thinking of?'

'Picked it up for a song,' said Kemp absently, as they searched for the right path through the dunes. But he said nothing else, and eventually Penelope became impatient of his silence. She had drunk more than was usual for her, and the heat of the sun which earlier had been comforting and benign now made her feel scratchy and irritable.

'Well,' she said at last, 'so that's your Mrs Snape. I

can't say I'm impressed. After all, she's got a baby son . . .'

'What's that got to do with it?'

'I suppose she's got a nanny for him. People like her do.'

'Prejudiced, Penelope?'

She recognized his tone. Kemp, always the reasonable man, never judging. Now it only fuelled her resentment.

'Don't fall for her, Lennox. She's no good.' It was unlike Penelope to be so outright in condemnation and the words had come out with a bitterness which surprised even herself.

He stopped and pulled her off the path on to the grassy turf.

'Come and sit down and tell me what's on your mind. There's more to this than Mirabel Snape.'

But once seated she remained silent. Her knees hunched up to her chest, she stared out across the estuary, peacefully ambivalent, blue-silver water, golden sand, the sky a milky haze. Her natural reticence put a rein on her tongue, and she was afraid of what she might say if it were left unbridled.

'Why'd you warn me about falling for Mrs Snape?' Kemp spoke lightly, sensing her unease. 'Do you think I'm so susceptible?'

She tried to match his jesting tone but the words tumbled out with a seriousness of their own.

'Of course you are. You get emotionally involved with all the women in your cases. You don't see yourself like that, Lennox. You think you stand aside, the objective eye, the rational man, so infinitely reasonable . . .' Once started, the effect of alcohol was to clarify her thoughts and lend her a loquacity

51

normally beyond her scope. 'But you're not. You get caught up in these women. Just look at them.' And she spread out her hand on a cushion of wild thyme, and plucked at her fingertips one after the other. 'Frances Jessica who was too good to be true, that odd Scottish girl you wanted to marry, Alexina something . . . You played uncle so much to Lettice Warrender that she got ideas about you . . . And, last of all, you'd have gone to bed with Frelis Lorimer, never mind whether she killed her husband's girlfriend or not. You still haven't got over that one yet . . .'

She stopped, not daring to look at him but squinting up at the sun as if to blame it for her outburst.

Appalled. The word had always rather amused Kemp. People said they were appalled when they were lost for words. Now he knew what it meant. He was appalled. Struck dumb.

Could it be true what Penelope had just said? He might argue that women inevitably entered his cases; you could hardly keep them out of matrimonial matters. And of course he met them in a highly emotional context; marriage and its ramifications were concerned with emotion, with instincts, with psychological needs, it wasn't a simple matter of contract like hire-purchase or buying a house. Was he trying to rationalize again, justifying himself to himself?

And what if it was true? He'd have to consider that possibility at length, but not now . . . All he could muster up at the moment was a brief – and he hoped dispassionate – review of the ladies in question, and he found that all but the last had already retreated into memory. Surely that was a sign that he was a rational being. All he had to do was to act like one now.

With this course in mind he changed the subject.

'Time the two of us had some tea . . . the cups that cheer but do not inebriate. I can never get hold of the tenses in that quote . . .' He put an arm around her, and pulled her to her feet. 'That was a nasty disturbance back there. There's something about this place, all this scenery on show, it's too like a stage set, it's unnerving.'

She caught his mood of reconciliation gratefully, and they went along the path together, their hands just touching.

'You wouldn't like to live in the country, then?' she asked him.

'Would you?'

'And become a lady of good works, join the Women's Institute, help raise money for charity? For that's what I would be, Lennox. That's my type. Competent, unflappable.' She nearly added, 'And boring,' but stopped herself in time.

'It would be a good life,' he reflected.

'But not for you,' she said firmly, 'you'd hate it.'

'Are you sure? I could easily join that practice in Westerbridge, convey second homes, and bungalows for the retired, make wills for farmers, defend local salmon poachers in front of magistrates who'd know every man-jack of them from boyhood . . . Could be great fun.'

Penelope shook her head.

'It's not for you, Lennox. Confess it, you actually like working in places like Newtown.'

Kemp considered something he'd never really given much thought to. Harlow, Stevenage, Milton Keynes, Newtown; they had sprung in hope after war. Like the people's aspirations, they had promised more, much more, than they could fulfil. Yet they called to him in a way this earthly paradise could not.

'I'm a town mouse,' he said truthfully, 'and perhaps I'm just afraid of the wide open spaces. Looking at that – ' he gestured at the shallow blue bowl out beyond the headlands where sky and ocean blurred – 'you can almost feel the earth turn. You know the sea will remain and the grass will go on growing on these cliffs long after mankind has packed its bags and left. I don't relish the thought that we don't count for much, and our lives are dwarfed in a place like this . . .'

'Then let's console ourselves with tea,' said Penelope, taking his arm affectionately to make up for the fact that she had, earlier, tried to take him down a peg. I wonder why I did it, she thought to herself as they went into the hotel garden. Perhaps he's right; the scenery does have its effect.

Chapter Five

When Kemp woke up the next morning a beam of sunlight hit him across the eyes. 'Busy old fool,' he muttered, 'just because it's up early . . .' The curtains were pulled back. Now that was something you couldn't get away with in Newtown or the neighbours would know exactly what you had for breakfast. Intrigued by the novelty of wide windows open to the sky, Kemp got up and leaned out into the fragrant air. From the tender green of the tamarisk feathers in the garden below, the golden-yellow dunes in the middle distance, out to the glimmering sea, the empty landscape lay breathless, waiting to be inhabited.

It was too much for him and, dressing quickly and with only a glance at the still sleeping Penelope, he slipped through the door and down the silent stairs. The clock in the hall said it was six o'clock.

He walked the whole length of the beach along the line of the incoming tide, through sandy runnels where the small waves frothed and fronds of bright viridian weed stirred among the rounded pebbles and broken shells, until he reached the point where the estuary turned to the ocean and the colour of the water changed to a deeper blue. Then he climbed upwards, and came back through the soft sand at the base of the dunes. Finding the going heavy, he threw himself down in a grassy hollow and let the beauty of the scene filter through half-closed lids and into his consciousness.

It was the spatial dimension he found disturbing. It must have been like this in the first days of the world, he thought, in the earliest morning of creation when the earth had received its frame and the hills in order stood – and of course before man arrived to give it vitality, and to pillage . . .

Across the estuary the truncated knob of Stepper Head was still darkly in shadow and between it and his view the light glanced off the bows of boats putting out from Padstow. Nearer the shore of Rocksea, indeed quite close in to the shore, a head moved through the water. Someone was swimming. At this hour. Kemp closed his eyes.

Stealthily the climbing sun drew the chill out of the morning air and warmed his face as he lay half asleep, lulled by the hum of insects browsing for breakfast in the grasses. A shadow and the soft sound of footsteps in the sand disturbed him. Only then, on opening his eyes, did he see above him on a clump of marram a towel, a pile of clothes and a pair of white sandals. He began hurriedly to scramble to his feet.

'I'm sorry. I didn't notice . . . I'm really sorry . . .'

Mirabel Snape stood above him, blocking out the sun. In a black swimsuit, wet hair flattened on her forehead, water droplets glistening all over her body, she looked sleek and smooth as a seal. He still couldn't make out the colour of her eyes.

But she was smiling. 'No, don't get up, please. You are so comfortable there. I can manage. That is, if you'll just turn the other way for a moment.'

She leaned over and snatched up the towel, throwing it quickly round her shoulders where the faint tan of her neck met the whiteness of her back. But not quickly enough; Kemp had already seen the ugly purple bruises that marred the whiteness above the low-cut line of her costume.

Embarrassed more by what he had just seen than by her sudden presence, he sat up, got out his cigarettes, and obligingly stared out to sea.

'It's a bit rough on you that out of a whole empty beach I should choose your particular spot,' he remarked conversationally. 'I must have been dreaming. I honestly didn't notice . . .'

It was quite unbearable, her closeness. He could sense every small movement as she dried herself, and dressed.

'I saw you from out there.' Her voice was muffled as she pulled something over her head. 'I thought your choice was deliberate.'

'Heaven forfend! That would have been an intrusion on your privacy and as such quite unforgivable.'

'You do use funny words, don't you?' Clothed now in sweater and shorts, she plumped herself down beside him. 'You wouldn't mind giving me one of your cigarettes?'

Lighting it for her, he saw at last that her eyes were the colour of the sea, blue with a hint of green, almost turquoise, and startlingly pale in her brown face. She had towelled her hair so that it stood out like black wires glinting gold where the sun struck through.

'Thanks. The first smoke after a swim is always the best.' She lay back, relaxed, her head on her bunched towel. 'You should try it . . . swimming, I mean.'

'It's not my proper element. Do you always come out this early?'

'When I can. It clears my head. And later, there's too many people on the beach. I like to swim alone.' She was silent for a moment, then went on in a dreamy kind of way: 'Sometimes I think it's only in there – in the water – that I'm ever really happy.'

It sounded as if she was communing with herself, but it was in Kemp's nature to respond even at that level.

'Are you so unhappy then, Mrs Snape, when you're not in the water?'

She took him, and answered him, seriously – as he had intended she should.

'At least I can't be got at out there . . . Everything's clear even when I can't see to the bottom. The water's my friend and I can drift away on it.'

'So long as you don't drift too far out.'

She sat up. 'Don't be stupid. There's no danger of that kind for me. I was brought up on this estuary. I know it like – like the back of my hand.' She caught her breath. 'At least, I thought I did. Now everything's confused . . . It's all spoilt . . . Even my own beach.'

'Spoilt? In what way?'

She stirred restlessly and ground her stub hard into the turf, watching until the trail of blue smoke ceased.

'Questions, questions. Why does everybody have to ask questions? What am I doing? Where am I going? On and on, endlessly . . .'

'If you know you are happy swimming, Mrs Snape, then you must know what it is like to be happy. You must have had the experience.'

She turned her amazing eyes on him.

'That's quite a sensible remark. Of course I know what happiness is. I had it before . . .' She suddenly registered something she had missed. 'You called me Mrs Snape, so you know who I am. Didn't I see you yesterday?'

'At the luncheon, yes. I did hear your name. I'm sorry if I've been presumptuous . . .'

'There you go again. What a fellow you are for feeling sorry. You don't have to worry about me. Everybody knows me, and talks about me. I'm sure you've heard it all . . .'

'Do you want honesty, or would you prefer the civil approach?'

'Oh, spare me the civilities. You really have a way with words, Mr . . .?'

'Kemp. Lennox Kemp.'

'I think I'll choose honesty, Mr Lennox Kemp, if it doesn't hurt too much.'

'Very well.' It must have been the sun, he thought afterwards, that made him so bold. The sun, the blasted scenery, and the lack of breakfast. 'I have heard that you drink more than is good for you, that you are having an affair with one Robin Adair, and that if you go on as you are doing you will be the death of your aunt.'

For the first time he heard her laugh, a ringing peal of almost jubilant laughter.

The sound seemed to surprise herself, for she broke it off abruptly and looked at him in astonishment. 'Nobody's ever talked like that to me in years. Who on earth are you, Mr Lennox Kemp?'

Now of course should have been the moment to tell her. I know your husband, Mrs Snape, and from him too I have heard about you. That you are happily married yet you linger on here in Cornwall incurring his displeasure. From another source, that you are not altogether a satisfactory wife, that you are highly-strung . . .

All he said was: 'A stranger on the shore. Someone of no consequence.'

'But you've heard all about me,' she persisted. 'They probably also say that I neglect my baby son, that I suffer from some kind of neurotic illness which the highest-paid physicians can't find a name for, never mind cure . . .'

Kemp heard the rising note of possible hysteria, and, feeling himself to blame, tried to lighten the atmosphere by quoting:

> 'They murmured, as they took their fees,
> There is no cure for this disease . . .'

Innocuous verses, useful to fill a gap. But at least they made her laugh, although not with the same merriment as before. Then she said quietly: 'It's why I came down here . . . being ill, I mean. We thought the change . . .'

'We?'

'My husband.' Mirabel shivered suddenly.

'Are you cold?'

'Of course I'm not cold.' She could be brusque when she chose. 'Stop worrying about me. There's plenty of others to do that . . . As I said I preferred honesty to civility, so let's be honest, then. It's true I drink. I like the feeling. It takes me away from things.'

'And the young man?'

'How persuasive you are. It's rather fun, though, you being a stranger I shall probably never see again. You're not local, you're down on holiday?'

Kemp nodded. He wasn't sure he wanted to hear any more.

'I shouldn't have asked . . .'

'You started it,' she said flatly. 'You heard things

about me and you want to know if they're true. Well, about Robin. I met him the first week I was here. I was so drained after my illness . . . life no longer had any meaning. They called it depression, as if any word could describe that grey void. But Robin made me live again. He gave me back something I thought I'd lost. Perhaps it was my girlhood.' She gave a short, bitter laugh. 'I'm nearly thirty – old enough to know better. Meeting Robin has done me more good than all the pills they keep giving me. Yes, I'm having an affair with him – if that's what they like to call it.'

'He's an antidote, you mean?'

She looked into his face.

'How sensible you are. Not many would see it like that . . . As for the other rumour, that I don't look after Simon properly, well, that's just not true. Even when I was ill I kept him with me all the time. Down here Aunt Susan insists on helping, and Tammy the maid loves taking him out, but I bath and feed and play with him, so that part of their story is all lies.' For the first time Kemp sensed anger in her.

'I had not heard that you neglected your son, Mrs Snape,' he said quickly. 'And as for the other gossip – for that's all it is – does it really matter?'

'Talking to you here like this, no, it doesn't. I wish I could always be so clear-headed . . . Sometimes I get so confused in my mind. So much has happened to me lately. Even with Robin . . .' She stopped.

'I have heard him described as high-spirited,' said Kemp cautiously.

'He can be . . . but there are times when I wonder about him too. Do you ever find things moving so fast that you can't take them in? As if the earth beneath your feet isn't stable any more. Do you ever feel like that?'

She had turned eagerly towards him as if to share some experience of her own.

'I think,' he replied slowly, aware that he was about to sound sententious, 'there are different levels of living. We go happily along on one plane and then something happens. The level doesn't hold, it crumbles, and we find ourselves on another layer where even the everyday world takes on the look of another planet. And that can be a pretty inhospitable one until we adapt and find our way through it. Perhaps your illness was just such an earthquake and you're still blundering about on a new level of living . . .'

While he had been speaking she had watched his face with the intensity of a lip-reader. Now she sat back. 'So it needn't just be in my mind,' she said thoughtfully, 'it needn't mean that I'm going mad?'

'Who says you're going mad?' Kemp spoke sharply.

'Oh, nobody's actually said it. They're all much too tactful for that. What was that word again? The civilities . . . the civilities must be observed. So they don't talk about it.'

'That's because they're not on your level any more. Yours has changed, theirs hasn't.'

'But you're talking to me on my level now. How does that come about? You're not a doctor, are you – not a psychiatrist, I hope?'

Kemp laughed. 'Far from it. I'm a lawyer, Mrs Snape.' Then in case the admission might cause her alarm, he added, more seriously: 'And that means that although we met as complete strangers on the beach this morning everything you have said to me, every word, will remain safely tucked up in my head, never to be repeated.'

'And never used against me? Have I got that right?' She broke into a fit of giggling. 'Imagine me picking a lawyer to bare my soul to! You might have been a plumber.'

'I know some very intelligent plumbers. But, seriously, I ought to warn you against talking to strangers.'

'I've never done it before. Well, I suppose I do when I've been drinking . . . or so they tell me. But this has been different because my head is clear this morning. What an odd conversation we've had.'

She sat up, groped in the grass for her watch, and strapped it on her wrist. 'It's after eight. Simon will be awake by now. I must get back to him. Do you suppose you and I will ever meet again, Lennox Kemp?'

'Across a crowded room?' he said wryly. 'Maybe . . . Would you like me to walk with you or would you rather go on your own?'

She was on her feet, one hand shading her eyes as he had seen her first when she got out of the car at the Yacht Club.

'Look, our little world has been invaded,' she said.

It was true. Where the beach had stretched bare and deserted, now it was dotted with tiny figures as people emerged, walking their dogs, jogging purposefully alone or in bunches, children were racing along and beach balls bouncing; the day had come alive.

'I think I'd prefer to go alone. It would only spoil things if we met other people and had to talk to them. But I'll remember what you said about levels of living.

I have to find my feet on a different one. Goodbye, Lennox.'

'Goodbye, Mrs Snape.'

He watched her go lightly over the dunes, and down to the shore. She went by the water's edge, her sandals swinging in her hand.

Chapter Six

Kemp waited until Mirabel Snape was only a dot among many on the far side of the beach, then he strolled slowly back along the path at the top of the sandhills. He found himself running out of cigarettes, so he took the road to the shop above the slipway where the fishermen were about their boats.

As he casually watched them, they gathered themselves into a knot around a dinghy which he had seen earlier crossing the bright strip of water from Padstow. The two men in waders who came ashore became the centre of the group, drawing the others to them. When Kemp came out of the shop they were still there but by now there was a small crowd as some of the yachtsmen from along the shore who had been tinkering with their craft, waiting for the tide, joined them.

Kemp was attracted by little gatherings of people; in Newtown it generally meant there had been an accident, or at the very least an altercation. In this sleepy place it was probably quite different; perhaps it was always this way when the night fishermen's boats came in. He realized he was ignorant of the comings and goings of the men who fished the estuary, or laid the lobster pots he'd seen from the cliffs bobbing on the waters outside the headlands. He strolled down the slipway.

But it was not of lobsters that they talked this morning. The faces that turned at his approach were grim, and the eyes bleak and withdrawn.

'Good morning,' he said pleasantly.

''Mornin' . . .' It was a bare growl, and the nods were perfunctory. The Cornish have a natural courtesy and his greeting could not be met with total silence, but, one and all, they closed ranks against the stranger. It was an awkward moment for Kemp. As he stood uncertainly he heard quick footsteps behind him as someone strode briskly past him and hailed the men.

'What's wrong, Mr Treglowan? Bert, and you, Trevor, what's the matter?'

Kemp recognized the person in authority he'd last seen in the resplendent blazer at the luncheon party.

One of the two men from the dinghy spoke up. ''Tis a bad business, Mr Seagrave. A bad business indeed.'

'What's that? What's happened?'

'They've found Steve, that's what.'

There was a muttering from the group as every man tried to speak at once.

'Steve Donray? What d'you mean – they've found him?' Mr Seagrave's commanding tone eventually brought a coherent response.

'In a manner of speaking, Mr Seagrave.' A short elderly man with a thick thatch of greyed curls was cautious.

'Out with it. Are you telling me they've found his body, is that it?'

The other rower of the dinghy stepped forward. 'It came up in the nets. One of the Padstow boats out last night got it caught up in their net.'

'Are they sure it's Steve Donray?'

The men looked at each other, shuffled their feet.

'Aye, they're sure,' said one of them, 'though it's only the head they've got . . .'

'For God's sake!' Mr Seagrave stared at them. He

became aware of Kemp's silent watchfulness. 'Did you hear that? Steve Donray's a local man, lives here in Rocksea. This is a terrible thing . . .'

'Indeed it is,' said Kemp. He turned to the grey-haired older man. 'You're saying only the head's been found? But they're sure it's Mr Donray?'

'Aye, it's him all right, God help him. The crabs were at it, but the colour of the eyes, and the hair . . . Besides, he's been missing for a week, isn't that a fact, Mr Seagrave? Seems they've spotted his boat – what's left of it – in Foxhole Cove.'

'But there's been no rough weather,' Seagrave protested, 'and Steve was an experienced fisherman.'

'The police have taken his brother over there. For identification, I reckon.' It was the young man, Trevor, who spoke. 'They won't put it on the news till the family's been told. Least said, soonest mended, I'd say until then . . .'

'Yes, yes, of course. Quite right too.' Mr Seagrave seemed at a loss for words. Kemp began to walk slowly up the slipway; the fishermen would not welcome further intrusion into what, in their close-knit community, must be a private tragedy. As if they felt the same, the holiday yachtsmen drifted away also.

Mr Seagrave caught up with Kemp, and seemed anxious to have someone to talk to. 'Dreadful thing. I could do with a drink after that news. What about you? Didn't I see you yesterday at our shindig? Come on and have one at the Club.'

Kemp followed him up the steps and across the wooden pier.

Seagrave poured himself a whisky, but Kemp contented himself with coffee from the dispenser; he didn't believe in drinking spirits before breakfast. He learned that Peter Seagrave was a retired naval officer and a widower. As such he liked company, particularly at a moment like this, having no other audience and being naturally shocked and upset. Within the space of some fifteen minutes Kemp had found out all Seagrave knew about the late Steve Donray. There were also hints of what he didn't know, but could only surmise.

'Of course we did wonder how Donray kept up his style of living,' Seagrave mused when his second whisky was low in the tumbler. 'It was a bit high for a fisherman. Must have had a sideline. Many of them do. The black economy . . . Can't say I blame them. There's little money for the lone fisherman these days with all the Common Market regulations, and when you think what it costs just to insure the boat . . .'

'Mr Donray had other interests? Do you know what they were?'

'Difficult to know for sure. He was getting on rather. I suppose you could call him a late child of the sixties.' Seagrave looked at the phrase, and seemed to like it. 'By Jove, that's just what he was. You see, Mr Kemp, the sixties came to Cornwall after they'd been around for some time, if you see what I mean . . . Youngsters didn't get their long hair and beards down here, and into the drugs racket as early as they did up-country.'

'Was Steve Donray into that kind of thing?'

'There's some say he was. But of course it's fizzling out now – and a good thing, too.' He shook his head vigorously. 'Spoiled a place like this . . .'

'It looks an easy coast to run drugs into,' observed Kemp. 'Are you so sure it's stopped?'

Seagrave drew himself up. 'We're not fools down here, Mr Kemp. We know our coastline's wide open, and difficult to patrol. But we've an alert Coastguard service, and a cracking good Drugs Squad. And the Customs are always on the lookout. They even have to search private yachts.' He seemed to find this a particularly unpleasant aspect. 'They boarded one recently in Falmouth. Found some fool running the stuff in from Morocco . . .'

'What about round this estuary?'

'Well, a funny thing did happen about a week or so ago. It's still hush-hush. Inquiries being made. You being a lawyer, I don't have to explain the kind of thing . . .'

Kemp pressed the buttons of the coffee dispenser. The resulting liquid was pretty revolting but perhaps only because he'd had no breakfast. 'What was it happened, Mr Seagrave?' he prompted.

'I only got half the story from one of the lifeboatmen. They'd been out on a routine practice when they spotted this craft hove-to without lights. Of course they hailed it, but they were given a plausible enough excuse – or so it seemed. But, do you know – ' he swivelled round on his seat, quite carried away by his tale – 'just about the same time a chap in a boat out from Padstow found a floating marker buoy where it had no right to be. He hauled it in, and do you know what they found?'

Kemp shook his head, though he could have made a reasonable guess.

'Attached to that buoy – underwater, you understand – was a plastic container. Drugs, of course . . . cocaine.' He gave a gruff laugh. 'Some of those substances . . . Well, what do you make of it?'

'Obvious,' said Kemp. 'A drop that went wrong. But it predicates someone on land to do the pick-up. Someone in the know.'

'That's what put everyone under suspicion,' said Seagrave gloomily. 'There's been a lot of talk. And, I understand, some very nasty phone calls. Least, that's what I heard from the police.'

'And some of the talk led to Donray?'

'For God's sake, the man's only just . . . I don't know. I shouldn't be talking this way. Hope you'll hold it in confidence?'

'I've got nothing to do with it, Mr Seagrave. And of course I'll respect your confidence. Thanks for the coffee. I must be getting back to my hotel. I imagine this bad news will get around fast . . .'

''Fraid so. And the media will make the most of it . . . Rather gruesome, don't you think, only the head being hauled up?' Peter Seagrave, despite or perhaps because of his naval training, regarded imagination as an obstruction, but he tried nevertheless to stare it through.

'If Donray's boat smashed up on the rocks and he was thrown overboard,' said Kemp helpfully, 'and he drowned, couldn't the propeller of a passing ship . . .?'

'Not a chance.' Seagrave was adamant. 'There's been no rough weather, and anyway Donray could handle that boat in any circumstances. He'd never get into difficulties anywhere near Stepper or Foxhole Cove.' He sighed. 'I just can't understand it. For all his faults, he was a fine seaman, and a popular chap hereabouts.'

Notwithstanding Seagrave's earlier disclosures, that seemed a fair enough epitaph, and doubtless one that would be shared by many along the estuary when the news broke.

Kemp took his leave, and arrived back at the White House at half past nine. Penelope was sitting over toast and marmalade. She finished a bite with a decisive snap of her lips, and frowned at him.

'So – here you are, at last.'

'Sorry, but isn't one supposed to get up early at the seaside? Now I'll have bacon and two eggs. I'm starving.'

He had no intention of telling her of his meeting with Mirabel Snape. If Penelope found him somewhat distracted, it was understandable when he gave her the news of Donray.

'His head? But that's terrible . . .' Her eyes widened.

'I know. Don't say it.' He knew they were both thinking the same thing. A severed head. A song-and-dance act. In fun?

'And the body?' asked Penelope.

'They'll be looking for it. They say the sea will give it up in its own good time. Mr Seagrave tells me there's one shore around here where bodies always come in . . . but it might take weeks yet.'

She shivered.

'How horrible it is. I don't think I want to go into the sea today.'

'Nor me. It's as if somebody had slipped an alligator into the swimming pool.' He remembered what Mirabel had said: 'It's all spoiled – even my own beach.' And he wondered what the connection was.

'We could go to one of the moorland villages,' Penelope was saying. 'There's a church at Blisland called St Protus and St Hyacinth where there's a remarkable modern screen . . .'

'You sound like a guide book.' Kemp grinned. 'But anything's better than being in Rocksea when the news breaks. And what a happy name, Blisland. Is the church all there is to it?'

'Don't fret,' she said, 'there's bound to be a pub as well.'

'I'm perfectly capable of higher thought,' he told her loftily, 'and who could resist such a misalliance of saints, Protus and Hyacinth indeed!'

The celebrated rood screen proved in fact to be well worth the visit, an astonishing artifact stretched between the cool grey columns of the church in an accomplished harmony of ancient and modern.

Afterwards, they wandered into the churchyard where the granite memorials demonstrated their endurance over centuries – even of Cornish winters. Kemp patted a little headstone commemorating Annie Symons, aged eight years, laid to rest in 1789. 'Don't worry, Annie,' he whispered, 'you didn't miss much.' It might have been bliss to Wordsworth in that dawn to be alive and to be young a very heaven, but to the child beneath the stone life had possibly been nasty, perhaps brutish, and certainly short.

A smile twitched Penelope's mouth. 'Stop brooding on mortality, Lennox,' she said. 'I see a fine-looking inn across the green.'

Chapter Seven

Despite the mullioned windows, pillared doorway and scarlet canopy over it, the Black Boar was in fact quite small inside; a jumble of dodgy little rooms, low-ceilinged and slate-floored. It was packed, not just with people but with objects; every wall was hung with posters, horse-brasses; mottoes jolly and pertinent, pictures old and new, every shelf, angled to knock the head of the unwary, was jammed with Toby jugs and tankards, chipped china and pottery jars, dusty grasses and desiccated flowerheads. From the rafters corn-dollies swung in the air like strangled children.

Kemp and Penelope ducked, and wove their way through to an inner room which seemed quieter. Penelope sat down on an oak settle beside the back window while Kemp made his way to the bar for drinks and a menu. The food was excellent: moist bulging prawn sandwiches on brown loaf, fresh salad, and afterwards, crunchy apple-pie with thick Cornish cream.

'I never really believed one smacked one's lips after a meal,' said Kemp when they'd finished, 'but I do now. Do you want coffee?'

'Not really. It might be a let-down.'

Muffled voices from the other rooms echoed down the stone passages like the roar of a far-off sea. The noise suddenly grew louder as an incoming party approached. Then there was one of those moments that happen over and over again in public houses, and inns, and even in the dining saloons of luxury hotels – the influx of a new set of people upon a company already bunched into some sort of comradeship by the mere fact of having eaten in the same place, and exchanged friendly glances. All eyes turn towards the newcomers, and conversation is suspended as the intruders are assessed, placed and assimilated.

This particular moment had its own disturbing quality, for the young people who entered were so blatantly intoxicated that their high-pitched gaiety cast a gloom over the other occupants of the room by very contrast.

A family with teenage children out for Sunday lunch turned their heads briefly, then drew together in whispered colloquy. Couples who had been conversing contentedly in corners fell silent, casting distrustful glances at the newcomers.

'Sanctuary? Have we found sanctuary?' There was no mistaking the high sing-song voice as Robin Adair followed his noisy companions into the room. There were three men and two women. One was Mirabel Snape. She wore a scant green silk dress, her legs bare and brown as they had been that morning on the sandhills. Trays of drinks were carried in from the bar, hers a large Pimms, greenery curling the brim – that blue-eyed borage Penelope had commented on to Kemp as it had stared out at them from the hedgerows.

'They're tight already,' she said succinctly, bringing her lips close to Kemp's ear. He sensed her disapproval, and was conscious of irritation.

'So were you after the Yacht Club lunch.'

He knew at once it was the wrong thing to have said. 'I mean it's easy to drink a lot when you're on holiday . . .' he finished lamely.

Penelope said nothing, but her eyes darkened.

The girl with Mirabel was a blonde of the outdoor sort, long-legged and tanned, with a haughty look to her features, and a loud neighing voice to match. Mirabel herself was dishevelled, her black hair, sun-dried, standing out in mock Afric style. Her shift had slipped down one shoulder, as she leant, giggling, against one of the young men. Indeed, the whole group were in high spirits as they settled themselves at a table across the room, Robin Adair dancing attendance, a leaping, cavorting, ageless elf.

'Even he is not that young,' remarked Penelope, 'not when you look at him closely. There's a lot of grey in that corn-coloured hair.' She said it with some spite, and Kemp reflected that there was something about the coterie surrounding Mirabel Snape which brought out the worst in people.

Certainly the atmosphere in the room was changed by the incursion. The noisy party effectively took over, chivvying the lone waiter who could only hover irres-olute as they quarrelled over the menu and indulged in that particular kind of mindless horseplay so private to the half-tipsy, so repellent to sober outsiders. Such geared-up jollity was not of the infectious variety which can embrace others, rather it evoked reluctant envy, and Kemp felt his own mood soured as he watched its effect on his companion. The high well-bred voices buzzing in their ears precluded conversation, short-circuiting the pleasurable contentment there had been between them.

'I never expected to see Hooray Henries in a place like this,' Penelope murmured, 'and I don't think much of . . .'

'"Gentlemen-rankers . . . out on the spree, damned from here to eternity,"' muttered Kemp before she could finish what was bound to be further opinion on Mrs Snape. 'Come on, let's leave before they see us.'

'What's it matter? They don't know us.' But as Kemp pushed back his chair and rose, she gathered up her handbag and followed him to the door into the passage.

It was too late. He heard the scurry of feet, the swish of her skirt behind him.

'Lennox Kemp. And it *was* across a crowded room. How prophetic you are!'

Her voice was only slightly slurred, her eyes were laughing at him.

He was conscious of Penelope in the doorway, turning.

'Mrs Snape. How are you?'

'High, and dry.' She stood close to him, sipping her drink. Her hand shook, drops spilt on his sleeve.

'Bring your friends over, Mira,' one of the men hooted. 'Come and join the party.'

'I'm sorry, but we're just leaving.' Kemp addressed himself to Mirabel alone. 'Mrs Snape, I'd like you to meet my fiancée, Penelope Marsden.' He watched them nod distantly to each other, saw the quick astonishment in the hazel eyes, imagined a clouding-over in the blue, then he turned away and followed Penelope down the dark stone passage, through the crowded bar-room and out into the sunshine.

They walked to where they had left their car beside the lychgate of the church. It lay now deep in afternoon shadow, the trees black, bereft of sun. A small chilly wind rustled the bushes round the gravestones.

They had not spoken since leaving the inn and the silence between them was in itself portentous. So far as Kemp was concerned rational thought had fled to limbo, and hovered now like Mahomet's coffin in some space between heaven and earth. There had been such an element of comicality about the scene in the grotesque parlour of the Black Boar that he would have laughed outright had he not also been aware of the deeper implications.

He had managed, by a few words thrown at random, to get himself engaged, geared up, as it were, for marriage. He had settled his future – their future – on a sudden impulse, and not a very creditable impulse at that. For he knew that in those seconds with Mirabel Snape standing at his elbow he had grasped at a means of escape, as a man hurled over a cliff might clutch at the nearest branch to save himself from the fall.

He was shaken by the experience – one new to him, since he considered himself to be sane in judgement – but one part of his mind said his reaction had been inevitable. The other part, which he would stifle if he could, told him he'd taken a lurch into the absurd.

As they got into the car, he was aware of Penelope's quizzical look. He automatically fastened his seat-belt and the routine act helped to restore sanity – at least for the time being.

Penelope was the first to speak. 'Did you mean it, Lennox . . . what you said in there? Or were you just trying to get out of an embarrassing situation?'

'Of course I meant it. And why should it have been embarrassing?' It seemed a trite word to cover what he really felt. Panic. Panic had made him jump for cover like a scared bunny-rabbit. Enough of that; he had chosen a path and must follow it. 'Of course I meant what I said, Penny dear.'

Her eyes searched his face but it gave her no sign.

'You could have asked me first . . .'

'And what would you have said?'

'That it's still too soon . . . Oh, I don't know.' She made a sudden, tired gesture. 'We thought it would be all so rational, this taking of a decision. Now it's become confused . . .'

He turned awkwardly in his seat and kissed her.

'I bet St Protus and St Hyacinth were confused too, half-Pagan, half-Christian as they must have been . . .' He unclipped his seat-belt and kissed her properly.

Her response was warm enough to dispel the darker thought, and brought them back to something of their morning mood.

But as they drove away she said: 'How did Mrs Snape know your name.'

Kemp shrugged.

'Names seem to get bandied about in these parts.'

'Like Steve Donray's?'

'Perhaps.'

Penelope was silent for a while as the peaceful fields slid by, the blue haze of afternoon gathering, changing the colours, cooling the air.

'You don't suppose they knew, did they? That set with Mrs Snape?'

Kemp swore as a tractor backed nonchalantly into their path from a field gateway. He braked, and swerved round it. He was rewarded with a cheery wave and a spatter of manure on the bonnet.

'No,' he said, gritting his teeth, 'no, they couldn't have known. They can't be that heartless. They've probably been carousing round the countryside since breakfast-time. It wouldn't be on the news yet, and they're not the sort to listen anyway . . .'

'You don't have to protect her, you know.'

'Who is protecting who? What are you talking about?'

Sensing his barely suppressed anger, her courage receded.

'I'm sorry, Lennox. Too much is happening too fast . . .'

He laughed. 'What? In this rustic solitude where every prospect pleases?'

'And only man is vile . . . We must stop this, Lennox, and get back to our own real lives.'

'I agree.' Kemp felt he was building a bridge and trying to cross it at the same time. It seemed to span a greater abyss than he had the materials for. 'Let's celebrate our engagement tonight, eh?'

But it was a muted celebration, for the news of the discovery of Steve Donray's head had been the main topic of conversation in the bar of the White House, and over the dinner tables afterwards.

Phyllis Morris came up to them when they were having coffee in the lounge. Although she and Penelope were old friends, Phyllis had been too busy with her other guests to allow time for the chat they both wanted.

'The Carradines are awfully anxious to have a game of bridge this evening. I know you play, Penny – what about you, Lennox?'

'Sorry. I'm uncivilized in that respect, but take Penny if she wants to. Do you, my love? I'm thinking of a walk, anyway.'

Penelope hesitated. 'I admit to being too tired for a walk. Besides, the wind seems to have risen. It's so comfortable in here . . . Yes, I'd like to play, if you wouldn't mind?'

She wondered if her decision was setting out a pattern of their future, their separate ways; they were being so tenderly polite to each other.

Phyllis glanced at them both, but as a hostess she was pleased nevertheless.

'Good. Then I'll ask Susan Trevanion to make a fourth. She's always delighted to come for bridge here in the evening, and she hasn't managed out much lately.'

She went to the telephone. Kemp rose. 'Be interesting for you to meet Miss Trevanion. The other side of the picture, perhaps.'

Putting on an anorak and warm scarf – for Penelope had been right, a chilly wind was blowing and the sunset had been an angry one, fighting black clouds piling up from the south-west – he met Phyllis Morris in the hall.

'Susan's glad to come. Apparently her niece has brought some friends back, and she's glad to escape.'

Chapter Eight

After two fast rubbers, the time being by then nine thirty, Penelope had found Susan Trevanion to be a brisk, intelligent partner and one who obviously relished the game.

'My roots may go back as far as Culbertson,' she explained in the gentle, precise tone of a lady conscious of her age and the advantages it carried, 'but I've also imbibed Acol to keep abreast of the times . . .'

As Penelope was to reflect later, there's nothing like a game of bridge to sort out character. Within the short time it takes to play a few hands all traits are revealed; the good losers and those who take it hard, the ones who like winning, the casual philosophers who don't care either way, and the superficially calm who betray an edge of steel.

Miss Trevanion had that edge of steel.

Penelope herself was a defensive player, adept at making the most of a weak hand to subtly destroy an overweening contract but she lacked the aggressive spirit necessary for the higher bids. That too was indicative of her true nature; she reserved her competitive side for her profession.

The Carradines were relatively new to the pastime. They had studied the books, learnt from experts, and had all the enthusiasm of the newly-initiated. They enjoyed the game for its own sake.

'You're terribly good together, you two,' said Sophie as she shuffled, preparatory for another rubber.

'Just the luck of the cards.' Susan Trevanion smiled.

Penelope smiled back. She found herself liking Mirabel Snape's aunt. It was not simply her courtesy and pleasant manner, but she also exhibited none of the affectations sometimes associated with country ladies of her class and breeding. In the inevitable chat between games she showed friendly interest in Penelope's work, as she did in the Carradines' search for a retirement home.

The next hand had been dealt when there was an interruption.

Phyllis Morris crossed the lounge to their corner, her face anxious.

'I'm sorry to have to break in but that was a phone call from your house, Susan. Mr Adair . . . he says your niece has been taken ill again.'

Miss Trevanion frowned.

'Mirabel? Oh dear, just when we thought she was getting better. I must go to her. Did Robin say whether he'd called the doctor?'

'Yes, he did, but apparently Dr Griffin was out on a call. A message has been left for him.'

Susan Trevanion had risen and was slipping her outer jacket over her shoulders.

'Mr Adair did seem a bit worried,' went on Phyllis. 'Mirabel's had some sort of collapse, he said, and Dr Griffin being out, they don't know what kind of medication she was having.' She glanced in Penelope's direction. 'I'm afraid we have to rely on the practice in Westerbridge and in cases like this it might be some time before he gets the message.'

'If you think I could be of any help, Miss Trevanion,' said Penelope, not wishing to intrude but feeling it to be her duty in the circumstances, 'I should be glad to go along with you – at least until the doctor arrives.'

For the first time Susan Trevanion seemed put out.

'Not at all, Mrs Marsden. I wouldn't dream of it. I know sufficient of my niece's troubles to deal with this.'

'At least someone should walk down the road with you, Susan. It's dark, and blowing a gale. I'll get Bob.'

'There's no need.' Susan was already swiftly going towards the door.

Phyllis gave Penelope a pleading look. 'Robin Adair sounded very agitated, and there's no one else in that house with any medical knowledge. I think you should go with her, Penny, if you wouldn't mind.'

'Of course I don't mind. My coat's hanging in the hall. I'll grab it as I go past.'

'Susan Trevanion may not look it, but she's nearly eighty,' Phyllis muttered as they went out together. 'I hate to see her trying to cope with this thing alone. I'm relieved you're going.'

Miss Trevanion had almost reached the end of the drive when Penelope caught up with her.

'Yours is the lovely grey stone house in that grove of pines, isn't it?' she remarked, falling into step and speaking casually to avoid any hint that her presence might be unwelcome. 'I realize it isn't far but there are times when one needs company.'

The other made an impatient gesture as if to repudiate any such suggestion.

'We are quite used to walking on our own in Rocksea. However, now that you are here I'd better explain that my niece, Mrs Snape, has recently suffered a nervous breakdown and there have been certain after-effects. Under Dr Griffin's care there has been considerable improvement, but he warned us there could be setbacks . . .'

Penelope made no comment. Indeed, she could scarcely hear Miss Trevanion's words against the sound of the wind, and the groaning of the high branches as the trees took its full force.

'. . . and they are not pines, Mrs Marsden, they're macrocarpels.' Miss Trevanion turned in to an entrance between stone pillars. Penelope followed her, feeling chidden. The old lady has her pride, she thought, and she certainly knows how to keep her end up. She doesn't want me to see her beloved niece lying dead drunk but outright refusal of my company would have been plain rudeness; good manners had prevailed.

Most of the dwellings in Rocksea had names relating to either their colour or their building material – sometimes both, as in the case of Greystones House. Even on this turbulent night it had a bland, ageless look, as if having faced the sea for so long it could never be surprised, and its wide-stretching lawns isolated it from any troubles beyond its thickset hedges.

That only applied of course to stones and mortar – there were troubles enough inside.

Even the hall, the pivotal feature of the interior, demonstrated a kind of chaos.

Robin Adair, his hair ruffled, his silk shirt open to the waist and stained with what looked like spilt wine, had been out on the porch. Penelope, drawing back, couldn't hear the muttered words that passed between them as he lowered his head to Susan Trevanion's shoulder. Whatever was said, he made way for the old lady as she walked straight across the hall and disappeared through an open door to the left. Then he followed her. He took no notice of Penelope. She wasn't even sure he had seen her.

She looked around her. The massive central table was cluttered with half-full pewter tankards, some beer cans and an empty wine bottle as well as a horse's bridle, a tin of saddle soap and a child's toy. Setting an upturned chair to rights, and stepping carefully through the various items of outdoor clothing and footwear scattered on the floor, she too made her way towards the open door of what was clearly the drawing-room.

It was softly lit, long windows open to the night sky, their chintz curtains pulled back neatly in their furnishing bands as though there was never a need for privacy. A fire, small for the vast fireplace, glowed and crackled opposite a sofa on which Mirabel Snape was reclining, her aunt by now faithfully at her side.

'We put it on because she was shivering,' the blonde girl with the high voice observed to no one in particular.

'It is a cold night, though,' said Penelope pleasantly, 'and Mrs Snape seems to have recovered.'

Robin Adair was leaning over the back of a chair. He looked at Penelope, and through her.

'I came with Miss Trevanion, and to see if I could help in any way.'

Susan Trevanion gave him a sharp look. 'Mrs Marsden's a nurse,' she said. 'She kindly offered to accompany me.'

Penelope was conscious of an awkwardness as everyone in the room looked at her, their expressions by no means friendly. She recognized some of the party who had been in the Blisland pub; they seemed to be more sober now.

Her professional training concentrating her mind, she went across to the patient.

Mirabel's appearance was startling. To begin with, there were her clothes; a T-shirt soiled and smelling both of drink and vomit, a brief cut-down denim skirt frayed at the edge in the fashion of teenagers but incongruous on her, dirty sandals exposing raw bones on grubby ankles, she might have been any washed-up punk on the streets of Brixton. If Lennox could only see her now! But the woman's face under the damp strands of hair banished Penelope's fleeting thought as quickly as it had arisen. For Mirabel Snape's cheeks were yellow-white, her mouth grey and twitching, while her eyes stared blankly into nothingness, unblinking, unseeing. She's in a catatonic state, Penelope surmised, and it's serious . . .

'What drugs is she taking, Miss Trevanion?'

Susan withdrew her arm from where it had lain protectively round her niece.

'Whatever Dr Griffin has prescribed. She has been taking them regularly. They are for depression . . .' She was looking, not at Penelope, but directly at Robin Adair.

As if on cue, he straightened up. 'It's got nothing to do with the pills she's on, Mrs Marsden. She's under proper medication by her General Practitioner, and her aunt and I have seen how much she has improved . . .'

There was an insolent look in his eyes despite the innocuous words, and Penelope was nettled.

'No form of medication should be taken with alcohol, Mr Adair. Everyone knows that.'

She felt her voice coming out fierce and disapproving, the voice she occasionally used with recalcitrant probationers and always regretted afterwards, even when it got results.

'I say, that's a bit steep. Nothing wrong with Mirabel today that I could see . . .' It was one of the men she'd been pleased to call a Hooray Henry earlier in the day. Penelope was suddenly tired of them all.

She turned on him. 'Okay. Then what put Mrs Snape into this state, you tell me that?'

It was the blonde girl who answered, her voice lowered an octave, and more hesitant.

'It's just as Henry says.' His name really was Henry. 'Mirabel was fine earlier today. We all went out for a bit of a celebration. Tony'd won a packet at the Bolventor point-to-point yesterday, so we phoned Mirabel last night and said we'd bring the champagne . . . We had a glass or two here, didn't we, Miss Trevanion? Then we went off to Blisland for a pub lunch . . .'

'Didn't I see you there?' Henry's globular, gooseberry eyes weren't as vacant as they looked. Penelope nodded.

'Well, then. And Cousin Mira was all right when we got back, wasn't she, Aunt Susan?'

'I'm afraid I saw very little of her. None of you were around at tea-time.' Miss Trevanion pursed her lips. 'And then I put Simon to bed.'

Robin Adair gave his high, tinkling laugh. 'We'd had a hilarious game of cricket on the lawn to amuse the little chap. Then some of us went for a walk on the dunes, didn't we, Sally?'

'You didn't get further than the Mariner's Arms, you lazy sod,' Sally remarked.

'Did Mrs Snape have anything more to drink?' asked Penelope, striving to keep her voice free of censure.

They all looked at one another.

'Well, I suppose after the sun was over the jolly old yardarm,' Henry drawled, 'and we'd had a bite to eat . . . Sorry, Aunt, the kitchen must be still in a mess . . .'

'Tamsin saw to that,' said Sally, 'and I heard her remind Mirabel to take her pills. For a Cornish maid she's quite smart, that one. Then we all sat around, I suppose . . .'

'At one point Mira was cleaning tack on the hall table. I remember she asked if there was any of that wine left we had at supper. I gave her another glass . . .' Henry became defensive. 'But she was okay – in high spirits, I should say. Nothing wrong with her then . . .'

'She went bonkers.' The lean, rangy Tony was a man of few words. Perhaps he kept them for his horse. 'Absolute bonkers.'

Everyone turned to him, and waited. It appeared that you had to with Tony, so Penelope kept her mouth shut.

'I was having a lie-down in that study room with the TV. Got a bit tired, you know, had to put the old legs up. Mirabel came in. Didn't see me. Some bloke droolin' away on the box . . .'

'What do you mean – she went bonkers?' asked Penelope.

'What I said. Started screaming her head off. Dashed for the door. Fell flat on her face in the hall. Certainly brought you lot running.'

Sally's hands were shaking as she lit a cigarette. 'I put a cushion under her head, and got her some water. She came round in a few minutes but she wouldn't talk. She just stared at me as if she didn't know who I was. It was dreadful.'

'That's when I called you, Aunt Susan,' said Robin. 'It didn't seem like any ordinary faint – more like a complete collapse. We were worried . . .'

'You did quite right. And I'm glad you left a message for Dr Griffin. When he's seen poor Mirabel, then I shall know whether or not to telephone Vincent in London.'

Robin Adair looked at his watch. 'It's nearly half past ten. Do you think you should worry him this late?'

'It will depend on what the doctor says when he comes.'

Penelope was surprised at this exchange between them, the rest of the company taking no part in it. She had already been trying to disentangle relationships: Henry called Mirabel cousin, and Miss Trevanion, aunt, so he appeared to be a relative, and Sally and Tony friends of his. Robin Adair also addressed her as 'Aunt Susan' but in a playful way to which she made no objection – indeed, she treated him almost like a member of the family. Penelope recalled the remark of the brigadier: 'Lots of our memsahibs go to his classes' – perhaps Miss Trevanion was one of them. To Penelope's honest mind, Robin Adair had all the makings of an old-fashioned gigolo . . .

Something prompted her to say: 'Have any of you people had the news on today?'

They stared. Susan was the only one to answer.

'I listened to the radio at one o'clock but I missed the six o'clock news because I was with the baby. We very rarely have the television on. My maid, Tamsin Jago, watches it of course.'

'It must have been nearly nine thirty when you were in the study, Mr – er – Tony?' Penelope tried to keep the question casual.

'Spot on.' He clicked his finger and thumb. 'Spot on. Announcer chappie. Wasn't really listenin' . . . Bit of shut-eye, you know. The national drivel was over . . . they'd got to the local stuff.'

Penelope was conscious of Robin's eyes on her. In the flickering firelight they were round and black, the eyes of a bad child.

Hurried footsteps sounded in the hall, and a small figure burst into the room. She had reddish hair, screwed into a knob on top of her head, and a freckled face the colour of an Orange Pippin. She wore a fluffy blue dressing-gown and her feet were bare.

'Why isn't Miss Mirabel in bed? I got up to Simon just five minutes ago and looked in her room and she wasn't there . . . Oh, Miss Trevanion, I didn't know you were back? She's going to be all right, isn't she?'

'What are you doing here, Tamsin? I thought you'd gone home hours ago.'

'I couldn't leave her, could I? So I phoned my gran and said I'd be staying over.'

She took no notice of anyone else as she knelt in front of Mirabel Snape, and pulled at the inert hands. 'She fell in such a faint, the poor lamb, and they'd have given her brandy but I said no, it had to be only water. Come on, love, let's get you cleaned up.'

'Tamsin did give us some help earlier on, Miss Trevanion,' Sally said, somewhat belatedly.

The maid, she couldn't have been more than sixteen, gave her a scornful look, then turned all her attention to Mirabel. She brought out a handful of tissues from her pocket, smoothed the black hair from the pallid forehead, wiped round the staring eyes, and scrubbed gently at the quivering mouth.

'The doctor is coming, Tamsin, he'll see to all that.'

For the first time Susan Trevanion seemed to find herself inadequate.

'He'll not see her like this,' said the maid fiercely, 'properly washed and in her bed, that's where he'll see her. Come along now, Miss Mirabel.'

Under the rough but tender ministration, Mrs Snape seemed to come out of her stupor, the stiffness fell away, and her limbs relaxed. Only her eyes remained blank. She allowed herself to be lifted from the sofa, and between them Susan and Tamsin held her limp body upright. Only then did others rush in to help.

'Let her be, she's all right now.' Tamsin wanted no help, but Penelope stepped forward and relieved Susan from the burden of her niece. She and Tamsin went towards the door, half-carrying Mirabel, who lurched like a sleepwalker at every step.

Fortunately the staircase was wide with shallow risers. Penelope was used to supporting patients, and though Tamsin Jago was small she was sturdily built and knew what she was doing. Penelope speculated grimly that perhaps this was not the first time she had put Mirabel Snape to bed.

'Bathroom first,' she whispered to the girl, and Tamsin nodded. 'In here.'

When Mrs Snape was in bed, washed and in a clean nightgown, Penelope went back and took a look in the bathroom cabinet. She showed a small bottle to Tamsin.

'Is this the medication prescribed for Mrs Snape?'

'Yes, she's down to only two tablets night and morning. She forgets sometimes, so I remind her . . .'

Penelope looked closely at the label. She knew the drug, she'd come across it on the wards when she had done her psychiatric training. A bit strong, she thought, for simple depression, particularly for a patient not hospitalized, and the last thing one would take with even the smallest amount of alcohol. Were they all completely mad in this house?

'You a nurse?' asked the girl as they went back to the bedroom to see if Mirabel was settled.

'Yes, and you'd make a good one, Tamsin. You know the right things to do, and you've plenty of common sense – that's the basis of nursing.'

'I'd have liked to do nursing,' said Tamsin, 'but I haven't even got the "O" levels. I did three months at The Respite Hospital – that's a place up the valley where they take private patients, mostly them that's not quite right in the head . . . I liked the work. 'Course I was only cleaning up and that, but I got on really well with the residents – that's what they call them. They were all right. I've met dafter folk outside.'

Penelope looked in at the door of Mrs Snape's bedroom.

Their patient was not asleep, but there was a little more colour in her face now, although her eyes were still staring, unseeing.

Penelope went across to the bed as she saw Mirabel's lips move. She leaned over to catch the muttered words.

'Robin . . . it was real, that head. It was a real head. That was a joke about kicking it . . . into the sea . . . wasn't it? Robin . . .'

Penelope was thankful when the lids slowly came down over the blank eyes, shutting out the horror in them.

Chapter Nine

'And did you stay long enough to meet the amazing Dr Griffin who wields such power in that household?'

Penelope and Kemp were lying in bed. It was the end of a very long conversation and in a place made for more pleasurable activity than mere talking and listening.

She grimaced. 'You may be right about the power, not about the person. I met him briefly on the doorstep as I was leaving, and introduced myself. He wasn't impressed – and neither was I.'

'How come?'

'A furtive, seedy little man. Not my idea of a country physician at all. He was creepy and self-important at the same time. I didn't stay to see how he was received . . .'

'Sounds as if he was awaited like the Second Coming.'

'That's about it. Even Robin Adair, usually so light-some of tongue, used the term general practitioner as though it were some kind of totem pole.'

'What a fascinating evening you had, Penny. The only excitement in my dull walk was losing my scarf to the wind . . . It's probably in Padstow by now.'

Penelope turned to him. Her voice changed.

'Hold me close. I'm frightened.'

'No more talking, then.'

The closeness of their bodies, skin to skin, lapped them in a warm security, as individual desire reached out from one to the other, merging in blissful content – a night-fire to keep demons at bay.

But the demons were back by morning.

Penelope was the first to give voice to nagging anxiety.

'Let's have breakfast up here. I can't face Phyllis yet – she's bound to question. Should I tell someone what Mirabel said last night?'

'Only you heard it?'

'I think so. Tamsin was over by the door. And it was just a whisper.'

Kemp busied himself ordering from the kitchen downstairs. It gave him time to think. He found it both difficult and distressing trying to reconcile Penelope's graphic picture of the sick woman, the pathetic ugliness of its implications, with the shining figure that had come from the sea, or the laughing face under the wild hair that had taunted him at the inn. Intoxicated she may have been even then, but still tantalizingly beautiful.

He cursed such romantic images, but some emptiness inside himself must have been waiting for them, and now would not let go.

'Vincent Snape. You heard Miss Trevanion mention him?'

'She only said Vincent, but Robin Adair knew who she meant all right. I think he tried to put her off phoning him. Funny, that. You'd have thought the husband should have been the first to know his wife was ill.'

'Her aunt told you of a nervous breakdown, and of an improvement. That sounds as if it was some time ago. Presumably she came to Cornwall to recover.' Kemp was steering a cautious path. 'If Mr Snape

94

wanted me to assume he had a happy marriage he's hardly likely to mention that his wife's had a nervous breakdown.'

'From a professional point of view,' said Penelope impatiently, 'I never know quite what people mean by a nervous breakdown. In Mrs Snape's case she's just got a drink problem. No wonder your client didn't mention it. And those bruises on her body aren't new . . . They're fading. She must have been falling about in her London home before she ever came down here.'

'What bruises?'

'All down one side, and on her back. I told you last night.'

Kemp hadn't wanted to hear; the disclosure had struck at his own nerves. But now his curiosity overcame other feelings.

'What did you make of them, these bruises?'

'There could be several explanations. A fall downstairs, or against heavy furniture. People made insensible through drink or drugs tend to fall about even in their own homes. I've seen plenty of cases like that.' She hesitated. 'And of course women who've . . .' She shook her head. 'But that certainly wouldn't be possible here.'

'What wouldn't be possible?'

A discreet knock on the door signalled the arrival of breakfast, and over it they discussed their own plans, for the day ahead and for the future.

Penelope was uneasy. 'I feel we're rushing things, Lennox, or rather you are. I've never known you so impulsive. It's almost as if you were afraid of something.'

'Being left on the shelf. Travelling towards old age on a single ticket.' Spooning up grapefruit and trying

95

not to think too hard, he responded with a lightness he didn't feel.

'That can't be it. You've been a loner too long to let that worry you. All the same, I'm not going to rush off a letter to Uncle and Aunt saying you and I are going to be married. After all, we've still got another ten days down here.'

'Perhaps that's what I'm afraid of.' As quickly as he said it, he knew it was true. He nearly added, 'Let's get the hell out . . .' Suddenly he wanted to be back in London, in Newtown, in familiar territory, with people he knew and the work that could engage his mind to the full instead of letting it wander about chasing shadows. He was out of his element in this place of empty skies – he preferred rooftops – and the rolling fields that waited for something to happen, the long sinister beaches and the never-ending tides that swept in and out careless as to whether they bore crab-eaten bodies or harmless beach balls. There were things here he couldn't handle – and one of them was Mirabel Snape.

Penelope spoke and brought him back sharply to reality and its problems.

'You haven't answered me, Lennox. Should I tell anyone what I heard last night?'

His mind swung in another direction. Hadn't he made it part of his job these last few years to track down murderers, setting his own path through deception and ignorance to satisfy his innate sense of absolute justice. Why not exercise that talent now?

So he answered her firmly. 'No, not yet. Not until I've had the chance to renew acquaintance with an old song – Robin Adair.'

Penelope was dispatched to question Phyllis Morris.

Robin, an artist of sorts, had been around for some time. Possibly six years. At least for as long as the Morrises had owned the White House. He had come originally from London. Oh, his credentials were all right, he had studied at St Martin's, had exhibited in small galleries, sold paintings, and appeared to have income, although erratic, sufficient to keep himself. He had been for a few months part-time tutor in Art at a local college – Falmouth, Phyllis thought. Anyway, he'd given that up, and now held private classes around Rocksea and in Westerbridge. Quite recently there had been some surprise when Miss Trevanion offered him accommodation in one of the outbuildings at Greystones where he now had a studio.

'I think we ought to avoid the house today,' said Penelope, as she and Kemp passed the entrance and continued as directed along the dunes to where a sand-road led to the rear of the premises.

There was a notice tacked on to what had originally been a carriage-house. It said 'Adair's Studio' and beside it hung a seascape, brightly if crudely painted and representing a watery view of the ocean and headlands.

The door was open. Inside the place was neat. A table held specimens of the local pottery, dun-coloured with blue markings, which Penelope had admired in the Westerbridge shops. There were pictures on the walls, some framed, some simply on canvas. Others were stacked against the walls. It was a surprisingly spacious area with a good northern light and was obviously a workshop, no frills.

On a bench among mugs holding brushes, and bottles of spirit, turpentine and linseed oil there was another notice: 'Please look around. If you wish attention, ring', and a small bell stood beside it.

Kemp pressed the bell and it echoed in a further room. There came the sound of a closing door and footsteps. Kemp gave Penelope a nudge: 'Out,' he whispered, 'he's already met you. I'm the prospective purchaser, and lover of art.'

She slipped out, strolled down the path and waited round the corner of the hedge.

Kemp turned.

'Good morning. It's Mr Adair, isn't it? I was told by Mrs Morris at the White House that you might have some local paintings for sale.'

Robin Adair looked fresh and mettlesome today. He was dressed casually but with calculated effect in skin-tight black jeans and a big mohair-and-lurex jumper as irridescent as newly-caught mackerel. It gave him bulk and accentuated his slimness. He moved like a ballet dancer, and even when at a standstill he kept rising on the balls of his feet as if about to take off into an arabesque.

'I do some local views, yes. You're very welcome to look round my humble abode. Staying at the White House?'

'Yes. Down for a couple of weeks. Like the neighbourhood a lot. Wanted something to take back to remind me of it.'

'Are you interested at all in modern art, Mr – ?'

'Kemp. Lennox Kemp. Well, no, not really. I just wanted something pretty to hang up at home.' Kemp spoke apologetically, as if he'd asked Michelangelo to paint his bathroom ceiling.

Adair had small darkish eyes that glittered like his

jersey. Some of the glitter went out of them now, but a sale was still a sale.

'Most of my local stuff's on the walls. Take your time, Mr Kemp. If there's nothing there you like perhaps I could rustle one up for you. I'm about to have coffee. Care to join me?'

'That's very kind of you.' Kemp walked up to the pictures, examined them closely, stood back. 'I like some of these.'

'All right in a mug?' Robin called from the inner room.

'Fine for me.'

Kemp went round pulling back some of the canvases stacked against the wall. Most of the pictures were much the same as the others, some much better. The artist was certainly prolific.

Over in one corner were smaller ones, covered in old torn wrappings and dust. They obviously hadn't been touched for a long time. Kemp flicked through them. They were all abstracts, experiments in form, shape and colour. They were good. He drew one out: concentric curves, blue, white and silver, a breaking wave over black rock sliced into stern triangles. He'd seen something like it before. He peered down at the corner: 'R. Adair 1979'.

Robin came in carrying a tray with coffee mugs.

'Sugar?'

'No, thanks. I say, I like those over in that corner, and particularly this one.'

The artist looked at it. 'And you said you weren't interested in modern art!'

'Well, I know what I like,' Kemp defended himself stoutly. 'Do you do many like this?'

'Not any more. It was a phase I went through. We

all go through it. Mine didn't last. To be quite honest, Mr Kemp, it didn't pay.'

Kemp brought the small canvas over to the table, sat down and sipped his coffee.

'It's got a date on it, 1979. When did you stop painting like this? I thought artists developed into abstracts when they'd grown tired of the representational kind?'

Robin gave a short laugh.

'Well, I went the opposite way. These date from my college days, or just after. When I finally settled in Cornwall I found if I wanted to make a living I had to make the sea look like the sea, and a field of corn had to have the ears shown, and every cow had four legs. People want views of things they can recognize. It's what sells.'

'Don't you ever sell any of your abstracts?'

Robin looked at the canvas on the table as if reassessing its merits.

'Haven't sold one in years. Pity . . . it's really good now I look at it again.' He shrugged. 'But what's the use? All that the tourists want is a pretty picture of their favourite cove, and a blue sky over all.'

'Ah yes, tourists like me, Mr Adair.' Kemp smiled.

Robin's face took on an impish look. He placed his brown spatulate finger-ends together in an attitude of prayer.

'"I am poor Brother Lippo, by your leave!"'

There was no doubt the man had charm, and if the early abstracts were anything to go by, he had wasted his talents. But it could be of course that he had others, not wholly artistic.

'I'll take both of these, Mr Adair. The little abstract and that view of Rocksea over there.'

'Thank you, thank you, kind sir, for these mercies.' Robin Adair was skipping about finding paper and string. 'A man after me own heart, to be sure . . . You haven't even asked the prices!'

He named a not extortionate sum, and Kemp wrote him out a cheque.

They finished their coffee in amiable conversation and the desultory exchange of opinions on art in general. If Robin Adair realized he was being subtly quizzed he gave no sign, but drawing people out without their being aware of it was Kemp's forte. He discovered that for all his public frolicking Adair was serious in his own field; there was no cheap sniping at the enthusiastic amateurs who attended his classes.

'Most of them are retired. It's a relaxing hobby, but some have a genuine gift. Take Miss Trevanion now, you'd think she'd go in for dainty watercolours like she probably did at school . . . But no, she's a strong painter in oils, with a good eye for a composition. And some of my other elderly pupils are also surprising. Probably wasted their lives in the pursuit of money.' He couldn't resist the gibe.

'We all have to live,' said Kemp equably. 'What about her niece, Mrs Snape?'

'She doesn't come to my classes,' Robin answered, without change of expression. 'She's just a visitor, only been here a few weeks.' He got up, and handed Kemp the wrapped pictures. Kemp tucked them under his arm, and pushed back his chair.

'Pretty woman,' he observed slyly, as one appreciative male to another. 'I suppose there's a husband somewhere?'

'He toils in the City, I understand. I've never met him.' Robin's eyes narrowed. 'And if I were you, Mr

Kemp, I'd lay off Mrs Snape . . . She's not some kind of local tourist attraction.' His full lips curled back over white teeth, but there was no warmth in the smile.

Kemp immediately took offence as it was intended he should.

'My dear Mr Adair, I meant no disrespect to the lady . . . Nor would I dream of trespassing on another man's property.' He accompanied the words with what he hoped was a sufficiently salacious leer to signal knowledge, and even complicity, in the other man's affair. 'Like the Prior's niece, eh, Brother Lippo?'

Kemp often found that people who make literary allusions can't stand them being hurled back. Robin Adair had been rendered speechless but his stance, weaving slightly on nimble feet ready to spring, looked dangerous. Kemp went quickly through the studio door.

Damn it, he thought, I never brought up the subject of Donray's head.

Chapter Ten

Although it was some six years since Lennox Kemp had worked at Prendergasts, the Westerbridge solicitors, the tempo of life in the Duchy was such that he was not surprised to find Albury Prendergast still in the same room overlooking the river.

'And still working on the same case,' Kemp remarked cheekily, squinting at the name on the file.

'Not so,' Albury admonished, 'this doesn't refer to Poacher Perryman but his offspring, young Reggie. And when you were here last Reggie was only a ten-year-old pinching sweets from the supermarket counter, but deemed by law to be in that twilight zone of infancy when he's capable of knowing right from wrong but exempt from full criminal responsibility . . .'

'And thus safe from prison, transportation or the gallows?'

'Or the probation officer, the foster parent or the approved school,' added Albury, laughing. He and Kemp had done their legal training during the same period.

'And Reggie's now following faithfully in Father's footsteps?'

'Don't we all?' Albury looked round complacently. 'Adrian has retired but I like this room better than his.' He swept the file aside. 'It's good to see you. Are you looking for a job?'

'No, I'm nicely placed, thank you. And your elegiac

landscape unnerves me. I don't think I could work in all this pastoral simplicity.'

After chatting for a while over coffee, which was rather better flavoured than that from the machine in the Yacht Club, Kemp brought up the subject of the recent drugs find off the estuary.

'So far as I know they haven't traced that boat which wasn't showing lights,' said Albury. 'Probably scarpered when it was challenged. But there've been repercussions – nasty phone calls to some of the lifeboatmen, and their wives. Even threats to rough up their children on their way to school. That's pretty serious around here, with the distances they have to travel . . .' Albury sounded concerned. 'And the police haven't had much luck in tracing such calls. The whole operation's possibly being orchestrated from far off. Drug-running's big money, as I'm sure you know. Somebody's attempting to shut mouths. Why're you interested?'

'I'm staying at Rocksea. A head's come up out of the sea. Chap called Steve Donray.'

'Yes, I heard. I used to go out in his boat but not for a year or two. Mr Donray was after bigger fish than pollock – or so they say.'

'What was he like?'

'Grew up in Padstow and lived there all his life. Seafaring family from a long way back. His great-grandad had the name of being in with the wreckers. Some Padstownians still think they've the right to take more than just fish out of the sea . . . Donray would be getting on a bit – he would be nearly fifty by now. Got a taste of the good life a while ago, and liked to throw his weight about. Not the brightest of men, except at the helm.'

'Could he have been in on drug-running exploits?'

'That's my surmise, but don't quote me on it. Curiosity still your vice?'

'That's me,' Kemp laughed, 'even on holiday.'

'Then why not have a word with Mr Gudgeon if you really want to follow this up?'

'Inspector Gudgeon still at Bodmin?'

'Yes. Like me to give him a ring? So far as I know, they've not yet pulled anyone in on the drugs haul, but they're working on the hypothesis that there must have been a local connection. Bound to have been someone along the coast with a boat to fetch the drop in from the buoy, and it's probably been a regular run.'

Even Sergeant Ivell at the police station in Bodmin remembered Kemp.

'Well, well, if it isn't Mr Kemp. Not down on business, I hope?' For Ivell could recall the last time;* they preferred police business to be kept on an even keel at their station, and Kemp on that other occasion had demanded a somewhat unorthodox approach. Still, it had got results, solved one crime and prevented several more.

Kemp shook his head. 'Nice to meet you again, Mr Ivell, but no, I'm only a tourist.' He had found this form of self-deprecation to be the accepted norm.

'Great weather for it. Mr Prendergast said you'd like a word with the Inspector.'

'Just a social call, renew acquaintance, you know.'

But Gudgeon wasn't as easily taken in. After initial courtesies were over he asked: 'What do you really want?'

Kemp came straight to the point. Even in this law-abiding area detective-inspectors are busy people.

* *The Sitting Ducks.*

'I've heard of two odd happenings since I came to Rocksea, and I wondered if they're connected. A haul of drugs, and the disappearance of a fisherman.'

'If it's Mr Steven Donray you're talking about, he's been found.'

'So I gather – or at least a part of him has . . .'

'It's Mr Donray all right. His brother's identified the – er – the remains.'

'The body's not turned up, then?'

'The sea'll give it back in its own time.' There was nothing folksy about Detective-Inspector Gudgeon despite his turn of phrase. 'What's your interest?'

'Sheer curiosity,' Kemp said, with relish. 'I've not got a client, if that's what's worrying you. I'm not here on business.'

Gudgeon relaxed.

'The coastguards have been suspicious for some time about goings-on out beyond the estuary. There've been too many fast motor yachts spotted closer inshore than they've a right to be all along the north coast, but with limited resources it's the devil's own job to challenge them. That night they got lucky, thanks to the lifeboat, and the chap who found the marker buoy.'

'What was in the package?'

'A mixed bag. Which is unusual. Normally when there's a haul it's all the one substance. This was mostly cocaine – good quality, the Drugs Squad tell me – but there were other things too, amphetamines, LSD, that sort of stuff. All neatly wrapped, all watertight. It's been done before.'

'Would the late Mr Donray have been mixed up in it?'

The Inspector's round blue eyes gazed at him in mock horror.

'You know I can't answer that, Mr Kemp.'

'Any idea when he lost his head – and I don't mean metaphorically?'

'I can't answer that either,' Gudgeon growled. 'There'll be a medical report in due course. Postmortem can wait for the body. It's not our concern anyway, unless there's been a crime committed.'

'Yes . . . but I'm sure Dr Mordaunt must have had a chat with you,' Kemp coaxed gently. He knew the Medical Examiner was a friend of Gudgeon's. 'It's still Dr Mordaunt, isn't it?'

The Inspector cleared his throat. 'You being who you are, Mr Kemp, and interested, like . . . I don't mind telling you that Dr Mordaunt finds that head fascinating. Might well get a footnote in the books on forensics. Just having that, and not knowing when the rest will turn up. From his preliminary medical examination he says that head was sheared off after death, possibly some time after. Sheared off – that's what he said.'

'Could Donray have drowned?'

'Ah well, that's yet to be determined, isn't it? The head had been in the water some days, there was a lot of sand in the orifices, and the features had been disturbed by crabs . . .' The balanced rhythms of Gudgeon's West Country accent lent perhaps a little too much colour to the words. '. . . the hair was all caught up in seaweed, and the neck was torn.'

'Torn? Could it have been up against rocks?'

'Could have been. Sharp and slatey they are round about Stepper Point. Nasty, pointed slabs as any fisherman'll tell you. Dr Mordaunt did say as there were bits of slate found, driven in, like.'

'So Donray could have gone overboard, fallen on rocks and the sea did the rest?'

'Except that we've had nothing but fair weather these last weeks, Mr Kemp, and where's the *Polly* been till it was found?'

'The *Polly*? That was his boat?'

'Smashed up in Foxhole Cove. But it hadn't been there long. There's a footpath goes right past, and folks walk there. Steve Donray must have been in the water long before the *Polly* landed in the Cove.'

'But if he went overboard – maybe through drink or whatever cause – surely the boat would just drift about, maybe for days, before the tide took it in?'

Gudgeon gave him a pitying look.

'Shows how little you know about the sea in these parts, Mr Kemp. A drifting, unmanned fishing-boat like the *Polly*? Someone would have spotted it. These are busy waters. There's the other fishermen who knew that boat well, there's the yachtsmen from the estuary, there's pleasure craft in and out from Padstow every day to Seal Island off the Cove, not to mention the coastguards whose job it is to keep watch. No, it's a real mystery how the *Polly* got where she's lying.'

'Anything aboard to give you a clue?'

'What's left of her? Nothing but spars. She was smashed on those rocks. And what you said about Donray might have been drunk and fallen overboard, his brother says he wasn't a drinking man, even if that makes him about the only one in Padstow who wasn't . . .'

'So, until the body turns up and a proper post-mortem can take place, all you've got is a head. And nothing to connect Mr Donray with the smuggling of drugs. To take it further, if no body ever turns up it'll be assumed that he drowned as a result of accident, and it won't be a police matter even if he was mixed up in drug-smuggling?'

'Inquiries are continuing into the drug business along the lines taken before this other mishap,' said the Inspector stolidly, reverting to official phraseology. 'If Mr Donray died by accident, God help him, then we'll not blacken his memory . . .'

Very commendable, thought Kemp, let him lie unsullied in his watery grave.

'Now, have I fully satisfied that curiosity of yours, Mr Kemp?' The Inspector was already turning to the papers on his desk, and he spoke with a trace of sarcasm.

'Up to a point.' Kemp rose, sensing dismissal. He looked down at the top of Gudgeon's head, at the implacable parting of the greying hair, at the stiff shoulders bulging the shiny blue suit, and was seized with a rogue desire to give this embodiment of the law a good poke in the well-upholstered ribs.

'Just supposing – ' he put it negligently – 'just supposing someone happened to have seen that head before it ended up in the sea?'

The Inspector glared up through bushy eyebrows like a Cornish Oscar Homolka. 'If that's more than just a supposition on your part, then why isn't that someone standing where you are now, and telling me about it?'

'I might just find that out,' murmured Kemp as he swung the door shut behind him. He sighed. He would have liked to keep the friendship of Detective-Inspector Gudgeon but there were circumstances here which could upset the delicate balance Kemp usually tried to hold between the police and his own unorthodoxy.

The trouble was he'd no idea where to turn next. He

wasn't working on a case. He didn't even have a client; his work for Vincent Snape had been accomplished and anyway seemed a far cry from drug-running on a Cornish estuary – the banal modern equivalent of smuggling and wrecking. Distance lends enchantment to the view. For the excise officers of old there had been nothing romantic about 'brandy for the parson, baccy for the clerk' . . . they'd had a job to do just as tiresome as that of the present authorities with the occasional reward, now a publicized haul of the new contraband. 'Watch the wall, my darling . . .'

Against all reason, the word linked itself in his mind to Mirabel Snape, and as he parked his car in the drive of the White House his eyes turned inevitably to Greystones, half-hidden in its dark grove. He wanted desperately to see her again – if only to rid himself of illusion, to come to rational terms with the pictures already etched into his memory, somehow to fit into the scheme of his thinking the disparate views heard and seen: Vincent Snape's happily married wife, Robin Adair's light of love, his own sleek lady from the sea, Penelope's terse professional exposure . . .

It was Penelope who recalled him to reality.

'Come on, Lennox. You're late.' She was calling from the steps, and he followed her in to lunch.

Penelope had had a pleasant morning with her hostess. Now that the weekend visitors had left, the hotel was quiet, and Phyllis Morris had been anticipating this talk with her old friend.

'And you're really engaged to Lennox?'

'If you mean his calling me his fiancée makes me that, then I suppose I am. Such a quaint old-fashioned term. But it takes two to become engaged.'

110

Phyl had persisted. 'But you're going to marry him, aren't you, Penny?'

'I don't think either of us is sure about it.'

'Aren't you in love with him?'

Penelope evaded the direct question. 'We're not youngsters, either of us. We have a pleasant enough relationship as it is.'

'You mean it would be spoiled if you get married? You're not making a lot of sense.'

Penelope tried to put her doubts into words.

'I just can't see Lennox and me as a married couple. I've tried, but I can't. Sometimes I feel I don't really know him, and perhaps he feels the same about me. No, that's wrong. He does know me – he's very acute about people. He makes things easy for me because he sees that's the sort of person I am. I can't bear stress in relationships, although I can take it in my work. There's a wild side to Lennox . . . I couldn't cope with that.'

'Your first marriage wasn't without stress,' Phyl reminded her.

'Oh, but that was illness, something I could face – even when he died. But the time we had together . . . When I look back, it was so perfect between us. We knew each other so well, there could be no unpleasant surprises, nothing to shock . . .'

'And you feel with Lennox there's room for surprise? You don't think it might be fun finding out?'

Penelope had laughed, but still shaken her head.

'I'm too set in my ways for that. I want life to run evenly for me. If it doesn't, well, I have my bitchy side – I suppose most women do – and if that surfaced it could be disastrous for us both. I have thought this thing out, Phyl. I'm old enough to know my limits. I've had my happy days, and now I'm content with my life as it is. I see myself going on with the work I love, it fulfils me somehow. As you know, I'm well provided for. I can eventually retire to the country, and cultivate a garden . . .'

'You sound just like Miss Trevanion,' Phyl Morris had said, 'except for one thing . . .'

This part of the conversation – and for obvious reasons, only this part – Penelope now repeated for Kemp's benefit.

'You know, Miss Trevanion doesn't own that lovely house, Greystones? It was left to Mirabel by her father, who was Susan's brother. That's why Mirabel was brought up there. Her aunt always lived with them, and went on living there when both the parents died. Mirabel was under age then, but the house and all the money were left on trust until she was twenty-one. Poor Susan Trevanion hasn't a bean, apart from her pension. It doesn't seem fair . . .'

'Oh, come on, Penelope, you've seen old-age pensioners in far worse circumstances. What about the loneliness of the tower blocks, and the Council estates in Deptford you're always going on about?' He spoke in a rougher tone than his normal one, irked by something intangible in his own thoughts. 'You've been hoodwinked by the scenery down here . . . I don't trust it. It's too like those cardboard sets they put up for pantomimes, all flowers and fields and fairy woods, with glimpses of sparkling seas. Then the pirates come, and hob-goblins jump out of the bushes and eat up all the children . . .'

Penelope stared at him. She had her code of sympathies, and was irritated to find them not shared.

'You're talking in riddles,' she said pettishly. 'I just

think it's a shame a nice lady like Susan Trevanion should have to be dependent on the whims of someone as wayward and disturbed as Mirabel Snape. From what Phyl Morris tells me, there's been nothing but trouble for Susan since her niece arrived.'

'Miss Trevanion seems to turn a blind eye to some of it . . . the lyrical Robin, for instance.'

'Mr Adair was no trouble until Mirabel came along. His art classes are popular, and Miss Trevanion has been attending them for the last two years. She can hardly cut him off just because her niece has set her cap at him.'

Kemp looked at Penelope in bewilderment.

'I thought you didn't like Robin Adair?'

'I didn't like his histrionics the other day. That was in bad taste . . .'

'It was more than in bad taste in view of what's happened since.'

Penelope looked unhappy but stuck stubbornly to her view.

'I still think you're wasting your sympathy on the wrong person. Miss Trevanion is clearly in need of it. Mirabel Snape is not. Where's your normal sense of fairness?'

It was said with such asperity that Kemp felt his hackles rise. He told them to lie down while he tried to get things into proportion.

'You and I, my dear, are on the verge of quarrelling on a minor issue over people who are really no concern of ours,' he said mildly, at the same time aware that he was seeing Penelope with a fresh eye. They had had their differences before; they stood, for example, on either side of a political divide, but such divergence had been easily bridged by mutual affection. The present spat was by comparison a small matter, yet here they were tossing the crust of it between them with rancorous undertones. He couldn't understand it.

Penelope understood it all too well, and chastized herself for the fault. She had been surprised by jealousy. Such a base emotion, yet so powerful. That terrible nagging doubt, it infused all her words with its insidious poison . . .

'It's not a minor issue, Lennox,' she burst out. 'You're in danger of being bewitched. Mirabel Snape . . .' She said the name as if it was nettle rash.

'She's nothing to me,' he snapped back, 'but it may be she's in need of help.'

'She has plenty of that. She has doctors, she has her aunt, she has a lover and she has a husband. It's already a pretty crowded scene without you butting in.'

Kemp changed direction. 'Aren't you at least curious about that thing she said? And why she should collapse when she heard that Steve Donray's head had been found? We know that was the item on the local news . . .'

Penelope recognized his attempt at diversion. She was regretting the spiteful note she had brought into the conversation, and knew it was due to the confusion in her own emotions. The doubts she had expressed to Phyllis as to whether she should marry Lennox were genuine, yet here she was so upset by his interest in another woman that she was playing bitch in the manger – as if they were already married!

'I don't think I want to know anything more about these people,' she said wearily. 'They've come between us. I'm not cut out to be your Dr Watson. I don't share your curiosity.'

'Would you like us to go back to London today?' he asked her gently.

She was shaken by the suggestion.

'I thought sleuths always stayed on the trail. That's what they do in books.'

'This isn't a book, Penelope, and I'm not sleuthing.'

'But you went to see Albury Prendergast, and Inspector Gudgeon.' She shook her head. 'It's no use, Lennox. I know you. You won't rest till you find the answer. I'm just being silly. Of course we'll stay. After all, it's our holiday.'

There were a lot of words Kemp could use. Words were his coin; sharply pointed for Court use, bread-and-butter words with just a sprinkling of brown sugar – 'may it please Your Worships'; staccato words to gun down a hostile witness, wheedling words to draw out a reluctant one. But now he could summon none to bridge the gap yawning between himself and Penelope on the subject of Mirabel Snape, so he abandoned the attempt, and said: 'We're on holiday. Let's go walkies.'

Chapter Eleven

'You'll need wellies,' said Bob Morris, meeting them at the front door and peering out gloomily. Kemp indicated their waterproofs and shunned the proffered boots. 'She says she's going to walk me round Pentire Head – whatever that means.'

'In this weather, hot baths when you get back.'

He was right. They hadn't gone far along the cliff path when the rain sluiced down as if it was the water going over Niagara, and in no time the yellow-brown slabs of rock on the headland were glistening like spread oilskins.

It wasn't weather in which to talk, struggling against the wind took away their breath. And even when the rain eased off – with that deceptive break in the sky common at the seaside – and they rounded the Point in a burst of wary sunshine which turned the waves to gold, they still maintained a silence, companionable enough but unlikely to advance either of their aims. In Penelope's case to put into words what was in her mind; in Kemp's an apprehension of what she might say, and how he was to meet it.

When the next shower came they sheltered in a cave on the north side, out of the wind, where they could watch the play of sun and shadow along the rugged line of coast from Pentire to Tintagel. In the foreground an Iron Age fort showed up black and brave against the curtain of rain.

Penelope handed out chocolate.

'People talk about the elements,' said Kemp, munching contentedly, 'but you have to be out in them to know what it must have been like when the elements were all you had. Like down there.' He nodded towards the ancient outpost.

'Fire is the only one we haven't got,' said Penelope. 'There's plenty of earth and air, and a deal too much water.'

'I could light you a match. Is that all you women think of, the hearth and home? A hovel under the wall of the great man's castle? A little house in the suburbs? An executive residence in Newtown?' He was watching her face.

Damn him, she thought dispassionately, he would bring that up. It was a point of controversy, where they would live if they married. It had been discussed before without satisfactory conclusion. He had never asked her directly if she was prepared to give up her work.

'Of course I could always move to Clement's Inn,' he was saying now, as he shook the raindrops from his hat. 'I don't think this headgear is as waterproof as they say . . .'

He was being deliberately casual. Working with Gillorns in London would mean giving up some of the independence he cherished in his Newtown office. Why should he be the one to make the sacrifice? The suggestion irked her. She would dislike having to be grateful to him for that. Yet she knew she did not want to abandon her post as Sister Tutor, she had striven so hard for it, and she wanted to continue in what to her had become a dedicated profession.

Receiving no answer from her, Kemp had suddenly bounded away across the short, wet turf, and was now clambering up the slippery ramparts of the fort where natural rock and man-made artifact had long merged into simple mound and craggy outcrop. She walked slowly towards him. He was looking strangely exhilarated.

They stood together on the ridge and gazed down at the churning blue-black water and the lines of foam creaming the base of the sheer walls.

'I like it,' he said, 'it's real.'

'Suits your romantic notions better than the inland scenery you disparage?'

'It's never still. It's always changing. I think I can see what Adair was trying to catch in that abstract of his . . . And there are times when change, even sudden unexpected change, is good for us.'

She looked at him, sharply.

He's not thinking of us, she thought, but of something else. He knows I'm afraid of change. I would like things to go on as they are, that we should remain pleasant companions, no more. But in her heart she knew they could not; it was in the nature of things that there should be change.

As if by tacit agreement, they talked only of the weather and the scenery on their way back to the hotel.

'We have reached a watershed,' Kemp said at one point, and she knew he was not referring to the terrain but to their relationship. His thoughts too had been running on change; something in the surge and flow of the sea against the black teeth of the rocks had stirred in him a yearning for it. Romanticism, Penelope would call it, and although he knew she would not lightly scoff, she wouldn't understand either . . .

Enjoying a hot shower, and relishing a kind of victory

in the challenge the walk had made on a body disin-
clined for such activity, he thought wryly: We're not
even married yet, and already I'm wondering if my
wife is going to understand me . . .

Chapter Twelve

They had hardly begun dinner when Phyllis Morris came up to their table, her eyes anxiously seeking Kemp.

'Bob wonders if you could give him a hand in the cellar,' she said, breathlessly. 'A consignment of wine's come in late . . . I can't go down. I'm needed in the kitchen.'

Kemp was surprised. Phyl was usually in the kitchen at this hour, and Bob Morris was perfectly capable of running the hotel single-handed if need be. But he rose and followed Phyl, who scuttled in front of him through the baize door leading to the private premises.

Steps led downwards into the vast basement which served as cellar and store-rooms, levelling off to the back entrance giving access to a stone-paved yard at the rear. Phyllis paused at the top of the stairway.

'It's not Bob . . .' she whispered hurriedly. 'That was just an excuse. There's someone here . . . She's come from Greystones. Tamsin Jago. Miss Trevanion's maid. She's asking for you. Says no one else must know. I couldn't think what to do. She's out in the yard . . . I must go back.'

Bemused, Kemp walked slowly down the stairs.

The cellar was in darkness but there was light coming from the open door at one end where a pale sky showed itself. As Kemp walked across the slate floor a figure came fleetingly against the light.

'Mr Kemp? Mr Lennox Kemp?'

'Yes. I'm Lennox Kemp.'

She was standing out in the yard beside a crate of bottles. He recognized her from Penelope's description, the screwed-up hair, the round face, pale in the glow from the hotel windows above, wide eyes scrutinizing him. He took her hand which was trembling, indeed her whole body was shaking.

'What is it, Tamsin? Come over here and sit down.' He drew her over where he could see her properly, and sat her on a stone bench by the cellar door. 'Now, you wanted to see me?'

His action calmed her. There was excitement in her voice, but not fear.

'I had to find you, Mr Kemp. Mrs Snape sent me, but at first I didn't know where to look . . .'

'You've come from Mrs Snape?'

The knot of hair bobbed up and down vigorously.

'I'd have come sooner if I'd known where you were. All Miss Mirabel said was find a Mr Lennox Kemp. She made me repeat the name to make sure I'd got it right. We only had a minute. They wouldn't let her out of their sight. But she managed it . . . She outsmarted them . . .' Tamsin gave a chuckle. In her own way she was enjoying herself, indulging a natural taste for adventure to which her life so far had yielded little scope.

'Tell me from the beginning, Tamsin. You're a friend of Mrs Snape?'

'Oh yes, from when she came. We got on like a house on fire. None of this Miss Mirabel stuff that Miss Trevanion's so keen on . . . Miss Mirabel this and Miss Mirabel that . . .' in a fair mimicry of Susan Trevanion's prim voice. 'Call me Mirabel, Tamsin, she said right at the start. Said she didn't hold with all this maidservant

121

thing . . . Well, she and I agreed the way it would be. I was to help with little Simon. There's little work in that, he's so sweet and good . . . Oh, she mustn't be taken from him, Mr Kemp. It's all wrong . . .'

The round eyes were on his face, blinking back tears.

'Take it easy. Simply tell me what has happened at Greystones.'

Tamsin Jago wasn't short of words. She came from a large family where she had had to hold her own in a great babble of talk, and she had a native intelligence beyond her years. She proceeded to give Kemp a graphic description of the events that had brought her to him.

Mirabel Snape had been seen by Dr Griffin after Penelope had left the previous night. Tamsin was not as impressed by him as the rest of the household seemed to be. 'I wouldn't go to him,' she said stoutly, 'not for a bee-sting. He's not like a proper doctor at all. Spends half his time out at The Respite with the private patients. None of we goes to him.' Kemp took it that that meant the indigent population of the area.

Dr Griffin had stayed some time with Mrs Snape, then there had been a long consultation downstairs, the result of which had been a telephone call to London to Mr Snape. Although Tamsin had been packed off to bed by Miss Trevanion and told that she would not be required as Mrs Snape was quietly sleeping, Kemp surmised that the little maid was not above a spot of eavesdropping and like a mouse under the floorboards had missed nothing.

In the morning she had been told by Miss Trevanion that she was to take charge of Simon as Mrs Snape wasn't well, and that his father would be arriving by lunch-time and would wish to see that the child was being properly cared for.

'As if he wasn't always, the poor lamb. Mirabel saw to that, whatever the rest of them say . . .'

'Was Mr Adair around in the morning?' asked Kemp.

'Jolly Robin? Oh no, he melted away all right. Down to that studio place. Miss Trevanion saw to that. And those noisy cousins and their pals, they were seen off early. And all the mess they left cleaned up. Everything neat and proper for Mr Snape's coming. Of course Dr Griffin came back about nine with his horrid little black bag. He went straight up to Mrs Snape's room. I wasn't allowed in to see her . . .' Tamsin gave a sniff, and dabbed at her eyes.

Mr Vincent Snape had arrived about midday. He'd driven down from London. In Tamsin's view he must have been very concerned about his wife to have started so early; to her London was a far-off place, she had been no further than Plymouth in all her seventeen years. By Kemp's reckoning, however, London was only five hours away – probably less for Vincent Snape, who would have a powerful car and was the kind to put his foot down hard and keep it there.

Tamsin Jago had been impressed by Mirabel's husband. Very calm, he was, she said, and stern. She had not seen much of him, however, beyond his coming into the nursery and picking up the little chap.

'He was ever so anxious about his health. No need to be, I said. He's on the beach most days with his mother, and he's fit as a fiddle. Mr Snape's ever so fond of his son, though, you could see by the way he held him. Not like some fathers I know . . .'

After lunch, at which Mrs Snape did not appear, Tamsin had been told to take Simon out for a walk.

'That was just to get me out of the way, Mr Kemp. But I could see rain coming so we didn't go no further than the garden. There's a summerhouse at the bottom and I took his toys down there. I suppose everyone thought we'd gone out . . .'

There seemed to be a lot of activity at Greystones all afternoon. Dr Griffin came and went, then he arrived about four o'clock in a big car with another doctor.

'How did you know it was another doctor?'

''Cos I'd seen him before. When I worked out at The Respite. I think he's the psych-psychiatrist in charge . . .' Tamsin made a good stab at the word. 'He runs the place. Dr Sylvester, I've heard him called.'

Tamsin had arranged a picnic tea for herself and Simon in the summerhouse, and she seemed to have trotted back and forth between the kitchen and the garden for this purpose – or, more likely, for her own purposes – and kept herself unobserved.

'I was dodging the showers,' she said blandly. 'Simon wanted his tea down there, it was more fun than in the nursery, and it kept him happy. I was hoping to get a glimpse of Mirabel.'

'But you didn't?'

'Not then. I think she was still upstairs. Of course I couldn't keep Simon out there for ever, so we came in about five o'clock. They were all in the drawing-room with the door shut but I could hear their voices. They were terribly solemn. Then Mr Snape came out and told me they were going to take Mrs Snape into hospital. He must have seen it upset me but then he got angry when I said I wanted to see her for myself, and that she would want to see me. I wasn't thinking what I was saying because he told me not to make a scene . . . that I was to take Simon up to the nursery and stay there . . . Well, Mr Kemp, I didn't go. I stood my ground.'

Kemp could see her, a small, determined maid standing up to Mr Vincent Snape.

'Go on,' he urged gently.

'Miss Trevanion came out then. She was very cold to me. Like ice she was. Ordered me to go to the nursery and not be so foolish. Dr Griffin and this Sylvester went upstairs and into Mrs Snape's room. Then I heard her shouting at them. Proper yelling, she was, saying she wouldn't go. Mr Snape went up, and it was quiet for a while. I was tidying up Simon's toys when I saw Mrs Snape coming down the stairs behind her husband. She looked awful, so pale and scared-like. My heart bled for her. They had her suitcase and they'd put a coat over her nightie. I couldn't believe she really was going . . . I cried out to her. That seemed to bring her out of a daze . . .'

By now Tamsin was breathless. She stopped, gulped once or twice, then went on.

'Mrs Snape, she looked over towards where I was standing, and she said, very firmly in that comical way she has with her when she's all right and not half-drugged like they keep her, "I want a pee" . . . that's what she said.' Tamsin giggled, self-conscious about the word. '"I want to go to the bathroom. Right now, and Tamsin is to take me." Well, you should have seen their faces! But there was nothing they could do. I was up those stairs in a flash, I can tell you, and got hold of her and we walked along the corridor to the bathroom. She held on to me so tight. They were all worried-looking, they nearly followed us in, but I slammed the door in their faces and locked it. Then she said to me: "Tamsin, you've got to find a Mr Kemp. Mr Lennox

Kemp. He's somewhere in Rocksea." Then she said: "Find him, and hire him." I thought that funny but there weren't time to say any more because by then they'd got Miss Trevanion at the door, and she ordered me to unlock it, that Mrs Snape's health was in danger and that if anything happened to her it would be my fault. What could I do? I had to open the door. Mr Snape took his wife in his arms. He was very gentle with her, but firm . . . and he carried her down the stairs . . . and I heard the car go . . .'

Tears were flowing now, the excitement drained away.

'Tell me again, Tamsin. The exact words Mrs Snape used.'

'She said: "A Mr Lennox Kemp. Find him, and hire him." And that I wasn't to tell no one.'

'I'm sure you've got it right, and I think I understand.' He didn't, not quite, but he'd work it out later.

The girl was quiet for a moment, twisting her fingers.

'Then I had the most terrible row with Miss Trevanion. They'd all gone, you see, there was only her and me. I must have carried on a bit. Perhaps I said things I shouldn't have. My tongue sometimes runs away with me, my gran says . . . Miss Trevanion got ever so angry. Then she fired me.'

'What?'

Tamsin nodded, biting her lips.

'She said I was to pack my things and leave right away. She would see to Simon, and that anyway his father would be back from the hospital as soon as Mrs Snape was settled in, and other arrangements would be made. That's when she let out that it was The Respite they'd taken Mirabel to . . . I shouted at her that that was no place for someone like Mrs Snape. It was then she ordered me out of the house, said she'd send my things on. I didn't know what to do. I rushed out of there. All I could think of was what Mirabel said. I kept saying it over and over. I went to my gran's. She could see I was upset but I told her it was because I had lost my job. Then I had a think. I had to find you, so I asked round the village. Most of them's family anyway. My cousin Molly works here part-time in reception and she said there was a Mr Lennox Kemp staying at the White House, so here I am.'

By now she was drooping with tiredness.

Kemp helped her to her feet. 'You've done wonders, Tamsin. You're a very bright girl. Now you go back to your gran's and get a good night's sleep. Don't talk about this. You understand?'

She nodded.

'I'll come and see you tomorrow.'

'It's Mrs Jago's. Myrtle Cottage, next to the Post Office.' She gave a wan smile. 'I'm near passing out on my feet.'

'Want me to see you home?'

'It wouldn't be right, Mr Kemp. She said to tell nobody about you. I won't let Mirabel down.'

He watched her slip down the path, and out at the gate of the yard. She would be all right; it was her village.

Chapter Thirteen

By the time Kemp returned from the cellar it was too late to continue with the fictitious excuse since Bob Morris had been plainly visible for some time at the other end of the dining-room patiently lending an apathetic ear to an elderly couple's dissertation on wines they had known and loved.

'You're not built for lugging crates around on your own,' observed Penelope. Kemp had to say something, perhaps half the truth would suffice.

'It was your little Tamsin who wanted to see me in private. She's just lost her job, and wanted some advice.'

Penelope raised her eyebrows.

'Why come to you?'

Kemp shrugged. 'Perhaps someone told her I was a solicitor.'

'And what's the news of Mirabel Snape?' asked Penelope, just keeping tartness at bay.

'She's in hospital. Her husband has arrived at Greystones.'

'Are the two events connected?'

'I thought you didn't want us to go on discussing the home life of the Snapes.'

It wasn't like Kemp to use a snub direct and he had spoken lightly, but Penelope could recognize a barrier when she saw one. She evaded the dangerous ground, commented on the excellence of the fish and suggested Kemp should have the same. If there had been a moment of consensus between them earlier, then it had been reached, and passed. But she felt resentment; once again the incursion of the people at Greystones had clouded the air, upset the delicate balance of the relationship between herself and Kemp – and at an awkward time. She had fully intended, in a kindly manner, to tell him of her decision. Now that too was spoiled.

The remainder of the meal was taken in silence, or only stilted conversation, and afterwards, in sudden petulance, Penelope pleaded tiredness and went upstairs early.

Aware of her changed mood, and not wishing to deliberate too finely upon the cause, Kemp sought the company of the Morrises who liked to relax with their guests in the evenings. Although not Cornish themselves, they had been accepted in the district and allowed to know as much as was good for them about the local families.

'Tamsin Jago has been upset by a rather summary dismissal from work,' he told them, an idea formulating in his mind. 'She wondered if I could advise her as she'd heard I was a lawyer. She's a very articulate girl.'

'Like her father,' said Bob. 'Dick Jago gets the name of being something of a charmer.'

'He certainly has a way with the ladies,' said Phyl, 'at least that's what I've heard. They say he has a golden tongue.'

'So has his daughter,' said Kemp. 'She's not short of a word. Pity she didn't curb it at Miss Trevanion's – seems to have got her into a spot of trouble. I'll see what I can do for her.'

'I wish you would,' said Phyllis. 'I'm sorry she's lost her job. There's not much down here for a bright girl like Tamsin. I understood Miss Trevanion had been very pleased with her. There does seem to have been a lot of trouble at Greystones these last few weeks . . . well, since Mrs Snape came. Poor Miss Trevanion must be very worried.'

'Mrs Snape has been taken to hospital. The Respite, I believe it's called. Mr Snape has come down from London.'

Bob and Phyllis Morris looked at each other, averting their eyes from Kemp. Then Phyl said hastily: 'I'm sure it's for the best. We'd heard rumours, of course . . . She'll get proper treatment at The Respite Hospital, it's very highly recommended for people with – er – problems . . .'

'I'm only interested in Tamsin Jago,' said Kemp smoothly. 'I understand she's gone to her grandmother's.'

Phyllis was glad to be rescued from further talk about the Snapes. 'You'll find old Mrs Jago a rare specimen. She's supposed to have had the same trouble with Dick's father, he too had an eye for the ladies, but she sat it out. You had to in her day. There's not much escapes her attention in this village . . .'

As he approached Myrtle Cottage the next morning Kemp could see why. Mrs Jago was out front in a wicker chair ostensibly shelling peas but so strategically placed that most of the street was open to her view, and many of the passers-by within earshot. People coming and going at the Post Office next door greeted her, and some stopped to chat. For a veteran newsgatherer the spot was perfect.

She must have singled Kemp out long before he touched the latch of the gate but she kept her head down. She wore a white apron over a long dark skirt, and with the bowl on her lap she looked like a peasant woman in the corner of a Dutch painting, and Kemp wondered if she knew it. The scrap of garden was scant earth strewn with slatey shards from the beach but up against the cottage wall stood, astonishingly, a great clump of Madonna lilies.

'How do you grow them like that?' asked Kemp, pausing by her chair.

She turned and looked at the flowers as if she'd never seen them before.

'I don't grow 'em. They're just there.'

Mrs Jago had a creased brown face, neat features and round black eyes that stared out unaided by the glasses half-way down her nose. 'You lookin' for someone?'

'Your granddaughter, Tamsin, if she's about.'

The old woman was out of her chair like a jack-in-the-box. She was slight and wiry with no excess of flesh and she moved quickly.

'In here.'

The tiny parlour straight in from the door was deep in shadow. Tamsin was at a round table in the window, the only source of light, where the green and white trumpets of the lilies pressed excitedly against the glass.

'Hello, Mr Kemp,' said Tamsin, nervously rattling teacups on a tray. 'Would you like some coffee?'

'Make us a pot of tea, there's a love,' said the old lady, with a sideways glance at Kemp.

'Tea would be fine,' he said, taking the hint and wondering if Mrs Jago meant to sit in on their conversation.

Tamsin started for the kitchen which looked even darker than the far corners of the parlour, but with the benign illogicality of the aged her grandmother changed direction. 'No, you sit down there, maid, with your visitor. I'll get the tea.'

She moved so fast across the floor she might have been on runners. The kitchen door closed behind her.

Tamsin grinned.

'She's supposed to have arthritis. She goes like Speedy Gonzales just to prove she hasn't. But she does have her bad days. This isn't one of them.'

Kemp sat down on the other side of the round table and scrutinized the girl. Her cheeks were rosy this morning, and her eyes clear. The resilience of youth, he thought.

'Sleep well?'

'Like a log. I'm glad you've come early. I was just beginning to think about it again.'

'Don't think too hard. There's nothing more you can do for now.'

Her eyes were like a chipmunk's – bright, brown and inquisitive.

'Oh, but there must be. We can't leave Mirabel there . . . Not in that place.'

'Tell me about it.'

It was as well for Kemp that he had learned of her father's word-spinning propensities (perhaps simply a manifestation of the old Celtic belief that truth was too precious for everyday use and must be hung about with garlands), otherwise he might have been caught out by Tamsin's hair-raising account of The Respite being somewhere between Bluebeard's castle and Fawlty Towers, grisly but with a comical aspect not wholly confined to the patients.

'They're all a bit looney out there,' she ended, 'even them that runs it.'

'All right for them as can afford it,' put in Mrs Jago, as she thumped down the tray. She added nothing more, however, and whisked out with her own cup, presumably to take up her watch on Rocksea.

Sifting the wheat from the chaff, and allowing for the girl's imagination which he suspected was fuelled by more than her native scenery, Kemp gathered that an old run-down nursing home had been recently bought, renovated and reopened by money from up-country, darkly hinted at as a London source, and certainly not the National Health Service. Kemp guessed some entrepreneurial foresight had been at work; the influx of retired people of means into the neighbourhood would underline a need for private medical care. Nothing necessarily wrong in that. Whatever the source, the funds spent had been lavish enough to arouse local suspicions as to the purpose of the Hospital.

According to Tamsin, with the healthy scepticism of the young, most of the patients were rich and their reasons for being there wealth-related. There were units for the treatment of the milder disorders of age such as obesity and dietary problems, as well as for alcoholism and nervous breakdowns, and, at the far end of the spectrum, senile dementia.

'It's ever so well organized,' she said, giving Kemp his second cup of the strongly-brewed tea, 'but creepy.'

'How long were you there?'

'Two months in the winter. Then I gave it up. I really wanted to go in for proper nursing but they won't have me without the O-levels.'

'Get them,' he said absently, his mind elsewhere.

'Could I?' Tamsin took him up eagerly.

He looked at her bright, unnerving eyes. She was

worth more than just casual attention. 'I know someone who might help. I'll talk to her. Now, to get back to The Respite, you say Dr Sylvester is the man in charge?'

'He's the one they all kowtow to. But Dr Griffin's in and out a lot. All the local patients are his.'

'Which brings us back to Mrs Snape.'

'Can't we get her out, Mr Kemp? It's no place for her.' Tamsin shuddered. 'I can't bear to think of her in there. I've seen those others . . . they're like zombies. They can't do that to Mirabel. And she's away from Simon . . .' Sudden feeling filled her eyes.

'If she's under proper medical supervision there's not much we can do – ' Kemp began, but Tamsin could not contain herself.

'We could get her out. I know the layout of the place, and one of the night porters is a friend of mine. I can find out which room she's in and you could help me smuggle her downstairs, or out of the window . . .'

Kemp looked at her upturned face with amazement.

'Tamsin, what on earth did you read at that school of yours?'

She blinked, stalled in the track of some imagined adventure.

'I liked *Jane Eyre*,' she said, 'but since I left I get detective stories from the library. I think Chandler's super, don't you?'

Kemp gave a sigh. 'Look, my girl, Mrs Snape isn't the mad wife of Mr Rochester, and I'm not Philip Marlowe. I don't shin up drainpipes and rescue damsels in distress from sinister nursing homes. I have to know a lot more before I can be sure there's anything I can do to help Mrs Snape. Do you understand?'

'Yes, Mr Kemp,' she said meekly. 'I've overrun

myself again. I'm always doing it. Like with Miss Trevanion.'

'I want to ask you about that. Can you remember just what it was you said which made her so angry?'

Tamsin sat back, twisting a strand of hair. 'I was ever so upset. I said things I shouldn't have. About the way she let Mirabel drink when she knew she was on drugs . . . Well, no, I didn't mean drugs of that sort . . .'

'What sort?'

'You know . . . the things they write about in the papers. There's a difference, isn't there, between them and the proper kind the doctors give you?'

'Yes, there is. But the difference is hard to see sometimes if you don't know much about either.'

'That's what Miss Trevanion said – I was an ignorant girl and should mind my own business. I don't know about these things and I shouldn't have spoken like I did. But when they used to say Mirabel had too much to drink I didn't believe them.'

'Why not, Tamsin?'

'I know about drinking,' she answered flatly, 'I've seen plenty of it. My grandfather got drunk, often, and I'd help Gran to put him to bed. My dad when he lived with us got drunk regular. Mother was ashamed, but when we were all kids it was only a small house and you couldn't help knowing what it was like. Drinking and getting drunk's nothing to me. I grew up with it. 'Twasn't the same with Mrs Snape. She didn't drink that much . . . Lots of ladies drink like she does. She only gets merry, and skips about, and laughs a lot. Seems to cheer her up. But when she'd collapse of an evening, or just sit staring at nothing . . . that weren't drink, Mr Kemp.'

He looked at her with renewed respect. She might

have been a country girl and by some regarded as ignorant, but she had the acute perception of a child, and such perception was grounded in reality. Her imagination might soar, her tongue take off on her father's golden wing, but in the things that mattered she would remain earthbound.

'You and I have to have a base from which to work,' he told her. 'The best I can think of at the moment is this: you've come to me because I'm a lawyer and you think you might have been unfairly dismissed. There's a law about that.'

She nodded. 'I've heard my brothers talk about it. Never happened to me.'

'Well, perhaps it has now. So let's go about it in the proper way.'

He took out his notebook.

'Who actually engaged you at Greystones?'

Tamsin had been in several jobs since leaving The Respite, and was still doing part-time at the local grocer's when she'd heard that Miss Trevanion wanted someone a few days a week to clean. Tamsin had been taken on, and apparently given such satisfaction that when Mrs Snape arrived she'd been asked to do full time.

'It was Mrs Snape herself who asked me if I'd be willing to live in, and help with the little chap. Miss Trevanion seemed pleased with the arrangements, and I was given a good rise in wages.'

'Who paid you?'

'Well, Miss Trevanion, like she always did. But I think – I don't know for sure – I think the money came from Mirabel. Miss Trevanion's not as well off as she pretends to be . . . Of course it's her house I was employed in.'

'Never mind that. All I'm really looking for is a reason for me to talk to you without it being remarked upon, and you can tell people quite openly why you are seeing me. We don't want gossip, do we?'

Tamsin's eyes sparkled. 'You mean they might think I fancied you?'

'My dear child, I'd be flattered but it wouldn't do either of our reputations any good. Now what I'd like you to do is this . . .'

Chapter Fourteen

Leaving Myrtle Cottage, Kemp felt all the eyes in Rocksea watched him up the village street. It was something to do with the harsh light, for the sun had broken through and as it climbed towards noonday it was snared by the mirror of the sea so that rocks and houses, quays and idling boats, stood flat and shadowless like a picture postcard.

A stage set he'd called it, and as on a stage he must move without camouflage. Everything here would have to be played out in the open; he longed for the grey anonymity of the Newtown streets.

They would have to meet sooner or later, he and Vincent Snape. Word would spread quickly, and names had already been bandied about. He must take the situation head-on – not a method he liked. Kemp preferred to emulate the mole and nose his way underground. It would not work in this blatant landscape.

He took the path through the dunes, and entered the pillared gateway of Greystones.

Tamsin had obviously been swiftly replaced – a hint here of a *coup de main* – and Kemp was met at the door by a stranger, an ageless woman with a girlish face, dressed in a cream blouse and navy skirt that suggested uniform, the effect softened by a frilly apron picked up from her predecessor.

'I'm sorry,' she said, 'there's no one at home.'

Kemp frowned in disappointment. 'I'd hoped to see Mr Vincent Snape.'

'He's out, I'm afraid.' She turned her head at the sound of a child's running footsteps. A small dark-haired boy appeared at her side, and stood staring at Kemp from wide sea-blue eyes.

'Hullo,' he said, 'I'se got a new car.'

He thrust it up for Kemp to see. Kemp knelt so that they could examine the vehicle together and Simon showed how it could run down the stone steps. The woman meanwhile was unable to close the door as she might have wished to do.

Kemp straightened up, took a card from his pocket and handed it to her.

'I've been doing business with Mr Snape in London,' he explained. 'I'm down here on holiday and heard that his wife had been taken ill . . .' Kemp put on the expression of one anxious to be of service. 'And Miss Trevanion's not in either? Perhaps I could leave a note?'

The woman's prim features relaxed as she read the card, reassured by the profession of the visitor and by his obvious knowledge of the household. She said apologetically: 'You'd best come in for a moment, sir, I have to shut the front door or Master Simon'll be off down the drive.'

The little boy looked up at her. 'Not go out? Nanny says Simon not go out?' But he let her draw him away from the door as she shut it, and once inside the hall he darted off.

'I'm just getting his lunch. If you'd care to come in here you could write your message for Mr Snape.' She led Kemp towards the small room on the right which he guessed was the one used by Tony to put up his feet in. It was furnished vaguely as a study with an old desk in one corner, a sofa in the centre, and a telephone on a chest by the latticed window.

'That's very kind of you.' Kemp smiled at her, and took out his pen. 'I can see you have your hands full with the little chap. It will only take me a minute to write a note.'

She was well-trained. Despite his credentials, she took a careful look at the desk-top to see if there was anything lying about of a private nature before she began to search for writing-paper.

'Don't put yourself to any trouble,' Kemp told her, 'I'll use a loose page from my notebook. Simon seems to have taken to you, Miss – ?'

'Brenda Arbuthnot.' She was disarmed by his pleasant manner; Kemp had a way with him, when he chose, of presenting an easy amiability which was hard to resist, and the nursemaid, although adjured to keep strangers at a distance in her calling, had a natural instinct to respond to friendliness. She had to spend so much of her time alone or in the company of toddlers that she sometimes wondered if she would forget normal conversational practices. 'The Agency only sent me this morning,' she said now as if to explain any failure of etiquette on her part, 'so I'm just finding my way about. Of course, Mr Snape and Miss Trevanion have had to go to the hospital, and I've been left in charge of Simon – and the house if it comes to that. . .'

The telephone by the window purred softly, twice. Miss Arbuthnot looked towards it but made no move. 'Oh, that's the extension to the Studio,' she said briskly. 'Miss Trevanion did tell me about it. There'll be someone down there to answer it. It rings properly when it's for the house. Now, if you'll excuse me, I must see to Simon.'

She pulled the door to behind her, and Kemp heard her soothing the boy who had set up a cry for attention.

Kemp tiptoed quickly across the room and carefully took the receiver from its stand.

A conversation was already in progress. He recognized Adair's voice: '. . . and I don't know why you're phoning me . . . It's too dangerous . . .'

'For you it is, buddy boy. You know the score.' The other man's voice was rough. 'You've been trying to lie low, haven't you? We don't like that. We've got business to discuss . . .'

'It's not convenient. Something's happened. I can't meet you yet . . .'

'You'll meet us when we say so. That's an order. Who do you think's calling the tune this time, Mr Robin Adair?' A laugh grated over the line. 'A tune, that's what your mate finally got out . . . he's called for a tune. And he sang like a dicky-bird, your mate did, when the time came . . .'

Adair's voice came stammering, a note of desperation in it.

'I didn't . . . I didn't know . . .'

'You know now. You know far too much. He named you at the end.' There was a moment's silence, as if over a grave. Then a whisper: 'When the sand was in his mouth and he could see where the tide was coming in.'

Adair's indrawn breath rasped in Kemp's ear. 'Don't . . . don't . . . All right, I'll meet you. I swear I didn't know . . .' There came the sound of a sob.

But also of footsteps in the hall. Kemp replaced the

receiver gently, and when Miss Arbuthnot came in he was seated at the desk writing briskly.

'Thank you,' he said, rising. 'Perhaps you'd be good enough to give this to Mr Snape when he returns. I'm sorry to hear of his wife's illness. It must have been very sudden. I mean his having to call you at such short notice to take charge of the little boy . . .? I presume Mrs Snape's gone in for an emergency operation?'

'Oh no, Mr Kemp, nothing like that. The London Agency told me some time ago that I might be required in Cornwall, and it was then that I was interviewed by Mr Snape. I've been staying in Bodmin so as to be near at hand. Of course I'm used to these cases. There's usually a breaking-point and that's when I'm needed.'

'And you're coping very well.' Kemp followed her into the hall. Through the open kitchen door he could see Simon perched on a high-chair solemnly eating. 'He looks happy enough.'

'I'm a trained nanny,' she said severely, 'it's my job to see that the children in my care are kept happy. Of course he doesn't realize yet that his mother . . . we've told him she's not very well – but I expect he's used to that, poor little soul.'

'Very sad these cases must be,' Kemp responded, 'and how fortunate Mr Snape is to have someone like you to take charge. I had not realized that Mrs Snape's illness was so serious . . .'

But although Nanny Arbuthnot had been forthcoming enough with the details of her own engagement, it was strictly against her professional code to discuss her employer or his wife with a stranger, no matter how presentable. There was no more information to be gleaned here, so, with further effusions of sympathy and discreet flattery, Kemp took his leave.

It was not simply curiosity this time that drew him towards the Studio. Robin Adair was being threatened and in a peculiarly nasty way. Not only had there been menace in the obscenely whispered words, there had been cold-blooded knowledge behind them, and their implication chilled Kemp's backbone as he hurried across the garden. 'Sand in his mouth . . . and he could see the tide coming in.' If someone could see the incoming tide, that meant . . .

The nebulous image taking shape in Kemp's mind robbed the sun of its warmth, and he thrust it from him and concentrated on the effect the words had had on Robin Adair. He'd been reduced to tearful surrender.

And a quick getaway. For the Studio was empty, a notice hanging askew on the door said 'Closed', and although Kemp walked several times round the building peering in at the windows, there was no sign of the artist.

Running scared? Or had that meeting already been arranged?

Kemp went back to the White House and put in a call to Inspector Gudgeon. Although he held no brief for Adair, the man had to have some protection. Of course alerting the police might put Adair in greater peril; he'd have to take his chance on that.

'The Inspector's not in at the moment. Station Sergeant Lobb speaking.'

It wasn't Kemp's day for finding people in.

'Please give him a message. Tell him that Lennox Kemp phoned.' He waited, knowing the man was laboriously writing. 'Tell him to find a Mr Robin Adair.

He's an artist, lives in the Studio at a house called Greystones in Rocksea. Tell the Inspector to keep an eye on Mr Adair. He might possibly have information on Stephen Donray's death. Got that?'

The Sergeant checked the message back for accuracy, but before he could ask any questions Kemp had rung off.

Perhaps it had been as well the Inspector wasn't in; Gudgeon wouldn't have let him get away with putting down the phone like that. Of course there were plenty of unanswered questions, they drummed in Kemp's mind as he went in to lunch with Penelope, determined, if only for her sake, to behave like an ordinary solicitor on holiday and not like one of Tamsin's fictional heroes. He had salved his conscience by the phone call to the police – the dutiful act of any citizen who might suspect skulduggery afoot in Rocksea.

Self-righteousness tended to make his rather cherubic features look smug. Penelope was suspicious.

'What have you been up to?' she asked, straight out.

'Oh, this and that . . . Thought it was time I saw Vincent Snape – before he got any wrong ideas.'

He told her of his polite reception at Greystones but not of his impertinent misuse of it; even if Adair were a villain he had the right to some privacy in his affairs. And it would hardly be prudent to extend the field of eavesdroppers. Kemp had no desire to bring Penelope within the shadow cast by that cold, knowing whisper.

'So we can forget the Snapes for the rest of the day,' she said nicely. They had finished lunch and were gazing out of the hotel window at the estuary. The tide was at its lowest, exposing the sandy flats, the river now only a trickle of silver over towards Padstow.

'Looks as if you could walk across. Are there quick-sands, do you think?'

'Bob says there aren't. Those sandbanks are firm. Look, there's people out there on one of them playing cricket. They've landed from that little sailing boat. Do you want to go and swim? It's hot enough.'

'Not here. I don't like the estuary when the tide's so far out.'

Neither did Kemp. Indeed, he viewed the scene with some distaste. Inshore, the scumbled black and green sea-weedy wastes laid bare by the tide's ebb looked like an ocean floor from which the waters had been rolled back by some primeval cataclysm, a spongy desert where eyeless things spawned in the pitiless sun, and spiny crustaceans scuttled to and fro on ragged claws, feeding on sand. No, he didn't want the estuary today.

'Phyl says there's a pool built into the rocks at Treyarnon where you can swim even at low tide,' said Penelope. 'We'd have to go through Westerbridge to the other coast.'

'That's where we'll go. I'll even swim with you if the water's warm.'

Chapter Fifteen

The pool had been formed by the forces of nature in a rocky basin on a small headland jutting out to sea. Its original outlet had been roughly concreted, so that although the pool filled up each high tide it held its depths when the waters receded, providing an ideal swimming bath for those not put off by the rubbery brown bladderwrack clinging to its edges, nor the shadow cast by the overhang of cliff at one end which prevented the sun ever reaching the deeper levels.

Most people preferred to dangle their feet in the cool seaweed curtains, or probe the shallow end for bright jellied anemones. Others were content to stretch out on the surrounding slabs of warmed rock, and simply absorb sunshine. After a cold swim Penelope and Kemp were thankful to join this bare-limbed tribe.

'Like kippers,' said Kemp contentedly, taking out cigarettes. 'Ah, the first smoke after a swim is always the best . . .'

Penelope sat up. 'Whoever told you that? You haven't swum anywhere since you came out of the Ark.'

'I guided the dove on the first peace-keeping mission to the Middle East,' murmured Kemp, remembering who had said the words and trusting flippancy would keep the memory at bay.

Penelope paused in the act of brushing out her hair to dry.

'Can we be serious for a moment, Lennox? I think we ought to talk . . .'

'Why do people always have to say that in films?' said Kemp lazily, watching the white line of the incoming tide lap the pool's man-made ridge. 'They do it when the scenery gets boring.'

'I'm serious, darling. I have to tell you something . . .'

'You don't want to marry me. That's it, isn't it?'

'How did you know?'

'I'm a detective. I have extra-sensory perception . . .'

'You're not a detective, and you haven't . . . Oh, but I'm serious,' she said again.

He took her hand.

'I know you are, Penny. But I've felt your hesitation these last few days. It was rash of me to say what I did at that pub in Blisland. I shouldn't have taken it for granted that you would . . . Damn it, I do want to marry you. You know that. There is a kind of love between us. We like each other's company . . . We could have a happy future.' He was playing devil's advocate, and knew it.

'It wouldn't work.' Penelope had rehearsed what she would say but now the carefully thought-out phrases refused to come to order; instead she found herself spilling out jumbled feelings, self-justifying, regretful, and making no more sense than the screech of the gulls around them.

Kemp put his hand over her mouth. 'It's all right, Penny dear, I understand.'

He could be persuasive when he tried. He had only

to counter her objections, assure her that the problems of their work, where they would live, were mere practical matters which sensible people could easily sort out if they put their minds to it. He knew he was losing something precious, something he might never be offered again. An end to loneliness. In his wilderness years – as he himself thought of them – deprived of professional colleagues, home and money, he had been kept going by the dream that one day the little door would open, as it had for Alice, and he would squeeze through into that rose-garden which promised happiness. Penelope's stability, her straight view of life, her essential goodness and her love, these had seemed to open that door.

But another part of his mind was already rejecting such simple analysis. Hadn't he too had doubts? Perhaps a tranquil rose-garden wasn't his natural habitat, contentment not wholly within his scope.

'And I wouldn't want children,' Penelope was saying, her hazel eyes solemn and concentrated; for this was something she really had thought through. Marriage would disturb her orderly life, pregnancy would shatter it. She was not too old in age, but too old by her very nature, to have a child now. It was only fair to tell him so.

Kemp was staring up at the sky through half-closed lids. Unbidden, there came as if on the retina of his eye the blurred image of a dark-haired boy who had his mother's colouring. Kemp sat up and rubbed his eyes.

It was an area into which his thoughts had never ventured. He was a man who lived now from day to day; never look beyond tea-time was a lesson he'd learned long ago. Since the débâcle of his first marriage when all plans for the future had fallen about his ears like debris from a landslide, that maxim had been his guide; never to think ahead, never to say 'next year things will be better' or that in a few years' time all would be well. He'd had no faith in the future, never built on its promise.

Even now Penelope was striking at that vulnerable spot.

'You've never talked much about Muriel,' she said with some hesitation. 'I know you took that money from the trust funds to pay her gambling debts . . . You must have loved her a lot to do that for her, and risk your own future.'

He narrowed his eyes in the sun's glare and tried to answer truthfully. 'I think love had gone by then. Pity can be a stronger urge. Pity is something you can't talk yourself out of. I couldn't bear seeing Muriel so frightened . . . terrified at what they would do to her if she didn't pay up. Gambling was like a drug, an addiction . . . When they threatened she went to pieces. She tried to kill herself. What else could I do? The money was there and I took it. It was the only practical solution . . .'

'But you were the one to suffer. And then she left you.'

He moved restlessly.

'Muriel came out all right in the end. She's re-married, and lives in the States. Old, unhappy, far-off things, Penelope . . . If I don't believe in the future, I don't believe much in the past either.'

She looked at him with something very like love in her face.

'You never really make proper plans for yourself, Lennox, do you?'

'Perhaps it's just as well,' he said with a rueful smile, 'now that you're turning me down.'

'Do you really feel like a rejected suitor?'

'I feel like a smoked mackerel, and these rocks don't fit my contours.'

She sensed his withdrawal from any further personal probing, and she offered him her suntan lotion. He refused, and began to look for his shirt. 'I have a sensitive skin that can't stand exposure,' he said lightly but perhaps with oblique reference to the former subject, and she saw that she too must resort to levity.

'You mean you're too conscious of that paunch of yours.'

'Now, now. Just because the body has become middle-aged before the spirit is ready for it, there's no need to remark on it. Come on, it's nearly tea-time . . .'

Driving back to Rocksea they were both quiet, partly the rather stupefying effect of sun and sea, partly the result of their conversation. Each felt that there was nothing more to be said on the level at which they had talked, certain essentials had been revealed upon which they might ponder but nothing could change. The situation between them had to be accepted.

The practical aspect engaged Penelope.

'Uncle and Aunt will be disappointed,' she observed, 'but don't worry, I'll tell them when we get back. And the blame is all mine . . .'

Kemp laughed. 'Archie Gillorn is no longer in the firm, and he'll always be a friend even if I don't marry his niece. Did you think he'd have me fired?'

'You're far too valuable, Lennox, you know that.' Then she realized how ridiculous she sounded, how little she really knew about his work.

Their mood that evening over dinner was relaxed. It was as if they had come to a dangerous corner, and somehow avoided taking the wrong road. Neither would have admitted to feelings of relief – that would have been no compliment to either of them – and they still wished to retain some self-esteem, so they slid into their earlier pleasant relationship, but warily this time, recognizing it had no future.

But they were thus able to present a united front to Vincent Snape who arrived in the lounge of the White House about nine o'clock.

'I got your kind note, Mr Kemp. Good of you to call on me. What a coincidence that you should be here in Rocksea . . .'

'Blame Penelope, she chose it,' said Kemp, rising to greet him and introducing his companion.

'I'm glad to know you, Penelope. And it's Lennox, isn't it?'

Vincent smiled expansively upon them, as if getting on first-name terms bestowed a benison. Perhaps it was a spin-off from the special relationship Snape enjoyed with the American clients of whom Mrs Forbes had spoken. Indeed, Vincent Snape was looking rather American tonight in his holiday casuals – but not too casual, that light jacket had been carefully cut to take his breadth of shoulder and the open-necked shirt was silk. He brought his drink over to their table, and eased himself into a chair.

'I've met your wife,' said Penelope, 'I hope she is better?'

'Mirabel is making slow progress, I'm afraid, but she is in excellent hands. A local private hospital called The Respite . . . Quite an apt name, don't you think?' Without waiting for their comment, he changed the

151

subject as smoothly as if he were controlling the agenda of a meeting. 'I gather your uncle is a friend of Father's. He has often spoken about Archie Gillorn – a lawyer of the old school, eh? Up North that still means a lot to a firm like mine in these changing times . . .'

It was an effortless lead-in to a discussion on some City matters recently highlighted in the Press. Snape was not only a man who used words well, he had the additional merit of directness and the ability to simplify complex issues for eager listeners such as Penelope. Like many people, she was intrigued by the jargon of finance and anxious to understand it better.

Kemp sat back and said little, though he felt he should be applauding the performance. He watched Vincent with increasing interest. The man kept his power under tight rein, but power was there, the power to manipulate and the skill that can produce facts and figures at will. That was the name of the game in Snape's line of business. Kemp judged him to be one of the few people he had met who possessed the knack of being able to synthesize rapidly; Snape would get to the nub of an intractable subject while other men of equal intelligence were still floundering. He wondered if that was what Snape had done with his own report.

Now Vincent was amusing Penelope with comments on some of the more pi-faced City moguls, a degree of homespun Northern humour giving pith to such remarks. He was a many-sided man, this husband of Mirabel . . .

At a pause in the conversation Penelope asked after young Simon.

'He's a great little chap. Sturdy, like me. He'll be a credit to the family. Chip off the old block . . . Well, maybe only a splinter right now . . .' He smiled the indulgent smile of a father who sees in his son the tiny mirrored image of himself, and not the alien creature older, more realistic parents might have to recognize as individual and not wholly theirs to command.

'I hope he visits his mother,' said Kemp, stung by Snape's sense of property in his offspring.

'Not wise at the moment.' Vincent pressed his stubby fingers together and let his chin droop upon them. 'The doctors say Mirabel is too disturbed. Oh, I know what you're going to say – ' he was quick in his turn towards Penelope – 'that the child suffers if separated from the mother . . . But, believe me, Simon is quite used to that. There have always been people to take him off Mirabel's hands when she couldn't cope. Now he has good old Aunt Susan, and I've engaged a trained nursemaid. What more can a poor father do?' He was appealing for sympathy and approbation.

Kemp wondered what, in so short a space of time, had happened to the premise of the happy marriage. He felt the need to jab Snape with a reminder of it.

'Looks as if I shall not be dining with you next month, then?'

'My dear chap, how could I know how ill my wife was becoming during her time here? We spoke of stress then, did we not?' He smiled at Kemp as if to assure him their previous discussion was still on file. 'Perhaps it's not only we men who are affected but our wives also, eh?'

Adroitly he switched the trend of the conversation away from the personal and on to more general terms, deftly bringing Penelope within its scope. He inquired about their holiday, and complimented them on their choice of the Cornish countryside as if he had had a hand in sponsoring it.

'The scenery is nice enough,' said Kemp. 'I've even bought some paintings of it. By a man called Robin Adair. Do you know his stuff?'

'Susan Trevanion's tutor? I've heard his name but I've never met him. Doesn't he have that studio place in her grounds? But I'm afraid I know nothing about art.'

'I thought you did. You have some nice pictures in your office.'

Snape gave his warm, full-throated laugh. 'Don't put me in the tycoon class, Lennox. I don't paper my walls with masterpieces. I leave all that kind of thing to Mrs Forbes. She chooses the decor, including the pictures.'

He went on to explain his secretary to Penelope, stressing her devotion to the firm, her Manchester origins, her age, as if to put a stopper on any speculation that his office was full of nubile young women.

As he was about to leave, he politely but firmly scotched Penelope's tentative suggestion that she should visit his wife during his absence in London. 'Complete rest. She's been ordered complete rest, and no visitors. I'm sure you as a Sister can appreciate the need for her to be kept quiet.' Penelope noticed how sharp his eyes were; behind them lay full knowledge of how she had found Mrs Snape the night she had gone with Miss Trevanion to Greystones. Not only that, but he had gauged exactly her professional reaction to the signs and symptoms she had observed, and he was satisfied by it.

After Vincent Snape had crossed the room, a bulky figure but light of step, and the door closed behind him, Kemp turned to Penelope.

'Well, what do you make of him?'

'I like him,' she said. 'I think Mirabel Snape's a lucky lady. He's worried about her, under all that smooth talk. Why'd you have to needle him?'

'Did I?'

'Of course you did – and he knew it. Why on earth did you bring up the subject of pictures? The poor man probably knows all about his wife's fling with Robin Adair.'

'I'm sure he does,' said Kemp drily, 'and probably before he came down here . . .'

'Well, then. There was no need to rub it in. What a fool Mrs Snape is! She's been caught playing with fire, and now she's been burned. Do you think that's why she's taken to drink? Or has she had a drink problem for some time, and they euphemistically call it depression?'

The expression jarred on Kemp.

'It's all much too pat. Like a romantic novel. Good husband, bad wife, lightsome lad for a lover. Breakdown, remorse, guilt, finds solace in drink or drugs. Do you think she's on drugs, Penny?' He shot the question sharply.

Penelope considered.

'Difficult to tell. Remember I only saw her once, and then for such a short time. Certainly no hypo marks that I could see, but then I wasn't looking for any . . . But those pills she was taking were strong – in the amphetamine category. Of course I only saw the prescription name on the bottle – that's no guarantee of what was actually in them. A combination of those tablets and quantities of drink could well have knocked her over the edge . . . and if she really saw something nasty in the woodshed, as it were . . .' Penelope wasn't sure where her thoughts were leading, and didn't want to follow them. 'Anyway,' she finished on a brisker note, 'The Respite Hospital sounds just the place for her – at a price, of course. It says a lot for Vincent's concern for her that he's willing to pay it.'

'You've been hearing about The Respite?'

'Professional interest. I asked Phyl. Seems it's properly staffed with highly-qualified personnel. They do take some National Health patients but the majority are the crème de la crème – soured by real or imagined ills. I'd like to have visited Mrs Snape if only to have a look at how a place such as that is run. Phyl says they keep it tightly buttoned up. Presumably to keep patients from wandering off.'

'Or entry by unauthorized persons, eh?'

Kemp went off to make a phone call.

Chapter Sixteen

Even in the best of institutions, however, there are always mice, and they have their own means of entry.

Tamsin Jago, just after eight o'clock that night, was sitting in the cavernous kitchen which underpinned and serviced the building spread out above, the wards and corridors, the private rooms and discreetly curtained cubicles, that squatted like a vast iced cake in the centre of The Respite's older lawns and shrubberies. Tamsin's companion, and the target of her evening's endeavour, was one Tom Rickard with whom she had attended the village school and subsequently the local Comprehensive. They were old mates, these two, understanding each other without deeper involvement in much the same manner as they had ganged up on unpopular teachers or teamed with their fellows in the limited sports curriculum designed to exercise their growing bodies and keep them out of mischief.

Mugs of coffee had been provided. Tom was keen to talk.

'Bloody boring, most of the time,' he observed gloomily, 'now you've left. At home they say I'm lucky having the job, but I dunno . . . Youth opportunity, my eye. What's it lead to, I ask myself? Years of cleaning up other people's messes, washing windows, hauling great bags of potatoes, raking out the boilers so that them upstairs can be kept cosy as rabbits. Bloody porter, that's all I am. Up Londonways they'd give the job to a blackie . . .'

'What's it like upstairs, then?' asked Tamsin, slipping easily into his idiom. 'Same like when I was here? Forever sloshing out pails and getting the antiseptic up your nose?'

'Worse, I reckon. There's more inmates . . . Least, that's what I calls 'em. Supposed to be patients. Come in here like it's an hotel. It's Tom, bring those bags, hoist them bales – get a little drunk an' you land in jail,' he carolled. 'Fat chance of gettin' drunk, though, with all their booze locked up.'

'You've got a new one. Mrs Snape.'

Tamsin sipped her coffee, and examined the brown stains on the mug.

'Yeah. Got a right slave-driver for a husband . . .' Once set in a groove Tom's mind tended to stick there. 'Bring up that luggage, Tom, and look sharp about it.'

'Where's she been put?'

'Alcoholics anonymous. Private wing, Room 3. What'd you want to know for?'

'I used to work for her. I want to get in to see her, Tom.'

'Fat chance. You know better than that. No one's allowed into the private wing. No, siree!'

''Cepting staff, of course. When's the time for late night drinkies?'

Tom glanced across at the trays of cups and mugs on the dresser.

'Same as always. The Ovaltinneys come on at nine, that's in about quarter of an hour, the pill-pushers meet them upstairs and dispense sweet dreams like when you was here, Tammy.'

'Who's doing private wing? The ancient Annie?'

'Naw, she's on the sick. We've got Susie Sparks this week standin' in for her. Gosh, you remember Susie from school, Tam. Thick as two short planks an' not even pretty with it. She's only on temp, she won't last. Doesn't take a genius to put on saucepans but they're already complainin' about skin on the top of the milk.'

Tamsin got up from the table and went over to a tall cupboard.

'Uniforms still kept in here?'

'Sure. What've you got in mind?'

Tamsin didn't answer. She rummaged in the cupboard, and in a few minutes stood clad in white overalls, neat cap and flat soft shoes. 'Will I do?'

'Looks like you never left. What're you goin' to do about our Susie?'

'Leave Susie to me. And not a word out of you, Tom Rickard, or I'll not go to the disco with you Friday.'

Susie was a podgy, good-natured lump of a girl who'd been a great admirer of Tamsin at school, and she was easily persuaded to take the weight off her feet and go home to watch the telly.

A short time later at the door of the upstairs dispensary Tamsin balanced her tray of milky drinks on one arm as she received the medicaments from the night sister. The nurse was new to Tamsin but, obviously resigned to the fact that temporary help came and went like the tide, she was in no mood to query someone properly attired and conversant with the routine.

'I'm on the private wing,' said Tamsin, edging in front of the others. She noticed that Room 3 got two pink capsules.

'Well, hurry up then, and no chatting to the patients,' said Sister, scarcely giving her a glance.

The first two calls were easily finished, and for once Tamsin obeyed the injunction.

She pushed open the door of No. 3 and closed it

smartly with her toe. There were two shaded lamps, one on a dressing-table by the window, the other on the bedside locker. The room was full of flowers, the air heavy with their perfume. Crimson roses stared down at Mirabel Snape who lay on the bed under a pink duvet which matched the draped curtains and the thick pile of the carpet. Her eyes were closed, her brown skin faintly yellowish under the scatter of black hair, but she was not asleep and she stirred at Tamsin's step.

'Your night-time drink, Mrs Snape.' Tamsin put the tray down on the floor and herself on the edge of the bed, a practice strictly forbidden to the staff. 'It's me, Tamsin.'

The eyes flicked open, then widened. They were dull as stones. A frown puckered the white space between the dark eyebrows. 'Tamsin? What . . . what are you doing here?'

'Working the night-shift. But never mind that. I have to be quick or I'll be caught. First, I saw your Mr Kemp, like you told me.'

'Mr Kemp?' Mirabel struggled to sit up. 'I don't remember . . .'

'Lennox Kemp. He's the lawyer. Oh, do try, Mirabel, please.'

Tamsin put both hands on the woman's shoulders and gave her a shake. Then, because of her own excited anxiety, her movements became rougher and her small hard palms began to slap at Mrs Snape's cheekbones until she raised a flush of colour, and the clouded eyes shone blue and angry. Mirabel struck out at the slapping hands, and Tamsin stopped, grinning.

'That's better. More like your real self. Now, Lennox Kemp. You must remember him?'

Mirabel gave a croak, near enough to a laugh.

'That man on the beach . . . You found him?' She pressed her fingertips tightly against her forehead. 'Oh, my bloody head . . . They said I had to go into hospital. I can't remember anything else . . .' She tried to push at the bedcover with her feet. 'I seem to be limbless . . . I'm a stranded fish.' She lay back, exhausted.

'It's just that rubbish they've been filling you up with. You're to listen to me. You're not to take any more of their pills. For a start . . .' Tamsin picked up the capsules from the tray and thrust one of them deep into the vase of roses, the other she concealed in the pocket of her overall. 'And don't drink anything they give you. Put it down the loo. Only drink water from the bathroom tap. Can you walk?'

'I'm not encouraged to try,' Mirabel said grimly.

Tamsin threw back the duvet and swung the patient round so that the thin brown legs overhung the edge of the bed. Then she stooped and began to massage the calves and ankles. 'Now, kick out,' she said, 'hard as you can. That's right. Now keep on doing it.' She looked round the room, and nodded. 'There's an electric kettle. I've smuggled you a tin of instant coffee from the kitchen. Hide it and make your own. Lots of it, very strong . . .'

Mirabel stopped waggling her legs, and stared. Then she burst out laughing. 'Where'd you learn all this, Tamsin?'

The girl was disconcerted. 'My gran,' she said, off-hand.

'Your gran knew all about drunks,' said Mirabel drily, 'but I'm not so sure that's what's wrong with me – whatever they may say.'

'You've got to be fit to get out of here,' said the girl fiercely, 'that's what Mr Kemp told me. You do your part and he'll do his. Here's a letter he wrote you. There's no time to read it now, but when you've done, flush it down the toilet . . .' She pushed the note under the pillow.

'You make this place sound like Holloway gaol,' Mrs Snape muttered.

'More like that Tenko series on television,' said Tamsin cheerfully, hiding the coffee tin under the lingerie in the bottom drawer of the dressing-table. 'And when you want a letter taken out, only trust Tom. He's the porter. Get him alone, tell them you need the windows washed or something . . .'

'Tom? Yes, I'll remember . . . I'll try and remember everything.' Mirabel's voice was fading. 'They keep on telling me not to remember . . . That if I do I'll make myself ill again . . .'

'I'll have to go,' said Tamsin, picking up the tray. 'That nurse will be here any minute.'

There was indeed a sharp knock on the door but Tamsin reached it before it was opened.

'Mrs Snape's drunk her milk and taken the tablets,' she said to the nurse. 'I was just going to put out her flowers.'

The nurse walked over to the bed. 'Everything all right, Mrs Snape?'

Mirabel had pulled up the cover and settled her head back on the pillows. Her eyes were closed. 'Yes, thank you,' she whispered, her voice slurred.

The nurse switched off the lamps as Tamsin gathered the vases on her tray, and followed her from the room.

At the end of the corridor a table was already arrayed with containers of other flowers, ferns and foliage turned out for the night hours, and in their collective banishment, having a funereal air.

'I'll get some fresh water for these,' said Tamsin, hearing the patter of the nurse's feet behind her.

'Be quick about it, then.' The nurse stopped to look at the roses, and sniffed – though not in appreciation of their scent. 'Those red ones are ever so expensive, but they're wasted on that Mrs Snape. Her husband brings them and she never so much as gives them a glance.'

She bustled off, calling over her shoulder once again, 'Be quick, now, you're the last on this floor.'

Tamsin watched the pink water flow down the sink, and re-arranged the flowers in fresh water. She would have liked to return to Room 3 but felt it would be pushing her luck, so she merely poked her head into the Sister's cubicle to say good night, then she ran softly downstairs to the kitchen.

'Five pounds you'll have, Tom, if Mrs Snape gives you a letter to bring out.'

Tom shrugged. 'All right by me. No one's ever said nought about carrying letters. It's not like it was a prison.'

'You'd be surprised,' said Tamsin darkly, her fertile imagination still running on hapless captives.

'And you'll not forget the disco Friday?'

'I'll dance your feet off, Tom Rickard.'

But as Tamsin scurried down the drive she had to step back quickly into the shadow of a laurel bush as a large car went past in the direction of the hospital. She caught a glimpse of Dr Sylvester at the wheel, and she suddenly shivered. Doctors were important, she had been brought up to respect them . . . What she had done tonight was against their rules. And the wishes of a man of power and influence like Mr Snape . . . Her sense of adventure faltered. What would happen if she were found out? There'd be the devil to pay – worse than Miss Trevanion's angry words and instant dismissal. Tamsin felt for the tablet in her pocket. Was taking it stealing? She began to feel very small and frightened as she crept out on to the gravel and looked about her. The sky had darkened, and the leaves whispered. There were so many shadows . . . One seemed to move out of the shrubbery up near the curve of the drive where the car had disappeared . . . Tamsin didn't stay to see whether the shadow was real. Clutching the stolen capsule she fled, the word 'stealing' pounding in her head as she ran. She had stolen something, perhaps it was a drug. She'd heard terrible things about stealing drugs. Could she be put in prison for it?

Because Tamsin Jago had only vague ideas about the law, and no real knowledge, the law itself loomed like a threat and somehow got mixed in her mind with the shadowy figure which had crouched, and moved . . .

Chapter Seventeen

The man who did have knowledge of the law was facing it head-on the following morning in official and wrathful shape.

'You sent my men on a wild-goose chase.' When Inspector Gudgeon was angry he dropped his soft West Country accent.

'I'd called on Mr Adair myself,' Kemp protested mildly, 'and he was out. How was I to know he'd scarpered? He might have been sitting on the dunes painting one of his landscape masterpieces . . .'

'Don't monkey with me, Kemp. What's the connection between this Adair and Steven Donray?'

'If I knew that, I'd tell you. All I know is that I heard him threatened.'

'And you won't say where you heard this telephone conversation?'

Kemp spread his hands, palms upwards.

'Does it matter? The words are what counts.'

Gudgeon brooded on them.

'Sand in his mouth . . . and the incoming tide. Sounds nasty, like he was going to drown. What do you make of it?'

'Even nastier than that. He was being made to talk . . . He sang like a dicky-bird . . . When the time came . . . The man who said it knew what he was talking about.'

'Torture?'

Kemp nodded. Both men were silent, leaving the ugly word hanging in the air.

The Inspector gave a deep sigh. 'It's a rotten business, drug-running. Too much at stake, too much money in it, makes people vicious.'

He pulled himself together, and rapped out: 'This call, was it local?'

'I'd no means of knowing. The conversation had been going on some minutes before I picked up the phone. At a guess, I'd say it was local. I understand there have been other threatening calls made to people in this area. Is that so?'

The Inspector moved restlessly. In an angry mood he'd asked Kemp to come into the police station first thing in the morning; now he didn't know what to do with him.

'There have been such calls, yes. They've not been traced if that's what you're asking. You know the impossibility of that.' He shuffled his feet. 'Look, Kemp, you and I know there are gangs out there organizing the running of the stuff but the really big men are well beyond our grasp. They're in Morocco or the South of France. All we can ever hope to catch are the little fish, and then only when something goes wrong.'

'Steve Donray was one of the little fish – but they got to him first?'

The Inspector was not to be drawn. Instead he returned to the offensive.

'When you were in here last you said something about that head being seen before it got into the water. Now I want an explanation from you . . .'

'Which I can't give. It was just a notion.'

'You're obstructing justice.'

Kemp shook his head.

'I don't think so. At present I know nothing that could help you land Donray's killer. We both know now that he was killed, and possibly in a most unpleasant manner. Looks as if Robin Adair's for the same fate unless he's found.' Kemp rose and pushed back his chair. 'Just to satisfy my curiosity, did you have anything on Steve Donray?'

Inspector Gudgeon hesitated. The lawyer might use orthodox methods, and he certainly had a devious way of investigating, but he had got results in the past; he could be trusted.

'We had our suspicions, yes. Shall we just say he was being investigated before he disappeared.'

'And if he knew you were on to him he'd do what they all do. Tell their masters in roguery that they want out. Ask for a final pay-off so that they can take ship for the rosy life in some South American haven. It never works, of course, only the big boys can play that game. The small fry end up in the pan, or at the bottom of the sea. Villains never learn, do they?'

'If they did, I'd be out of a job,' said Gudgeon heavily.

'Was Donray suspected of being the contact man here on the estuary when that unlit boat was challenged and the drop was discovered?'

Again the Inspector would not give a direct answer.

'Something of the sort,' was all he would say.

Kemp persisted. 'And if Donray had a private arrangement with Adair – something his masters knew nothing about until they squeezed it out of him – then our singing fool is next in line for the chop?'

Gudgeon frowned. 'We've only your half-heard conversation to link Adair with Donray,' he said irritably.

'I've checked up on Mr Adair. He's had no convictions for drug offences, in fact no convictions at all. As far as we're concerned, he's clean, and we've no reason to go looking for him.'

Kemp smiled. 'Of course you have. I've given it to you.' He knew Gudgeon. The Inspector was a great picker-up of trifles; Robin Adair would be quietly pursued through inquiries made in a proper manner. What worried Kemp was, would they be made quickly enough? There were other, more savage, hounds on that trail.

He was about to take his leave when a question from Gudgeon startled him.

'Do you know anything about this hospital place called The Respite?'

'I know of it, yes,' he replied cautiously.

'There was a break-in there last night. Report's just come in. One of the doctors got knocked on the head.'

'Should I be interested?'

'Thought you might be,' said the Inspector blandly, 'seeing as you're so concerned with drugs. There's a quantity missing.'

A tight knot formed in Kemp's stomach. What the hell had Tamsin been up to?

He slid the chair forward and sat down again.

'Tell me about it,' he said, quietly.

There wasn't much to tell from the short report on the Inspector's desk. One of the night sisters had found Dr Sylvester lying on the floor of his office about twelve thirty, and a drugs cabinet smashed. She'd called the police, and by the time they arrived the doctor had recovered consciousness but was still dazed and unable to recall exactly what had happened. He said he'd been working late on his medical records when he'd been struck from behind. No, he'd not seen his attacker. The sergeant and the constable had found no broken windows, locks or latches by which the intruder could have entered the premises. The smashed medicine cabinet had not contained dangerous drugs. Dr Sylvester appeared to have stressed that point, and anyway only a small quantity were missing. The doctor's view was that village youths were probably to blame. 'Thought we kept our patients high on heroin,' had been his comment, stolidly taken down by the sergeant and sounding sarcastic, which it possibly was. Dr Sylvester was also angry, and with reason, since it was he who had suffered assault. The weapon, an old-fashioned heavy round ruler from his desk, had been sent for fingerprinting. End of report.

'Dr Sylvester has been on the telephone to me,' said Gudgeon. 'He doesn't want a big thing made of it. Might encourage others, was the way he put it. Not the first time hospitals have been entered in the hope of finding drugs . . . Doesn't want too much publicity given to this.'

'Very accommodating of him.'

'Well, you know what doctors are. And The Respite Hospital has to keep up its image. Wouldn't do for their wealthy clientele to think their refuge could be broken into, eh?'

'I suppose you have to follow it up, though. It's on your patch. You don't think it could possibly tie in with your other business?'

It was Gudgeon's turn to look cunning. 'One of the patients out there is a Mrs Snape. I hear she's been running around with your Mr Robin Adair . . .'

Kemp decided it was time he left; he had urgent business to attend to elsewhere.

* * *

He made the journey from Bodmin to Rocksea only narrowly within the speed limits, and had to draw on reserves of philosophic patience to keep calm in slow-moving traffic. He parked as close to the small Post Office as he could, and made for Myrtle Cottage. Mrs Jago wasn't in her garden but she popped out of the doorway like a wooden weather lady as soon as she heard the click of the gate.

'Tamsin's just up. The maid was out late last night.' The glance she gave him had mischief in it rather than disapproval. 'I'm off to the shop.'

Tamsin was sitting in front of a boiled egg and a cup of tea. Both looked cold. She jumped to her feet when she saw Kemp.

'Am I glad to see you!'

'Eat up your breakfast, child.' He took the chair across the table from her. At the window the lily heads peered in like frustrated eavesdroppers.

'You sound like my gran. I can't eat a thing this morning.'

'Try. And while you're keeping up your strength you can tell me about last night.'

'I got in, Mr Kemp. I saw Mrs Snape, and she's got your note.'

The girl was nervous. She took up her cup and went into the scullery. She brought it back empty, and a cup and saucer for Kemp. 'Can't stand cold tea. But it's fresh in the pot.' She poured for both of them, then tackled her egg. Kemp waited.

Finally she said: 'I got that tablet for you.' She handed him a screwed up bit of paper which he put quickly into his pocket. Tamsin's eyes followed the movement. 'I've been ever so worried,' she said. 'I'm glad to get rid of it. Was it wrong what I done?'

'No, it wasn't, Tamsin. I was wrong to ask you to do it. But never mind that now. Tell me about Mrs Snape.'

With the pill safely in other hands the girl recovered something of her old spirit, and she gave a fairly coherent account of her visit to The Respite. She was anxious for his admiration for her exploit – to her it seemed well-earned.

'And nothing else happened? You only saw your friend Tom, and the nursing staff – none of the doctors?'

'I saw Dr Sylvester's car going in when I was leaving. He never saw me. I ducked into the bushes.'

'What time was this?'

But Tamsin was vague. Keeping note of time wasn't one of her strong points.

'I'd been excited at it all being so easy, like . . . But it was so dark in the drive, and I began to get scared. I s'pose it was seeing the doctor's big car made me think how angry they'd all be . . . I ran home.'

Traces of that fear showed now in her voice, and affected Kemp.

'I shouldn't have asked you to go there.'

'I'd have gone anyway to see Mirabel, honestly I would have,' Tamsin said fiercely, 'and I'll go again. Maybe she'll get a letter out through Tom . . .'

But Kemp had a twinge of conscience; he didn't want to involve these two young people further, certainly not now that the police would be investigating the break-in.

'Listen carefully, Tamsin. I have to tell you this straight because you'll hear about it anyway. Someone entered The Respite last night and struck Dr Sylvester on the head. Some drugs were stolen from a cabinet in his room.'

Tamsin went white so that her freckles stood out like brown blotches.

'I never went near the doctors' rooms, Mr Kemp . . . They're on the ground floor at the front. I was only in the kitchen and then up the back stairs to the ward. I never used the main stairway . . . And I only took that one tablet from Mrs Snape's tray . . .'

She was biting her knuckles, and her voice broke in frantic sobs.

Kemp rose, and put an arm round her shoulders. 'It's all right, Tamsin. No one's going to blame you. Tell me, what time does Tom come off duty?'

'Eight in the morning,' she gulped. 'Should I go and see him?'

'No,' said Kemp firmly, 'you keep out of it from now on. Leave Tom to me.'

'He lives over the cycle shop. It's his brother's place.'

'One more thing, Tamsin, then I'll leave you alone. You said you felt frightened when you were leaving The Respite last night. Think back. What made you frightened?'

Tamsin concentrated. 'It was creepy. The trees were rustling and there were shadows. After Dr Sylvester's car had disappeared in the direction of the front door I thought I saw . . . It was only like a shadow that moved out from the bushes . . . Oh, Mr Kemp, do you think I saw whoever did it?' She put her hand to her mouth, and spoke through spread fingers. 'And the time would matter?'

'It might.'

'I wasn't long in the kitchen with Tom once I'd come downstairs, then I slipped out the back and through the bushes to the drive 'cos it's the only way to the

172

gate.' Tamsin screwed up her eyes. 'It was well after eleven when I got home – Gran heard me come in.'

'So it would be about half past ten when you saw this shadow?'

Tamsin nodded. Her eyes were wide, and Kemp thought her imagination seemed about to take off.

'It sort of crouched, and ran . . . I think. I was scared.'

'Don't be. All this has nothing to do with you, Tamsin. I'm only sorry I got you involved. I'm going to have a word with your friend, Tom.'

But it was some hours before Kemp was able to speak to that local hero, who was reliving his brief moment upon the stage for the benefit of other youths gathered at the rear of the cycle shop.

'Kept us hanging about all the morning, they did, the fuzz . . .' Kemp guessed it was the first time Tom Rickard had used the term and he was relishing the opportunity. 'Bloody useless, the fuzz . . . Where'd I been, what was the time . . . Lucky for me the night staff had been in and out of my kitchen at all hours brewin' up their tea and gossip . . . And I never moved from there. Why should I? I'm only on call for emergencies like the lights failin', or one of the dipsos starts bangin' on the radiators . . . I could tell you things,' he finished, darkly.

Kemp managed eventually to draw him aside from his audience.

'My name's Lennox Kemp. I'm a lawyer acting for Miss Tamsin Jago in connection with an unfair dismissal case. You know Miss Jago?'

'What of it?' The boy's mouth took on a grim line.

'I know that Miss Jago visited Mrs Snape at The Respite last night, Tom. She had to see her because she'd been employed by Mrs Snape. Did you tell the police she'd been there?'

Tom continued to look sullen for a moment but Kemp's straightforward approach and friendly manner set him more at ease.

''Course I didn't. No business of theirs. She won't get into no trouble will she, Tamsin I mean?'

'No, she won't. It was on my advice she went. It's not normally a good thing to keep information from the police, Tom, but on this occasion you were right not to tell them. Tamsin Jago's call on Mrs Snape had nothing to do with the break-in. You have my word on that.'

Tom Rickard relaxed, dropped his tough attitude, and became the rather bewildered but honest young man he really was.

'Can't say it didn't worry me, her being there earlier, Mr Kemp, but seems the doctor was okay at eleven o'clock. Told the police he'd looked at the clock himself. Tamsin was gone long before that . . . Besides, she wouldn't . . .'

'Of course she wouldn't,' said Kemp briskly. 'Have you got any ideas yourself about this break-in?'

Tom looked at him in astonishment; he wasn't used to being asked for any ideas of his own.

'I dunno. It's a queer place, that. Not just because it's a funny farm . . .' He hastily tried to correct himself. 'I mean they take patients who're not right in the head. Well, you know . . . We've been told to keep quiet about it – to reporters and that . . .'

'I'm not a reporter, Tom.'

'Not that I've anything to tell them. Whoever did get in last night was some careful about it. I never heard nothing, nor did the nurses, an' they're flappin' around all the time . . . Do you want my opinion, Mr Kemp?'

'I'd be glad of it.'

'I don't think there was no real break-in,' said the boy, all in a rush. 'I mean a proper burglar breaks windows, smashes locks, that kind of thing. There weren't none of that. I know 'cos I checked all the places the fuzz never thought to look. And this business of trying to hush it up . . . What if it were done by an inmate – there's plenty of them daft enough?'

'An interesting theory.' Kemp smiled.

Tom's jaw suddenly dropped.

'I near forgot. You're Lennox Kemp. I've got a letter for you.'

He struggled with the pocket of his leather jacket, and produced a crumpled envelope. 'Mrs Snape. She complained her radiator leaked this morning, insisted I fix it, wouldn't wait for the dayman. Nothing wrong with the radiator, but she gave me this. No name on it but she said for Mr Lennox Kemp. 'Course the fuzz searched me – daft, I call that, if I'd taken any stuff I'd have stashed it in the kitchen flour-bin double quick. Anyway, this was in my wallet with my driving licence and some bills . . . No room there for capsules – isn't that what they're called? – of sleeping tablets.'

Kemp put the envelope into his pocket and asked thoughtfully, 'Is that all that was missing – sleeping tablets?'

Tom shrugged.

'That's all that's ever in that cabinet. The real stuff's kept in the safe.'

'Is that so? How very interesting.'

Although the break-in at The Respite seemed by now to be merely peripheral to Kemp's main quest, he had obtained more information about it than he had expected from young Rickard, and as he left the cycle shop he was as puzzled as he surmised the police were. He wondered just how hard Dr Sylvester had been struck to have recovered so quickly.

And for all that she had a fertile imagination, Tamsin was not one to be scared of the dark, nor jump at shadows. To have sent her scurrying home that shadow must have been real, the shadow that crouched, and then ran . . .

Chapter Eighteen

It was a small envelope of the kind used by florists to take a card, and the note inside was scribbled in pencil on thin paper that could have wrapped flowers.

I must keep my mind on you, what you said on the beach. All else is nightmare. Tamsin says you are real and your letter proves it. Finding it hard to distinguish what is real. There are things you ask I can't answer. Things swim in and out of my mind. I'll try. Try to remember. There was a head in the sand near the Point. Tide very low. He said (this was crossed out) They say I dreamt it, part of my illness like the other things. I think Robin was away a long time. He laughed, not nicely, then teased about my silly dream. Ask him, please ask him. Or is he with them? You sound sane, I wish I was sure I was but if I'm sane then it's worse, isn't it?

No visitors but Aunt and V. And they're different now . . . Tamsin is the same, hold on to that. I do what you say with the pills and drinks. I'm walking around. They don't know that. Yes, I'm fighting back. Who are you to tell me? I don't even know you. Don't know anybody any more. Are they on that other level you talked about?

Something's going on this morning. Nurses all shut-mouthed and rattled. Tom was the name Tamsin said. I'll give him this.

The writing was a scrawl, sometimes firm where she'd pressed the pencil hard, sometimes so faint he could scarcely read it. There was a curvy 'M', and underneath: 'I'd give anything for a smoke.'

Kemp could almost hear the croak of a laugh. She's all right, he thought, she'll come through. But come through what? He suspected the worst of things he didn't know; areas of ignorance. Time he found out.

He'd given the capsule to Penelope, who turned it over between her fingers. 'Looks like an ordinary sleeping pill to me. What do you want done?'

'Have it analysed. Do you know the kind?'

'Yes. Innocent enough but a bit strong, especially if there's a daytime dose as well. That would keep a patient fairly sedated if necessary. She's not on the rampage, your Mirabel Snape?'

Despite the words there was a kinder note in Penelope's voice. Let him go, she had been telling herself since the afternoon at Treyarnon, you've no right to hold him now.

'No, she's not on the rampage as you put it,' said Kemp firmly. 'I think she's been drugged nearly out of her mind, and I can only guess as to why and for how long. Someone somewhere has an interest in keeping her that way.'

'That's a serious allegation, Lennox, and anyway it doesn't fit the facts. I met Miss Trevanion this morning, and she actually discussed her niece's case with me. I think she was glad to talk to someone who could understand it from a professional point of view.'

'You mean your genteel lady at last opened up on the drink problem?'

'It wasn't mentioned. You know these things aren't talked about when they happen in the best families.

No, Mirabel's case isn't really that unusual. It started soon after Simon's birth, and her London physician diagnosed post-natal depression. That's common enough, even in well-heeled young matrons like Mrs Snape. But she didn't respond to treatment, and it seems she continued to suffer from bouts of depression. She had a bad one just before coming down here – Mr Snape and her aunt thought the holiday would be beneficial.'

'Instead of which she began playing around with Adair, and drinking more than ever?'

'That's about it. It was hearing about Steve Donray sent her into the catatonic state I saw her in . . . Did she really see that head?'

Kemp looked grim. 'I think she did.'

'And Adair was with her? Then why on earth . . .?'

'That's something I've got to find out.'

Gudgeon hadn't been pleased at the enigmatic message.

'What the devil do you mean – in the sand near the Point?' he'd barked on the phone.

'The Point where the estuary meets the open sea,' Kemp told him patiently. 'At low tide the sandbanks there are firm. I've had a word with a local fisherman who says it's only in a bad winter storm that the sand might shift. Then things sometimes get uncovered that have lain there for years, old ships' timbers and anchors . . . Otherwise they'd remain buried for ever. Look, I'm only an ignorant landsman, you must have plenty of people who know the estuary . . .'

'Ignorant's the word,' growled the Inspector. 'There's miles of sand out there. And I want to know where you got this information from.'

'Can't answer that. Be thankful for any hint. What's the news on Adair?'

'Neither sight nor sound of him. We've still got no good reason to look.'

'But you will.' Kemp had smiled to himself as he put down the phone. Gudgeon would take up any lead, no matter how fragile the thread. Robin Adair had made a hurried exit from his studio, he did not appear to have a car. As Phyl Morris told Kemp: 'Robin likes to play the barefoot beggar owning no possessions. Never stops him having the use of Miss Trevanion's car, though, when he wants it . . .' Gudgeon's force might be small but this wasn't London, inquiries would have been made at car hirers already, and with local taxi firms. Besides, Adair was well-known, someone would see him sooner or later. If he was still alive . . .

In the meantime, there was always Susan Trevanion who had looked with such indulgence on his playfulness. Would she have the same attitude towards her protégé now that his laughter had turned to tears?

Greystones House looked peaceful enough, smiling at the afternoon sun as if it was a visitor to whom the occupants were graciously at home. Miss Trevanion too smiled at Kemp, but frostily, when Brenda Arbuthnot showed him into the drawing-room. He had presented a card and reckoned that it was the writing on the reverse – 'About Mr Robin Adair' – which had gained him entry, if not any very obvious welcome.

Susan Trevanion seemed to have aged since he had glimpsed her at the Yacht Club luncheon; the pink cheeks were paler, the careful arrangement of grey curls could not hide gaunt cheekbones and a thinning scalp. She had grey eyes which she tended to narrow from time to time as if they might be hurt by light – or perhaps by the thoughts behind them.

'I don't think we've met before, Mr Kemp, although I've played bridge with your fiancée, Mrs Marsden.'

They sat and weighed each other up. On a table at Kemp's elbow bunched rosebuds spilled a little perfume. Smoke might spoil the fragrant air, nevertheless he took out cigarettes. 'May I?'

'Of course.' She indicated a cut-glass ashtray, and smoothed down her tweed skirt. It looked a little warm for the day but her blue cotton blouse was open-necked, giving her a girlish appearance and a resemblance to Mirabel which startled him.

He hoped the conversation would remain as civilized as the surroundings. She would keep to the niceties, it would be in her nature to do so, a protective screen while her mind ranged elsewhere. Kemp's tactics when faced with her kind drew on his experience of them. First, allay suspicion by soft words, acquiesce in the polite patterns of speech by which such people keep reality at bay, then when the going got rough, administer the shock which breaks the mould . . .

'Thank you for seeing me, Miss Trevanion. Yes, Penelope has told me about you, and how she wished she could be of some help. You must be very distressed by your niece's illness.'

'I'm afraid we saw it coming, Mr Kemp. Mirabel has a history of instability. It is of quite long standing.'

'I did some work for Mr Snape in London. He must have been upset by his wife's sudden collapse the other night – especially since she came on holiday, as I understand it, to regain her health. I suppose he's gone back to Town?'

'Mr Snape is a busy man, as I'm sure you know. But

he's left poor Mirabel in good hands. Dr Sylvester at The Respite Hospital is very experienced in cases like hers.' With a brusque movement Miss Trevanion dismissed the subject as something no longer to be discussed. 'But you didn't come here to talk about Mrs Snape.'

Kemp lounged back in his chair, put one leg over the other and scattered ash on the chintz upholstery. 'Oh, she interests me a lot, your lovely niece. Did she tell you we've met? No, I didn't think she had. She was in great party mood the last time I saw her. Likes a drink, doesn't she? But don't we all, these days, eh? Doesn't mean we qualify for that funny farm up the road.' He gave her a knowing grin which he hoped she would find insolent.

She did. The change in his demeanour struck her like a dash of cold water. She drew herself up, her nostrils pinched in disapproval.

'I will not have my niece spoken of like that.'

'Like what, Miss Trevanion? Everybody's doing it.'

She strove to control the situation. She still had his card in her hand. She looked at it with distaste.

'You indicated this was about Mr Adair?'

'Yeah. I'm interested in him too. Having an affair were they, your niece and this Adair chap?'

Kemp carelessly stubbed out his cigarette. Susan Trevanion's outraged eyes followed the trail of ash as it greyed the almond blossom of the Chinese carpet.

Of course at this juncture she should have risen in affronted majesty and shown him the door. That she didn't, in view of his barbarian behaviour, confirmed Kemp's belief that it was not mere curiosity which held her back.

Her figure was rigid, her face white, but her voice remained steady. 'You should ask Mr Adair that.'

'If I can find him. But the police will probably get to him first . . .'

Now I'm kicking old ladies, Kemp thought as he calmly lit another cigarette; at this moment he didn't like himself much.

'The police . . .?' His card fluttered to the floor as she put both hands before her face in an attitude of prayer.

'I'm afraid so, Miss Trevanion. Seems your Robin's been playing naughty games.'

Her thin fingers were on her lips as if to steady their trembling.

'What games?' she whispered.

'I think you know about some of them,' Kemp said softly. 'The one he was playing with Mirabel . . . the one you encouraged . . . Harmless, was it, that holiday fling to raise her out of depression?'

Kemp had drawn his chair nearer to her, to where she sat hunched now, her face crumpled, her eyes wide, staring into his with some spark behind them that might have been hope.

There was a silence before she spoke.

'I thought it was harmless. Robin said . . . he wouldn't go too far. Mirabel was so low when she came . . . she needed company. He was good for her . . . there was nothing in it . . .' Her voice trailed off.

'And no one put you up to it?'

Again something flicked in the eyes. But she shook her head.

Kemp got to his feet, and once again assumed his normal urbane self. 'I shall send your maid to you,

Miss Trevanion. You've had a shock. I'm sorry I had to do it.'

She looked up at him. 'Why do the police want to find Robin?'

'I think he had another game going as well as the one with your niece. A silly game, but a dangerous one. Drugs.'

Susan Trevanion shuddered.

'I . . . I didn't know.'

He watched her carefully for a moment. She was old, she had possibly seen little of the underside of life, and what she had guessed at she would draw her skirts away from as though such paths were too muddy for her to tread. She knew all right, at the back of her mind, what had been going on at Greystones; it simply didn't suit her to recognize the facts.

He wondered if she was really so fond of her niece. It is a mistake to presume that just because spinster aunts are sweet and homely-looking their affections should be taken for granted. If Mirabel Snape's life were to spiral downwards into a well of drink and drugs, if she were to become incapable of managing her own affairs, who would benefit?

He put the ugly thought from him, and only said: 'You must see that your niece gets better. You must insist that she leave that hospital, and comes back to her son. Do you understand me, Miss Trevanion?'

She didn't raise her head but he saw her nod.

'If you don't, I'll be back.'

He didn't altogether mean it as a threat but his parting words were sternly spoken.

He went into the kitchen, where he found Brenda Arbuthnot at the table with the little boy.

'I think your mistress would like her tea now,' he said, his eyes resting on Simon.

'I've the tray all ready.' She bustled over to the kettle. 'I'll make some fresh. I wasn't sure whether . . .' There were two cups on the tray along with the gleaming silver service; had his interview gone otherwise, he might have been allowed to stay and share the ceremony. As it was, he stayed for some time anyway, for Simon insisted that this nice man should see the new railway all set up in the playroom.

'Present from his daddy,' said the nursemaid before she went to the drawing-room with the reviving tea; Kemp hoped Miss Trevanion had recovered sufficiently to enjoy its benefit.

Had he been wise, as well as compassionate, in letting this elderly spinster off the hook? At least Robin Adair couldn't be hiding in the house – not with a prattling child about – but he had to be sure.

A casual inquiry of Brenda when she came to the playroom for her small charge drew the reply that she'd never seen Mr Adair from the studio down the garden.

'That phone keeps ringing for him, but he's not there. Miss Trevanion says not to answer it, that Mr Adair's gone away. None of my business. I've enough to do here.'

She stood watching Kemp playing on the floor with Simon.

'He's quite taken to you, Mr Kemp. I can always tell when people are good with children.' It was her highest accolade, and Kemp was inordinately pleased by it. He'd just been explaining why you shouldn't have two engines coming in opposite directions on the same track. 'That's no way to run a railway,' he said in mock severity as he scrambled to his feet. 'Although collisions can be fun.'

'Crash, bang,' said Simon, his face crinkling with delight.

Kemp laughed too as the child's hands tried to push the locomotives together. It was an elaborate layout for a two-year-old; Vincent Snape evidently expected his son to grow up fast.

Chapter Nineteen

When Kemp left Greystones the house was still smiling at the sun but a little uncertainly, for the shadows had lengthened, making bars across its indomitable front. Kemp's mind was in that disordered state which precludes concentration. All the same, a natural inclination to leave no stone unturned – or as Penelope called it, his unnatural habit of snooping – made him glance in at the garage. Miss Trevanion's car, the red one which had brought Mirabel into his life, was still there.

Kemp strolled down towards the Studio.

Someone was leaning against the closed door trying to look inconspicuous, a difficult essay when you're in uniform. He straightened up at Kemp's approach.

'Well, well, Sergeant Ivell. Can't you get in?'

The sergeant looked a bit sheepish.

'We've no good reason to break in, Mr Kemp. 'Tis Miss Trevanion's property, like. She's a lady of some esteem hereabouts. Wouldn't do, going upsetting her.'

'Then why're you here?'

'Orders. Keep an eye on the place. Not that I wouldn't like to have a look inside. There's talk of a search warrant but the Inspector's not sure he can show cause . . .'

Kemp had a moment's thought.

'If I were you, Sergeant,' he said carefully, 'I'd go up to the house right now and ask Miss Trevanion nicely for a key. As you say, it's really her property, and I'm sure she's got keys for all the outbuildings.'

Ivell's face brightened.

'That's an idea.' He hesitated. 'But the Inspector didn't want her upset . . . Won't she find it a bit odd having a policeman at her door?'

'She won't, Sergeant, take my word for it. And as a good citizen she'll be only too glad to cooperate.'

He watched Ivell stride purposefully off in the direction of the house, and he waited.

After about five minutes the sergeant returned, looking pleased with himself.

'Just as you said. Pleased to help, she was. That's a rare lady up there, never asked any questions. Handed over the keys without a murmur.'

They picked out the one that had a label 'Coach-house' crossed out, and 'Studio' written in precise capitals. The lock was fairly new, and the key turned easily.

The place looked much as it had done the morning Kemp had bought the pictures, perhaps a little dustier and more untidy. A coffee mug containing dried brown dregs stood on the table, alongside a bottle of soured milk, and on a plate a half-eaten saffron bun with a fringe of green mould.

'H'm, left in a hurry,' said Ivell sagaciously. Kemp made no comment.

They began a systematic search, the sergeant making no objection to Kemp's presence beyond a muttered: 'Suppose I should have contacted Gudgeon, but now you're here . . .'

Halfway through he remarked with some admiration, 'You do seem to know how to go about it, I'll say that for you, Mr Kemp. Shouldn't have thought it a lawyer's job, like . . .'

Kemp looked up from his task of examining a pile of

empty frames and mouldings. 'You'd be surprised what the legal profession can get up to when it's proof they're looking for.' He didn't add that his years with McCready's Detective Agency in Walthamstow had taught him more about turning over premises than it would be proper for the good sergeant to know.

Ivell went through to the bedroom, beyond which there was a mini-bathroom, complete with shower and a toilet. A brief glance had shown Kemp that the bedroom itself was neatly if sparsely furnished with a hanging wardrobe, dressing-table and comfortable-looking bed at present unmade. The bare floorboards were partly covered by a couple of rag rugs. Miss Trevanion had evidently provided her young friend with all he could reasonably require for an easy life – he was probably never even asked for something as mundane as rent. Kemp had averted his eyes from the bed, he didn't want to speculate how far Robin Adair had gone with that particular sleazy game.

He was busy scrutinizing the clutter of artist's working materials on the bench by the window when he heard a low whistle from the other room.

'You found something?' He went over to the bedroom door and watched Ivell. The rag rugs had been swept to one side and the sergeant was prising up a floorboard.

'Too bloody obvious,' said Ivell succinctly, groping in the cavity. 'Loose board, not even properly replaced. He's an amateur, this idiot . . .'

He drew out a narrow cardboard box marked 'Rowney Georgian'. 'Nice butterfly,' he observed, looking at the cover as he brought the box in and laid it on the table. 'Bet what's in it isn't so innocent. Got a plastic bag anywhere? This looks like evidence.'

Kemp found one and they carefully slid out the contents of the box: a shower of variously coloured tablets, too tightly screwed-up plastic packages, some small flat bottles, and a packet bearing the name of quite ordinary cigarettes. It was open, and Ivell gently rolled one out, and sniffed.

'Reefers. Well, what'd you know?'

'Nice mixture he's got there,' observed Kemp. 'Those white powders look dangerous. He's been trying a little of this, a little of that, our Mr Adair.'

His voice did not betray the cold fury he was feeling. A little of this, a little of that, a little drink so the medicine goes down, and, yes, you'd be ready for the funny farm in no time . . .

He watched the sergeant replace the contents in the box and place it in the plastic bag. Ivell handled it almost reverently. 'Only my prints on that,' he remarked. Kemp nodded. He was always ready to give the nod to police procedure; it was fair, tolerably impartial and dealt with facts as they came up.

However, when he had parted from Sergeant Ivell and was on his way back to the hotel his thoughts went further. To solve a crime in his opinion you needed more than procedure, you needed a knowledge of people as they lived their lives outside the criminal infrastructure. Policemen – particularly the younger element, full of zest and ambition – tended to view everyone as potentially if not actively criminal, or at the very least, on the make. That it was a warped vision seemed understandable, the media being so full of the rising crime figures – tacitly ignoring the fact that neither eighteenth-century nor nineteenth-century England had ever been a law-abiding paradise and the rates of detection in those times quite laughable by modern standards.

In Kemp's view – for he leaned to the long rather than the short – humankind had been beset by violence and chicanery of various sorts since the creation. There had always been exploiters of the weak, and pathological killers were not unknown to history though many would have escaped its pages. Thieves and robbers lurked then as now in the hovels of the poor and in the counting-houses of the rich, and there had always been upward-climbing entrepeneurs ready at the drop of a hat to capitalize on the misfortunes of plague and famine. Lazily, Kemp never questioned the whys and wherefores, neither did he allow himself to be surprised by the deviousness of the human mind given over to the pursuit of temporal power or the aggrandizement of the self. Once the premise was accepted that the mores of the age dictated an individual's needs and aspirations, it followed that such aims as they might have could be reached by fair means or foul depending on their moral sense, or lack of it. So crime had to be fought with cognizance of these floating aspirations, the personal element always to the fore when seeking the motive behind the unlawful act.

He brooded now on Susan Trevanion. He could understand, even sympathize with, her predicament. She loved her home, Greystones, in its superb setting by the sea, her garden and her way of life. She was the lady of the manor, deferred to by the native Cornish, one of them but superior by lineage, toadied to by the incomers – and who can resist being toadied to? – but she was growing old. She was only living in the house on sufferance as it were, and on a diminished income. Did she worry about her future? What if the Snapes' marriage broke up, and Mirabel were to marry again, this time not so richly? The niece might then want Greystones for herself, a new husband, a new family.

Yet Miss Trevanion had been playing a devious game with Mirabel, smiling upon, encouraging the liaison with Adair – surely that might have brought about the very thing she feared . . .

There was something deeper going on here. Kemp almost had a mind to return and shake the truth out of her. Just because you're an old age pensioner, he argued to himself, you should not escape censure. In the cities old ladies get mugged for their rent money, why should Miss Trevanion be protected from the evil upon which she had turned an unseeing eye?

But Kemp didn't go back. It's the scenery, he thought wryly. He would have acted differently in Newtown where the effects of crime impinged more swiftly upon the people concerned. Here, nature took over. The tide's turning and the changing colours, the slow procession of the skies, they all had a soporific effect on the mind. At least they had on his. From the steps of the hotel he looked back at the house; the dark trees above it waved nonchalantly at him. Damn it, he thought, I've disturbed her enough for one day. She'll have some explaining to do once Ivell gets his booty into the Inspector's hands. But she'll handle it in her usual patrician style: Mr Adair, such a nice young man . . . No, of course she had no idea . . .

Chapter Twenty

Having breakfast the next morning with Penelope, Kemp felt himself to be wasting time, as if he were sitting in the theatre at a play – possibly a Noël Coward comedy – while all the action was taking place out there in the streets. Indeed, his new relationship with Penelope had for him taken on an element of gentle farce for she had underlined it, tactfully perhaps, by sleeping last night in the other bed of their double room. Kemp had made no comment.

But now she was putting herself deliberately on his side as if to emphasize her allegiance – at least on a day-to-day basis.

'I'm off to Bodmin this morning,' she announced briskly, 'to see one of the sisters at the hospital there. I found out from Phyl that she's a Mrs Pengelly who trained with me at the London. I'll have a word with her about getting this capsule analysed in their lab, though I can't see why you don't just go to the Public Analyst . . .'

'Don't want to rock any boats just yet. As you say, it looks perfectly ordinary to me.'

'H'm.' Penelope had unrolled it from an envelope and now she inspected it more closely. 'It's a brand name, of course, but the trouble with capsules is that they can be taken apart. Do you think that's what Robin Adair was doing?'

'With that stockpile he had there, anything's possible.'

'But why? Just for kicks?'

'Something more serious. Adair doesn't need kicks. He's an artist.'

'What's that supposed to mean?'

Kemp tried to work it out. 'He needs money. Enough money to let him live and paint the way he wants to – the only way that gives him any real satisfaction. The days are gone when artists starved in garrets – even Parisian garrets. Adair has to have money. It's a common enough urge but in his case he'd go to any lengths to get it.'

'Such as running drugs?'

'That's for the police to find out, but I don't think Adair was into the main racket. He's much too light-weight for the big boys to trust, and not thick enough just to be used running errands. No, I'd say he got into it by accident through Donray. He probably guessed what Donray was up to and put a bit of pressure on to have small amounts of the stuff slipped to himself. He was genuinely surprised by that telephone call. If he'd been one of their regular runners he'd have been expecting it . . . It never occurred to him that Steve would ever mention their little sideline to anyone. In the circumstances mention is hardly the word – it was dragged out of him . . .'

Penelope shuddered.

'I can't help thinking of his play-acting, that sabre-dance thing he did.'

'He was on a high that day. Perhaps he'd been experimenting himself with the stuff he was feeding to Mirabel Snape. It's possible he too wanted to forget seeing that head but his temperament wouldn't let him. The image was there before his eyes, and he danced to its tune.'

Penelope didn't want to let her mind dwell on what was to her an unimaginable horror, so she changed the subject.

'And Mirabel Snape?'

Kemp looked grim but she knew him well enough to recognize that he was also nervous.

'I'm going to see her,' he said shortly.

'They won't let you in. Remember, no visitors.'

'We'll see about that. Thanks, Penelope, for what you're doing. You don't have to, you know.'

She looked at him squarely, her honest hazel eyes very bright.

'I'm just as interested in Mirabel as you are – but my interest's professional. Which is more than you can say for yours.'

With that parting gibe, albeit said with an understanding smile, she left him.

The weather was no longer halcyon and as he drove to The Respite Kemp found more people on the narrow roads between Rocksea and Westerbridge than there were on the beaches. However, few cars turned off into the wooded valley where the hospital sheltered its pampered clientele from rough sea winds and unwelcome attention.

It had been a fine house once, in the Edwardian style, crowned with those pepperpot towers that builders of the time were apt to set up with excess of zeal and fancy ironwork. There was a wide verandah where delicately perspiring ladies might well have rested after hectic tennis matches on the lawn. Today there were neither ladies nor gentlemen visible.

The front entrance had been solidly reconstructed, secure behind a steel-framed thick glass porch. Alongside, a panel of push-buttons gave Kemp a wide choice: Doctors, Staff, or Visitors. He chose the third.

Through the double-glazing he glimpsed a white figure, and the door was eventually opened by a primly-starched woman. He guessed she would answer all three bells.

'May I help you?' Her voice bore no indication that she would.

'I'd like to see one of your patients. Mrs Snape.'

'If you will come in, I'll inquire.'

She led him through the porch, and into a spacious hall. The floor was highly polished, with a square of glowing carpet, but there was little furniture save for the receptionist's desk, a few small tables and chairs, and pedestals of hothouse flowers. Closed doors marked each side of the room, and at the far end a handsome staircase rose and curved away into darkness.

The nurse gestured towards a velvet-covered swivel chair placed discreetly just out of earshot of the switchboard on her desk. After several minutes' conversation on the telephone, she turned to Kemp.

'I'm sorry, sir, but Mrs Snape is seeing no visitors.'

'So I understand,' he said, hitching his chair closer, 'but I should like a word with her doctor. It's Dr Sylvester, isn't it?'

Again a muttered colloquy took place of which Kemp heard not a word. Then she asked him: 'Who shall I say is inquiring?'

'Lennox Kemp. I'm a solicitor.'

She spoke into the mouthpiece, paused, then replaced the phone. 'If you will wait, Mr Kemp.'

At least five minutes passed before there was the sound of footsteps and one of the doors to the right of the receptionist's desk opened.

Had Kemp anticipated a sinister figure, bearded and

inscrutable – as he might well have done from Tamsin's account – he would have been disappointed. Piers Sylvester belied his name and calling by looking more like a farmer than any in the neighbourhood. Broad-shouldered and of a healthy, ruddy complexion, the effect of a countryman was heightened by his rough tweed jacket and corduroy trousers. He was not, however, hearty in his manner.

'I understand you would like to see me about one of my patients?'

Steely politeness with a trace of hauteur.

Kemp rose to his feet.

'Mrs Mirabel Snape. If we could have a few words?'

Kemp handed him his card. The doctor looked at it, and with some reluctance said: 'Very well. I'm rather busy, but . . .'

He took Kemp through the door to an inner corridor running the length of the building. At the end he showed him into what was obviously his office and consulting room. It was modern, and had been well, and expensively, equipped.

'Please sit down, Mr – er – Kemp.' He looked at Kemp's card again before placing it on his desk as if to remind himself of some trivial matter. 'What is your interest in Mrs Snape?'

'I represent one of her former employees.' Kemp took a chair and settled into it as though for a long stay. 'It's essential I see Mrs Snape as soon as possible.'

'Quite out of the question. Mrs Snape sees no one except her immediate family.'

'Come, come, Doctor, she's not that ill. She was hopping about quite merrily a week ago. People like her don't take ill suddenly unless it's appendicitis or something of that sort – and then she'd be in a proper hospital, wouldn't she?'

Kemp put as much insolence into the words as he could muster, at the same time noting how frosty the doctor's bright blue eyes were growing. 'I mean, this so-called collapse of hers . . . Now you and I know that kind of thing doesn't happen to healthy women.'

If the full frontal attack fazed Piers Sylvester, he showed no sign of it. Psychiatrists must get used to verbal assault, Kemp thought, but a bludgeon should get me results quicker than the polite scalpel.

'You know nothing of Mrs Snape's condition, either before or after her recent collapse,' the doctor was saying smoothly. 'I suggest you leave such judgement to those better qualified to make it.'

'Fully qualified, are you? I suppose you'd need to be to have charge of a place like this . . .' He waved a hand vaguely around, at the same time as his eyes took in the position of the filing cabinets, the range of glass-fronted cupboards, and the fact that the window had steel bars across it. 'Expensive layout all this . . . Doesn't come with the National Health, eh?'

'Mr Kemp, I'm a busy man. I don't think I have anything more to say to you.'

Studied politeness, no reaction whatsoever to blatant rudeness. Kemp was amused. A professional man himself, he could recognize and appreciate the doctor's attitude. It was one he also had cultivated, and often assumed when in the presence of a particularly blustering and ill-informed client.

He would have to use sharper weapons.

He sat back firmly in his seat to show he'd no intention of leaving it, and gave Sylvester a grin of pure comradeship.

'Nice little business, the private sector nowadays,' he remarked conversationally. 'You doctors must be raking in as much as some of my own professional buddies. Wealthy clients with tax problems, they come to us, we wind 'em up with the jolly old legal jargon, overload their precious little minds and they end up here for comfort and capsules. We've a lot in common, you and I, Dr Sylvester . . .'

It was good offensive stuff, and Kemp had the satisfaction of watching the reddish hue in the other man's cheeks rise to the forehead. The pen that had been idly held in one hand began a rapid tattoo on the surface of the desk.

For his part, Dr Sylvester saw a carelessly-dressed, rather scruffy individual with disturbingly opaque grey eyes who seemed to be relishing the absurd delusion that there could be some complicity between them. The doctor was used to persons with delusions but was not prepared to put up with them for long when there was no money in it. He began to get to his feet, in a signal of dismissal.

'I don't know what you hope to gain by rudeness, Mr Kemp,' he said coldly.

'Bluntness, please. No disrespect intended,' Kemp admonished him, then abruptly changed his tack. 'That was a nasty knock on the head you got from that burglar. Supposed to have been after the pills, wasn't he? You must get through a lot of these. Expensive to buy, are they, these uppers and downers, or should I give them their proper names, amphetamines and barbiturates?'

'What's that to do with you?' Sharpness in his voice now, but he sat down again. His clever blue eyes narrowed, and he studied his visitor more closely as though by such scrutiny he could draw out what was in his mind.

Kemp took his time fixing a particular arrow to his bow before he let fly; the preparatory bludgeoning had softened the target.

'But Mr Adair wasn't after pills, was he, Doctor? Quite the contrary, in fact . . . So, what happened? Did you have a row? You're more than a match for him in size. How come he bopped you on the head?'

Kemp's tone continued to be pleasantly conspiratorial, even genial. Piers Sylvester's icy composure was showing visible signs of cracking, a twitching at the corners of his mouth, a sudden movement of the hands, gave him away. In a patient he would have diagnosed the symptoms of a bad conscience, if not outright fear.

'I know Mr Adair, yes,' he said slowly, picking his way through a minefield. 'He comes here sometimes to help us with therapeutic art.'

'And runs a nice little sideline in drugs,' said Kemp cheerfully. 'Small stuff, but useful. Saves you buying from the proper sources for the quantities you need, and the drug companies aren't in the business just for the health of it, they've got to make their profits too. But I bet you balance your books so that it all looks above board.' He leaned forward, and assumed an attitude of serious commiseration. 'Look, Doctor, I'm not much interested in what went on in the past – that's for you to sort out. I can only warn you that if hard drugs were involved then you're for the high jump. All I hope for your sake is that Adair hadn't gone that far . . .'

Hope was far now from the bright, shrewd eyes, though the mind at the back of them had gone hunting it.

'Nothing like that ... I wouldn't take them. I refused.'

'So the hard stuff was on offer?'

Sylvester put both elbows on the desk, interlaced his fingers and brought them to his mouth as if to put a barrier against unwary speech. Kemp knew it was going to be touch and go. Most of what he had said was mere speculation, and all of it without possible proof – as yet.

But the doctor had dropped the guard of his hands, and was obviously about to squeeze out of reluctant lips some grains of disclosure.

'I had been doing some experiments – oh, perfectly harmless ones, I assure you – with some of my seriously depressed patients. Quite legitimate medical treatments, but they did involve small doses of hallucinatory drugs. You know that in hospitals before the First World War champagne used to be prescribed for post-operative depression? The quick lift, they called it . . . Well, I was working along these lines. No worse than hypnosis or some of the other idiocies of fringe medicine,' he ended, with a flare of temper.

Kemp remained unimpressed. 'I'll believe you,' he said drily. 'And where did Adair come into this research lark?'

Sylvester drew in his nostrils at the flippancy, but he continued, spacing his words with care.

'He was very interested in my work. An intelligent young man, if somewhat given to affectation and play-acting . . .'

'I know all about Adair's propensities,' said Kemp, 'let's hear about the drugs.'

'It seemed he had access . . . I never inquired . . . But he had access to a supply which was – er – useful.'

'For which you paid him well below the market rate. Go on, I want to hear the rest of it.'

The doctor was unused to his own methods of interrogation being forced upon him. He frowned. 'You must understand the dilemma I'm in. This place must be made to pay but it also has to provide a service – rather a lavish one. You talk about the private sector but you've little idea of the costs it takes to run. We must keep ourselves up to date in our methods, and all this, as you say, is expensive.'

Kemp's sympathy was muted. 'So, if any corners can be cut, you cut them? Good commercial practice. Now you let Adair in here the other night. He didn't break in, I know that.'

'He was skulking in the bushes when I drove up. He knew I often worked here late. He rushed up to me and said he had to talk to me urgently. Well, yes, I brought him in . . .'

'And what precisely did he want?'

'Money. He was always after money.' Dr Sylvester spoke as if it were an aberrant peculiarity like having webbed feet. 'But this time he was in a panic for it. He wouldn't, or couldn't, tell me why. Just said something had gone terribly wrong. Sounded as if he feared for his life, but he was a young man much given to exaggeration . . .'

'So, you had a row?'

'It wasn't a civilized discussion if that's what you mean. When I refused to have anything to do with – ' he searched for the ambiguous term – 'what he had to sell, he got into a rage.'

'What was it?'

'Cocaine,' the doctor brought out reluctantly. 'Told me he had a packet of the stuff worth thousands. I didn't want to know. Advised him to leave, well, actually I told him to get the hell out . . .'

It was the expurgated version but Kemp could see no way he was going to have it fleshed out into some kind of reality by the only protagonist he had to hand.

'There were tablets scattered about when you were found,' he said. 'Was that done to make it look like a simple burglary?'

'Of course not.' The doctor was nettled at being accused of such paltry deception. 'I didn't know he was going to attack me, did I? He smashed that cabinet. Said he was looking for something.'

Kemp got up and went over to the nearest wall cupboard where the door had been freshly glazed. 'Why should he look in here? What's normally kept in it?'

'You can have the key if you want to. It's only ever held the private patients' medicines, the ones prescribed for them by their own practitioners. They bring them with them when they come here, we check whether they're compatible with our line of treatment, and dole them out accordingly. You'll find all the favourite remedies there, for high blood pressure, constipation, obesity, insomnia and depression . . . They're just like pet foods.' Dr Sylvester was beginning to sound weary, and his prejudices were showing.

Kemp came back to the desk and stood over him.

'And what was missing after Adair had gone? I presume you or the nurse checked.'

'Of course we checked. All the contents of that cabinet are clearly labelled with the patients' individual names . . .'

'Go on, whose medicine was missing?'

'As I told the police, they were only sleeping tablets . . . There were no harmful drugs in there.'

'The name, Dr Sylvester, the name?'

'They were Mrs Snape's.'

Chapter Twenty-one

The sight of Dr Sylvester accompanying Kemp along the top corridor was enough to dislodge the nurse who had been leaning on the wall outside the door of Room No. 3, examining her fingernails for flaws. It looked suspiciously as if she had been on guard. At a brief nod from the doctor, however, she took herself off silently on her flat white shoes and disappeared into the cubicle marked 'Sister'.

Kemp felt a tightening in his stomach. So many images of Mirabel Snape had floated into his mind recently that he had forgotten what she actually looked like. He dared not let himself think of the worst that could happen, or had already happened . . .

Piers Sylvester opened the door without knocking. So much for bedside manners, Kemp thought, but perhaps the doctor might be excused such niceties on this occasion; Kemp was leading him like a bear on a chain.

Mirabel was sitting on the edge of the bed, swinging her brown legs. She wore a buttoned-up nightdress the yellowish-cream colour of buttermilk and her face was much the same shade, but her eyes were brilliant, startlingly light and very much alive. They were wary as she watched the doctor turn and close the door, then come over to the bed. But Kemp had already pulled up the only chair and now sat down on it, leaving Sylvester standing.

'Visitors first, Doctor,' he said cheekily, then he took

her hand. 'And how are we today, Mrs Snape? Better, I hope?'

She pulled in her legs, and drew up the covers.

'As well as can be expected,' she answered demurely; her voice was weak, but behind it there was more than a hint of laughter, 'since I'm starving, and dry as a salted peanut.'

It was clear that Sylvester was nonplussed, but felt he had to break up what appeared to him to be an unseemly exchange.

'But you have been eating good meals, Mrs Snape, and where is your barley-water?'

'Down the loo, food, drinks, pills, everything. I don't trust a soul round here,' she answered him, catching her breath on the words. Kemp squeezed her hand slightly.

'I came to see you about Tamsin Jago. I don't know whether your aunt has told you of her dismissal. It might possibly have been unfair, and I'm acting on behalf of Miss Jago.' He withdrew his hand, but the tremor of her palm against his told him she had got the message – other more lingering sensations had to be off the record.

'I'll be glad to talk to you about Tamsin, Mr Kemp, when I'm back at Greystones.' She looked up at Piers Sylvester. 'I'm going home today, isn't that so, Doctor?'

'My dear Mrs Snape,' Sylvester's tone was positively avuncular, 'that is quite out of the question. You are not well enough yet. When you consider the state you were in when you arrived . . .'

'I've done a lot of thinking about that. I've lain awake many nights thinking about that . . .'

'I put you under sedation deliberately so that you would not be troubled by such thoughts. Believe me,

206

Mrs Snape, you have a long way to go before you are well enough to leave us.' Kemp watched the doctor's lips as the soft emollient words flowed out like a soothing ointment. So that's how it's done, he thought; I almost believe him myself. If I didn't know him to be at least a halfway rogue, I too would be lulled by the patter. But words are my game, too.

He caught a sideways glance from Mirabel's eyes, those amazing eyes that held the changing colours of the sea, before she turned them steadily on Sylvester.

'I think I know why I was doped, Doctor. You call it sedation, I call it dope. You can't keep me here. I can leave anytime of my own free will.'

Sylvester shook his head. 'Your husband and your general practitioner put you in my care, Mrs Snape . . .'

'Dr Griffin's a nasty little man, he's not my real doctor. And Vincent . . . Vincent wouldn't . . .' Her voice had risen, cracked and broke. She turned darkened, stormy eyes on Kemp and her thin hand clutched at his sleeve. 'They can't, can they?' she implored him.

He gently disengaged her clinging fingers, and stood up. He spoke not to her but to Sylvester, and his voice was hard.

'As I understand it, Mrs Snape was neither a danger to herself nor to others. No order could have been made under the Act, there was no behaviour to warrant it, and you wouldn't dare hold her without one. You and I both know, Dr Sylvester, that you have no right to keep her in this place a moment longer, particularly in view of what's been going on here.'

The threat was plain, and Sylvester stood irresolute.

'I don't know . . . I shall have to get in touch with

Mr Snape, of course.' He had spoken quietly, and only to Kemp, but Mirabel heard him.

'I'm not a chattel,' she cried, 'you don't have to go running to Vincent as if I was a piece of lost luggage.' She pushed at the bedcover and began to get to her feet. But weakness overcame her limbs and she fell back, weeping now in frustration as her body refused to answer the fierce call of her spirit.

Dr Sylvester took Kemp's arm and led him over to the window.

'You see how it is,' he whispered, 'she can't leave in this state. She can hardly walk . . .'

'Neither could you if you'd been drugged, then half-starved yourself from fear you'd get more of the same,' said Kemp roughly. 'All Mrs Snape needs is a good meal, proper rest and a modicum of peace after the outrage that you've all put on her. But the less she knows about that for the moment the better.'

He walked over to the bed and put an arm round her shaking shoulders, pushed back the strands of damp hair, and turned her face to his.

'Trust me,' he said. 'No one is going to harm you now, even in here. I want you to eat and drink properly, get a good rest, don't talk any more . . . No, I mean it,' as she struggled to say something. 'Later I'll come for you with your aunt, and we'll take you home to Simon.'

Perhaps it was the mention of her child's name that did it, but her eyes cleared again, and a spot of colour came into her cheeks. 'I can walk,' she murmured.

He nodded. 'I know you can, but don't try. You're safer in here now than anywhere else.'

She frowned, puzzled, but accepted what he had said. He seemed to talk in riddles, this man whom she scarcely knew, but of one thing she was certain: he was on her side. She felt weary now after her outburst and on a more mundane level surprisingly hungry.

'I'd like something to eat.' She said it in a little girl voice which somehow wasn't quite her own.

'There now, Mrs Snape, that's better. I'll have something sent up right away.' Even Dr Sylvester seemed pleased with her, for the first time exhibiting heartiness. Kemp eyed him with disfavour, but he knew he had the doctor in his pocket.

'You do that. It's time Mrs Snape enjoyed this place like the five-star hotel it really is,' he said to Sylvester, his jocularity about as real as the doctor's new bonhomie. 'By the way, who actually owns it? Or does it change hands from time to time in the international merry-go-round?'

'It certainly does not,' said the doctor stiffly. 'It's part of a very reputable Foundation, and sponsored by the Northminster Trust. You must have heard of them – they're very big in the City.'

'A name to be conjured with, indeed. They've even got a bishop on the board. I suppose he brought his minster with him.'

The two men were walking to the door. Kemp turned back as he reached it. Was Mirabel simply waving him goodbye, or was she trying to tell him something? But Kemp's mind was on harsher things, things he had to say to Sylvester, and pin them right between the psychiatrist's bright, clever eyes. He waited till they were in the corridor.

He did it curtly, wasting no words.

'I want Mrs Snape properly looked after until I call for her. I want you to give immediate instructions to that effect to all your staff. And no funny business. If one hair of her head is harmed while she's in your care, not only will the police be informed of your involvement with Robin Adair, but the General Medical Council will be alerted to your little experiments. Do you get the message?'

Dr Sylvester got it.

'One last question before I leave this home of rest and repose: have you any idea at all where Mr Adair might be?'

'I wish I'd never heard of him.' The doctor felt he'd been beaten into the ground. 'No, I don't know. Nor have I any idea why he should take Mrs Snape's sleeping capsules.'

'Didn't he give any reason for smashing the cupboard?'

'Well, I wasn't going to hand him the key. He picked up the heavy ruler I keep on my desk and just smashed the glass. Muttered something about he was fed up being the tool of the Medici . . . Good Lord, that's just come back to me.' Piers Sylvester suddenly brightened. 'I was slightly concussed. Couldn't remember a thing till now. What else was he going on about? Poor Brother Lippo, that was it. He was pretty incoherent . . . I had my back to him. That must have been when he went berserk and hit me.'

Adair dancing mad; Kemp tucked his words away to sort out later.

'To come back to Mrs Snape,' he said. 'Why should an experienced medical man like yourself be taken in by her condition?'

When his professional judgement was attacked, Dr Sylvester could fight back. He did so now. 'What do you mean? It was a clear case of acute depression exacerbated by alcohol. She had a history of mental problems, brought to a head by severe post-natal depression. I've seen the notes of her London specialist. And a full account of her state of mind from the person who should know her best, her husband. Really, Mr Kemp, you go too far . . .'

'Could I make a guess? Was her London physician also employed at another of these foundations, as you call them, financed by the Northminster Trust?'

Piers Sylvester hesitated. It had been a gruelling day, and even his sharp mind was not functioning at its best.

'I think he was. Nothing unusual about that. A lot of businessmen use their facilities, that's what they're there for. You surely don't expect people in the City to wait in line for National Health services, even for their wives and families. Time is money. That's something the National Health has to come to terms with.'

'All right, let's not get political. I'm leaving now, but just remember, I hold you personally responsible as from this minute for Mrs Snape's safety and her full return to normality. You may not think much of my opinion since I'm only a layman and haven't seen her notes, but sometimes the onlooker gets a better view of the game. I think that lady's all right but she's been subjected to some very nasty experiences . . . And now, something else,' he said briskly: 'If you do have a visit from the police – ' he waved away the Doctor's agitation – 'it won't be because I've told them anything. They're only interested in finding Adair. Don't let them question Mrs Snape. Let her rest. She's been through quite enough. You're the man in charge here. You can tell them she's not fit enough – since it's obviously what you believe anyway.'

Dr Sylvester drew himself up and tried to look like someone in charge again.

'Naturally I shan't let anyone disturb my patient. And I stick to my opinion that she's unstable. All through the medical notes I've read there's a definite pattern of behaviour . . .'

'Even before she came down here?'

'Oh yes. She's often been in what they call a state of fugue.'

'I only know the toccata. Bach, isn't it?'

Sylvester looked at him witheringly. 'The term is used to describe a repetitive pattern – patients slip into it to avoid reality. They keep on doing, or saying, the same things over and over. In Mrs Snape's case she has certain – er – delusions. When she's shown how ludicrous such delusions are, she drinks to get away from them. She's a classic example.'

'Delusions like seeing severed heads?'

Sylvester shrugged. 'That's only a recent hallucination . . . there've been plenty of others in her medical history from what I can make out. It's all part of a certain pattern of behaviour in cases like hers.'

The doctor sounded more pleased with himself now that he had reasserted his professional expertise; Kemp left him to bask in it.

Kemp drove slowly from The Respite, taking time to recover. His health didn't seem improved by the visit; perhaps the drugs left a whiff of their ambivalent presence in the very air. He looked at the trimly-boxed escallonias bordering the drive and separating it from the overgrown lawn where vast clumps of untamed pampas grass bided their time; in the autumn they would sprout great feathery hands to wave about like crazy things.

It was that mixture of the clinically tidy and the downright disorderly which worried him. Dr Sylvester's costly set-up was so smoothly efficient, so grandly prophylactic on the surface, while underneath schemes were afoot as daft and dangerous as any from the early days of lunacy. Drugs, indeed! From the insane root that takes the reason prisoner to the modern panaceas for all ills, Kemp was fed up with the lot . . .

He switched his mind to another question: were Mirabel Snape's astonishing eyes so light because they were fringed by lashes black as her hair, or were the pupils artificially dilated? Yet on the beach that morning they had been natural enough though they still had had the same stare-right-through-you quality, and then had crinkled up in perfectly normal laughter.

The harbouring of such thoughts blunted any appetite for lunch, so he drove at random along unknown roads rather than return to the hotel and the rigours of holiday conversation. Inevitably these roads – like hedged canals, so little view they gave – led him to the land's edge, the track became grassy down the centre, and expired at an open gate. Kemp got out of the car and walked across the short turf, starred with white clover and yellow tormentil. A few feet only and he was on the cliff top.

Below, the water rose and fell lazily as if a giant were breathing but white spume already smeared the black rocks like spit. A storm was coming. It was heralded by high shredded clouds along the western skyline, and a wind that tore at the cushions of sea-thrift overhanging the cliff's edge. Not a day to be out on the sea. He watched a pleasure craft rounding the Point, heaving itself out of the troughs and running with the tide safely back to Padstow. Fishing-boats were further out, and away towards the darkening horizon other larger ships went steadily about their business.

Legitimate business? How could one tell? Kemp had had a word with the lifeboatman who'd spotted the yacht *Eurydice* idly drifting without navigation lights, and who'd challenged her. The excuse was that they'd had a rough voyage, a storm had damaged their batteries, they were afraid to make for harbour in the dark on a falling tide, and had simply hove to in the Cove to anchor for the night. It sounded plausible enough, but the man from the lifeboat had logged the conversation, and their position. Of course by the time the connection had been made between the *Eurydice* and the accidental discovery of the drugs attached to the buoy, the yacht had vanished.

On that occasion Steve Donray in his fishing-boat had been tardy in making the pick-up. Was that why he'd had to be punished, for missing the boat? Or was it because he was already suspected by the authorities, and had thus become a danger to the organizers of the smuggling venture?

So much money in it . . . Far more than the good old tobacco and wine trade had ever brought in, and far harsher measures against those who failed. Or got involved, as Adair had. No wonder he was on the run.

Kemp tried to follow his footsteps. He needed money to get away, to hire a car, get to London . . . He'd gone to Sylvester to sell what he had – it looked like the dregs of Donray's unsold hoard. Adair had known before anyone else that Steve Donray was dead. Did he also know where the fisherman had kept the stuff before it went 'down the line' and spread out among the pushers? The police would have searched Donray's place, but by then it would be too late.

Donray had been missing for a week, time enough for Adair to have got his long artistic fingers on the dead man's legacy of trouble, and transfer it to the hidey-hole under the floorboards.

But he hadn't known where to sell, he wasn't that far into the game, so when he was finally scuppered he tried the only possible buyer he knew – at The Respite. Kemp wasn't convinced by Dr Sylvester's denial that drugs of this nature had ever passed that way before, but this time the doctor refused to buy; perhaps Adair's panic signalled danger, perhaps the price was too high. At any rate, Adair had let fly in anger, and disappeared into the night.

Would he have been fool enough, desperate enough, to go to an arranged meeting point, try and bargain with them, offer to return the stuff and keep his mouth shut? They'd have soon shut it for him – with sand as they'd done to poor Donray, and the mocking-bird voice would be stilled for ever. Of one thing Kemp was certain: they would come by sea, and slip away afterwards into its vast anonymity . . .

The thunder of breaking waves interrupted his thoughts and deepened their melancholy. He'd glanced at a book back in the hotel. It was about the strange parson-poet, the Reverend Hawker of Morwenstow whose duty it was not only to bury the bodies washed up on this cruel coast but also to try and turn his parishioners – many of whom he'd found to be 'wreckers, smugglers and dissenters' – from their evil pursuits. He had known only too well his other enemy, that deadly destroyer, the Atlantic Ocean. Something he had written came now into Kemp's mind as he dwelt on the possible fate of Robin Adair:

And mockery followed after
The sea-bird's jeering brood,
That filled the skies with laughter
From Lundy Light to Bude.

There wasn't much laughter about today, only the screech of the rising wind, and a few small drops of rain. Kemp sought the comfort of his car. So this was what sailors meant when they said the weather's turning nasty.

Penelope was waiting on the steps of the hotel. 'Lunch is over,' she said, 'but Phyl's made us some sandwiches. We can sit in a corner of the bar. There's no one about.'

He looked into her face. 'That serious?'

'I think it is,' she replied tersely.

They sat at the window, now lashed by wind and drumming rain.

'Cocaine,' she said, 'not a lot, but enough when you consider a whole bottle of the capsules. Cocaine's only slightly soluble in water but it can be dissolved in alcohol or some of the volatile oils. It's been an amateurish attempt – if that's any comfort . . .'

'You've informed the police?'

'I had to. And I told them where that capsule came from. You'd have done the same.'

He nodded.

'Dr Sylvester's in for a bad time. Of course he'll say he didn't know. Mrs Snape's own sleeping tablets were brought in with her, they have a brand name, they're not in themselves dangerous. But I think the doctor's got a lot of explaining to do.' He said it with some satisfaction, and told Penelope about his visit to The Respite.

When he'd finished she looked at him with wide, serious eyes.

'But that's terrible . . . You mean Robin Adair's been supplying that man with drugs?'

'I think, I can't be certain, that they were probably the soft drugs, perhaps some cannabis but mainly the amphetamines – until this last time when Robin had got hold of the harder stuff.' Kemp ran his fingers through his hair. 'I simply don't know. Of course the police will find nothing out there. It'll all be most carefully accounted for.'

'What I don't understand, Lennox, is why Mirabel Snape? Oh!' She put her hand to her mouth. 'Because she'd seen that head, is that it?'

'That's obviously part of it but it's not the whole story. I wonder why Adair snatched back the bottle of sleeping capsules.'

'Perhaps he knew he'd gone too far. Inspector Gudgeon was going straight out there. He was going anyway. Apparently they'd just had the results of their fingerprint tests, and the prints found in Dr Sylvester's room and on that ruler match those in the Studio. You got there first in suspecting Adair was the one, but the police are on to it now.' She paused. 'Will they question Mirabel?'

'Not if I can help it.'

Penelope regarded him in silence for a moment. 'Still protecting her, Lennox?'

'If Dr Sylvester values my keeping quiet over certain matters, then I trust he'll do exactly as I've told him and keep the police away from her.'

'But if she saw something . . . If she really saw that awful head . . . Wouldn't it be useful to them to find out at least where it happened?'

'Maybe, but it won't bring Donray back to life. And it's her head I'm worried about. She's as brittle as a pane of glass. One knock and it'll shatter her again . . .'

Kemp felt pretty brittle himself. When Penelope departed for the kitchen to get a lesson in pasty-making from Phyllis Morris, he took his own confused head up to their room with a pile of books on the pretence that he might read them. He needed to think.

What the hell was he doing, he asked himself? He could win Penelope back if he really tried, if he really wanted to. How pleasant it would be to have a neat and tidy life ahead, to bask in the approval and delight of her uncle and aunt! Nor would such an alliance harm his prospects in the firm; Archie Gillorn still had considerable influence . . .

He was throwing it all away. For the sake of – what? A pair of blue eyes, someone he scarcely knew . . . He stared glumly out at the rain, recognizing the symptoms of obsession. He'd seen plenty of clients similarly afflicted and dealt with the disease briskly enough. Why could he not deal as intelligently with himself?

Cut and run. He'd very nearly done it that day at Blisland. He'd known then that Mirabel Snape was trouble. She was not a romantic damsel in distress, she was a lady with real problems, a neurotic, possibly an alcoholic. Also, she had a husband with whom it would not only be unwise to tangle but downright dangerous; he could snap Kemp's burgeoning career in two with a wave of his hand. And he, too, was a man obsessed – with his son. Kemp frowned. He got up and opened the window. Rain spattered over the sill. In the garden below the roses were tearing their hair; they didn't look very happy either.

Chapter Twenty-two

The deepening depression, winding itself up like a watch-spring, moved ominously in from the south-west about the same time as Vincent Snape came from the east, riding the fast lane with precision at ninety miles an hour. The feudal lord was looking to his lady.

If he had screeched to a stop in the drive at Greystones, he hadn't stayed long. He arrived at the White House asking for Lennox Kemp just before eleven.

The lounge was almost empty, Penelope and Kemp in a corner quietly playing Scrabble – a game designed to employ the wits and preclude conversation. It suited them at this juncture, giving rest to conflicting emotions, letting jagged edges settle, allowing both a temporary measure of companionship before the old life slipped away and left an uncertain future.

Snape was in a business suit – indeed, he looked as if he had risen from a board meeting, straightened his tie, and taken to the road, all in one swift, sure movement. His approach to the pair was, as ever, courteous and without undue fuss. Drinks were brought, civilities exchanged, but Snape had not come this far, nor at such speed, simply to engage in pleasantries. He came to the point quickly.

'You have seen Mirabel?' he addressed Kemp.

'Yes.'

'With Dr Sylvester's permission?'

'Naturally.' Kemp stretched his legs and lit a cigarette. Watching him relax, noting the vacant look that had come over the grey eyes regarding their visitor with blank, almost insolent, detachment, Penelope recognized danger signals. She glanced from one to the other, and finding herself irrelevant to whatever lay between them, she pleaded tiredness. 'It's the sea air,' she apologized to Vincent. 'I'll see you later, Lennox . . . if I'm not asleep.'

When she had gone Snape abandoned the subject of his wife for a moment and gave Kemp a sly look. 'So, that's the way it is? Quite a catch for you, Archie Gillorn's niece . . .'

'We're not engaged,' said Kemp curtly.

'Ah . . .' Snape put a lot of meaning into the syllable, as if the information had gone into storage but Kemp's private life was only of passing interest. 'I had a disturbing telephone call from Dr Sylvester. It seems you have been encouraging my wife to leave hospital.' It was a statement rather than an accusation but the flat Northern vowels lent it strength.

'I think she's sufficiently recovered to be allowed home. The doctor agrees.'

'I've not been to the hospital yet. I'm on my way there. I want to know what right you had to go and see her.'

Kemp explained his purpose, but baldly, adding nothing. At the mention of Tamsin Jago Vincent gave a short laugh.

'That's a very thin excuse. It could have waited. Anyway, that chit of a girl needs taking down a peg or two. I will not have my wife worried by such trivial matters. You don't seem to realize how ill Mirabel has been – still is . . .'

220

'I had other reasons.' Kemp was tired of going round in circles. 'Someone has been feeding your wife drugs, not strictly as prescribed by her doctors.'

'That's quite preposterous.'

'There's proof, Mr Snape. The police already have the evidence. A quantity of cocaine has been found in one of her sleeping pills.'

Vincent showed some agitation, not surprisingly since it was his wife they were discussing, but not enough concern to ask the most obvious question.

'Who would do a thing like that?' was what he did ask. Perhaps, thought Kemp, this is the way you deal with bad news in the City; never mind the reason for a falling market, find out first who to blame. He shrugged his shoulders but made no comment; let the other man do the talking, you learn more that way. Snape obliged.

'Mirabel has been on anti-depressants for some time . . . and I understand Dr Griffin prescribed sleeping tablets after she had this last collapse. Are you saying somebody got hold of these?'

'Somebody has been playing tricks. I think you know very well who we're talking about.'

Snape took a sip of his whisky. His hand was steady.

'I suppose you mean this young man she's been carrying on with. What's his name . . . Adair? Miss Trevanion tells me he's run away.'

The windows rattled as a gust of wind shook the building and there was a vicious burst of hail.

'Is that how she put it?' Kemp remarked with genuine curiosity. 'Was she anxious about him? Anxious that he should be found?'

'Naturally she is. I understand he's a bit of a protégé of hers. A pity, if he's one of these fools who get involved in drugs. And if he's tried to get my wife into that kind of thing I'll show him no mercy.'

'I think Robin Adair has troubles enough,' said Kemp drily. 'No one is going to show him mercy – if he's found.'

Vincent Snape sat, stroking the side of his glass with his carefully-manicured stubby fingers. He seemed now in no hurry to leave.

'And you think this fellow Adair was deliberately introducing Mirabel to hard drugs? What reason would he have?'

'You put it badly, Mr Snape. There's no suggestion she knew what was going on.'

'I know her better than you do – and there's no need to be so formal, Lennox . . . Mirabel has been in a very shaky state for some time. There's no telling what a woman in her frame of mind might get up to. This unsavoury character, Adair, seems to have been quite an influence . . . to the point of intimacy, from what I hear.'

So that's the way the tide is running, thought Kemp with a spurt of anger. It was surely time to counter-attack, and if they were to be on personal name terms then questions could get personal too. 'You told me your marriage was a happy one, Vincent. Has it become less so?'

'Of course we had a splendid marriage – until this affair blew up. But a husband has his pride . . .'

'I wouldn't know.' He'd found in his experience that when marital discord threatened the home, pride was best left outside on the mat.

'I understand from Dr Sylvester that your wife has suffered from depression for some time, a fairly long history of it, in fact.'

Snape frowned. 'He had no right . . . Well, yes. Mirabel is of a, let's say, neurotic disposition. She has fancies – what woman doesn't – but our marriage was happy so long as I could keep control of these passing bouts of . . . nerves, shall we call them? But after Simon was born, her condition got worse. I consulted physicians. Post-natal depression, they told me. But . . . two years of it.' He bowed his head and went on, heavily: 'I found it inexplicable. She said recently that she must get away, back here . . . like a return to her childhood.'

'Where she had been happy. And that's where Robin Adair comes in . . . At least that's your view.'

Snape spread his hands.

'What other view can there be? And now you tell me this terrible thing – that they were on drugs as well as having an affair. And my son was in the house!'

A flush had risen in the man's face. He took a gulp of his drink. Kemp watched him with interest. His son, of course, not Mirabel's.

'I said nothing about an affair,' Kemp said mildly. 'I would call it a mere holiday flirtation, something that lifted her from grey depression. It was harming no one.'

'It harms my marriage. You as a lawyer must be aware of that. If she's been sleeping with this fellow, that's adultery.'

'And forgivable. You've read my report?'

'Every page. Forgivable only if there's true repentance, and redeemable only if she's prepared to return as an obedient wife and mother.' The almost biblical language spoke for itself, putting Vincent Snape solidly in the line of his evangelical forebears.

Kemp stared at him.

'You are not surely contemplating divorce?' Further words failed him.

Snape stared back, controlled power behind his eyes.

'You may call it what you will, this adventure of hers. I call it an affair. There is her drinking . . . and now I hear of drugs. Is that proper behaviour for the mother of my son?'

It was Kemp's turn for discomfiture, his emotions thrown into flux by the implacable logic aimed at his head. It wasn't his head he was worried about, he could have countered with logic of his own. But his heart too was at risk in this game, and he might have spoken out from it – and unwisely – had there not been an interruption.

Two dull booms sounded, one after the other, masked by the howling of the gale but reverberating through the room so that the glasses rang.

Vincent Snape raised his eyebrows. 'Concorde? I gather they hear it over Cornwall.'

Kemp shook his head. 'Sounds more like the maroon.'

During the last five minutes he had been aware of some commotion round the bar. Bill Morris was there, and Phyllis, but they had been joined by what appeared to be quite a crowd considering the lateness of the hour and the emptiness of the hotel. He recognized Peter Seagrave among them, and the burly grey-haired fisherman whom he'd seen several times along the quay. Their conversation was animated, their expressions serious, and there was an undercurrent of excitement.

Bob Morris detached himself from the group and came over.

''Evening, Mr Snape. You've chosen a rough night. Did you hear the signal? That was the Padstow lifeboat being launched. There's a yacht in trouble out on the Doom Bar . . .'

Vincent Snape and Kemp got up together and joined the others who were now moving restlessly towards the door, as if drawn by a common purpose.

'I'm going out to have a look.' Seagrave sounded apologetic. 'I know it seems a bit ghoulish, but I can't resist . . .'

They all felt the same, and soon the little lobby was filled as men fetched mackintoshes, anoraks and boots, and they all streamed out into the night.

The wind was unexpectedly warm but blustering strongly from the ocean, with intermittent squalls of harsh rain. Bending into it, they fought their way on to the sandhills.

To Kemp it was an eerie sight, reminding him of some of the old paintings and photographs he'd been looking at in those books at the hotel. The Doom Bar, shelving across the mouth of the estuary, was as sinister as its name implied – although the word itself was only a corruption of 'dune' – and he'd read of the ships wrecked or stranded there, some three hundred of them, and of the men who had drowned in those treacherous waters.

'A summer gale and an ebb tide.' It was the grey-haired Cornishman speaking at his side. 'Every bit as deadly as a winter storm . . . Blows up sudden, like . . .'

'Surely a yacht would take warning?' As a devout landsman, Kemp had a healthy respect for wind and weather at sea.

The fisherman spat. 'They never take heed, these

modern yachtsmen. Think they know it all . . . and that powerful engines'll carry them over. What they don't realize is that on the ebb the sea going out and the flow of the river makes a proper millrace of the channel.'

'Well, I can't make out a thing, and that's a fact,' remarked Snape, peering into the whirling blackness.

'You'll not have walked around much in the dark,' said the Cornishman complacently, reading him for a City man. 'Wait a while till your eyes get used to it . . . Now, can you not see the two boats out there? One's the lifeboat, the other'll be the one in trouble.'

'It's a motor-yacht,' shouted Seagrave above the wind. 'I've just heard from somebody. She's a big one, ocean-going, out from Padstow this evening. Looks like they misread the tide, and ignored the gale warning.'

A sudden break in the clouds cast a weird yellowish light over the scene, illuminating the white-capped surf racing in flickering lines across the angry waters, and momentarily revealing the stark outline of Stepper Head and the bleak crags below it. But all the drama lay in the centre, in the maelstrom where the breaking rollers met the unyielding sand-bar.

Dimly, they could make out the yacht, heeled over, her masts askew, her hull pounded by the surf. The lifeboat was near but not quite near enough, its powerful motor edging it forward through the perilous cross-currents ripping across the shallows.

Then another squall set in, bringing blinding rain and a curtain of dark that hid the scene from the eyes of the watchers now strung out along the dunes, or standing below on the flat sands of Rocksea.

Kemp shuddered.

So it must have been in the old days; the watchers

by the shore, the helpless sailors out there as many a gallant ship had struck and foundered on the dreaded bar, or was driven before the wind headlong on to the black rocks at Stepper as they tried to run for shelter into Padstow on an ebbing tide. Many a fisherman's wife must have stood here and waited, waited for the hopeless dawn that could only bring drifting spars and pitiful wreckage . . .

'We'll see no more tonight.' The Cornishman was turning away. 'God grant they get them off . . .'

The small crowd who returned to the hotel were quiet, subdued by what they had seen, and not seen but only imagined. Phyllis had coffee ready. It was not a time for conviviality. Some talked of other wrecks they had witnessed, of ships run aground on those fair holiday beaches, of the heroic lifeboatmen who risked their lives yet still went out, as duty called them, to ships in distress off this terrible coast.

Kemp noticed that Snape had gone. He had heard his last remark to Seagrave: 'I hope that poor blighter's paid his insurance . . .'

It would only be a passing event for Snape, a story to regale a dinner-party with, he would talk of heroism and perhaps make a donation to the National Lifeboat Institution, but he would think no more about it.

Kemp on the other hand had been profoundly affected. Coming so soon on top of his conversation with Vincent Snape – a conversation which had stirred within him a turmoil of emotions alarming in their intensity – the violence of the forces at work out there on the estuary had heightened his sense of foreboding. It was as if he too stood on the planks of a sinking ship and must jump clear or go down.

That day he had walked with Penelope at Pentire

227

and reflected on the restless surge below the cliffs, he had felt the need for change; he had not anticipated how fast that change would come, nor that it would knock him flat as the wind takes the breath from the body.

Mirabel Snape. Her future was now in hazard, she could be in as perilous a plight as that yacht lying helpless on the Doom Bar. And his future, too . . .

Sitting on a chintz-covered armchair, drinking hot coffee, smoking the inevitable cigarette, half-listening to the murmured talk around him in this cosy haven of casual holiday, he faced the truth: he had fallen in love, as wildly and as recklessly as any hero of romantic legend.

He was recalled to reality by Peter Seagrave's voice. 'I've been on the phone to the Harbourmaster. Thought I'd better find out if any of our people are involved . . .' He was obviously thinking of the Yacht Club. 'But it's not a local craft, though she's well-known in Padstow. Came up from the Med. a week or two ago, put in for stores, and was outward-bound this evening for the Caribbean. They were warned about the tide but they insisted on sailing . . .'

'I think I've seen her at the quay,' said Bob Morris, 'expensive-looking vessel with a French name . . . the *Orfy* or something.'

'That's her,' said Seagrave. 'That's what Mr Hiller said, the *Orfée*. She's French, her skipper and two crewmen were aboard – all foreigners.'

There was no outward expression of relief among the company, but it was felt none the less; neither the close-knit fraternity of local yachtsmen or the fishermen were at risk. Yet they must not be sparing in their concern for others. 'There's a fine coxswain in that lifeboat,' said one, 'and the lads know what they're doing. They've taken many a survivor off a wreck before now . . .'

On that faint note of optimism people dispersed, some once again to the dunes to see if there was anything visible despite the darkness and persistent rain, others to their homes.

Kemp sat on for a while.

Orpheus and Eurydice, he thought, surely these two could not be separated? But it was Orpheus who had lost his head in the end.

'His gory visage down the stream was sent . . .'

Thankful that he could at least remember his Milton, Kemp went to bed.

Chapter Twenty-three

'There's two men lost, but thank God two were saved.'
Peter Seagrave had come to breakfast, it being a hard
time for a lone widower with news to impart and no
audience at home.

'I thought there were only three men on the yacht?'
Kemp frowned at a piece of toast. Penelope was
breakfasting upstairs.

'There's some confusion about that. Seems another
man was aboard . . . At any rate the skipper's drowned,
he went into the sea when the ship heeled over and
was lost in the surf. One of the crew was swept off the
deck just as the lifeboat got there but he must have hit
his head on the rail, for he was dead when they picked
him up. They got the other two out, they were below
decks when she struck.' Seagrave wiped his brow.
'Terrible tragedy. To think it can happen like that,
within sight of the shore . . . The *Orfée*'s a wreck of
course. They'll have to drag her off on the tide to clear
the channel.'

'Was it simply bad seamanship?'

'Who knows, now that the skipper's gone? The
crewman they saved is French and not very coherent.
The other man's unconscious and been taken to Treliske, so it sounds as though he's badly injured.'

Bob Morris approached their table, his face openly
excited.

'Have you heard? The second man they picked up

from that yacht last night, it was Mr Adair . . . You know, the artist fellow from Rocksea!'

'Good Lord! Now what on earth would he be doing . . .' Peter Seagrave's question was left unfinished as Morris addressed Kemp.

'Oh, Mr Kemp . . . a telephone call from Bodmin Police Station. Would you go over and see Inspector Gudgeon right away. Very urgent, they said it was.'

Kemp wasted no time, but when he arrived only Sergeant Ivell was there to greet him. 'The Inspector's gone to Truro. Treliske Hospital. Perhaps you'd better . . .'

'I think so too. But first, give me a brief rundown on what happened.'

'Adair was in the hold of that ship, all trussed up like a chicken for the oven. That's what probably saved his life because when she went over he just rolled . . . But he was in a bad way even before that happened, so he's gone to Treliske, and the Inspector wants to be there if there's any chance of him surviving.'

'What about the crewman?'

'The Frenchy was lucky. Got a bit of a ducking but he's not injured. All he needed was hot drinks and blankets, and some sleep. After that, well, perhaps they'll get something out of him. We've got an interpreter lined up, but in my opinion she won't be needed – Frenchy was fair spluttering with thanks to the lifeboatmen who hauled him out, and they slipped me the word that he's not unfamiliar with the English language . . .'

That had been shrewd of Ivell, thought Kemp, as he took directions from the sergeant and set off for Truro.

Twenty-five miles seemed a long way to have to travel if you were seriously ill, but the traffic was light and the roads good so that he covered the distance faster than he had expected. The sun shone calmly from a pale blue sky, clean-washed of all trace of storm; nature had divested herself of any responsibility for the night's disaster; let others face an inquisition, she would take no part in it.

He gave his name and made his inquiry at the hospital reception desk. The girl nodded, touched buttons, hummed to herself as she held on. 'An admission early this morning? Adair . . . Yes.' She listened. 'He's in the intensive care unit,' she said over her shoulder to Kemp. 'Who did you say? Inspector Gudgeon?' She spoke into the receiver, listened again, then put it down. 'You'll have to wait, Mr Kemp.'

Kemp waited.

A large hospital anywhere, but particularly one like this which has to provide medical care to a scattered population from birth to death, has an ambience which dwarfs the individual situation. Its environment evens out the disparities in the human condition, reducing the personal so that the whole can be tucked under the wing of the administration's unflurried but systematic direction.

Nowhere was this more apparent than in the waiting area – large enough for an airport lounge. People stood around in anxious groups, or relaxed and read the magazines, fetched trays of tea and chattered over the cups as if at home, or simply sat staring through the windows at further arrivals, or fortunate departures. At intervals a nurse would come and lead a party silently away, or a brisk attendant would call a name and someone stepped forward and was whisked off down one of the long grey corridors, towards what? News of a death, or of a birth? Or to be told the tests were negative and they could go on their way rejoicing?

Kemp waited.

Half an hour passed, an hour, another half-hour. He'd read *Country Life* and *Cornish Life*, a *Reader's Digest*, two National Trust periodicals with pictures of pretty castles, and was starting wearily on *Woman's Own* when he found Gudgeon standing beside him.

'Adair?' asked Kemp.

'We'll talk in the car,' said the Inspector abruptly, and he looked tired. 'Yours. You can give me a lift back to Bodmin. I came in the ambulance – just in case . . .'

'I can't see him, then? There's something I want to ask him.'

But the Inspector was already pushing his bulk through the revolving doors. Kemp followed him.

Manœuvring the car out of the hospital grounds and on to the by-pass round Truro, Kemp didn't speak. Neither did Gudgeon.

When they were out in the countryside, he said: 'Whatever it was you wanted to ask Adair, Mr Kemp, you'll get no answer.'

'He's dead?'

'An hour ago.'

'Did he regain consciousness?'

'For a while he did. When they'd made him as comfortable as they could. There was talk of an operation to relieve the internal injuries but he'd already lost too much blood . . . Kinder really just to let him go.' The Inspector's heavy features had a sad downward look. 'Kinder in the end.'

'But he was able to speak?'

'I took a statement from him.' Gudgeon pulled

himself back on duty. 'And a proper statement it is too. Clears up a number of things that puzzled us.'

It was a long road to Bodmin, and Kemp took it slowly as the Inspector talked, the softly-rolling accent of the Cornishman lending warmth and sensibility to what on paper would be a coldly factual tale.

Kemp knew Gudgeon's questioning would have been gentle but persistent, he would allow for the injured man's weakness and be patient with the ministrations of the hospital staff, but he would have probed away at the essentials until he had built up a coherent account.

Robin Adair had admitted knowing all about Steve Donray and the drugs traffic. A vessel would linger well offshore, Donray would get the word where the pick-up was to be – generally attached to a buoy so that his fishing-boat was never in contact with the other ship. For a lark – Robin's expression – he'd asked Steve to get him soft drugs, cannabis, amphetamines and the like for his own use, his 'dolly mixtures', as he called them. That little supply had been going for some time.

At that point the Inspector shook his head. 'We've still no lead on the organizers,' he said morosely. 'Adair swore he never knew – and any man who swears so near his Maker, I'd believe him . . . Well, maybe the Frenchman will tell us.'

Donray had grown careless; he spent money too freely, and talked too much. The Drugs Squad became suspicious. When he realized he was being watched, he panicked. He wanted out of the game, and begged whoever organized the delivery ship to take him with them on their next trip – to South America.

'They took him all right,' Gudgeon said sourly, 'in his own boat as far as Trebetherick Point. In the dead

234

of night they went ashore and buried him up to his neck in the wet sand. They wanted to know everything, who he'd told, what he'd done to get himself suspected. They were saving their own skins, of course. But out came the name of Adair.'

Kemp watched the sweet green fields go by.

Encased in firm, unyielding sand . . . and the tide coming in.

'A terrible death to die,' said Gudgeon, 'for a fisherman . . .'

He cleared his throat. 'They must have towed his boat far out to sea before cutting it adrift. The current brought it back, and it smashed itself in the Cove days later.'

'They told Adair all this?'

'Took pleasure in it, is my guess. He was for the same fate. A warning to others never to blab.'

What happened next the Inspector frankly admitted he found hard to credit, but Kemp with greater knowledge and a stronger imagination could not doubt it was the truth. He had known Robin Adair not as a weak, broken body taken from a wrecked ship but as the man with the gilded hair, a lively dancing figure with the voice of a crooning angel. That much of his behaviour could now be seen as the effect of his experiments with hallucinatory drugs did not alter the fact that he had been a singular man.

'He sheared off Donray's head with a piece of slate,' said Gudgeon bluntly. 'Oh, the man was long dead. There'd been at least one full tide over him . . .'

Adair had told the Inspector he'd found Donray's body one night while walking on the beach. He'd tried to loosen it from its imprisonment but the sand was firm. He didn't want it found, and knew the body itself wouldn't be if he left it there. But perhaps before the next tide someone would see the head. There'd be an investigation. He couldn't afford that, his connection with Donray might be revealed.

'So he cut it off, and threw it far out to sea. It was so heavy with sand and water it would be sure to sink . . . That's what he told me.' The policeman pondered the words, then went on quickly as though he couldn't bear them. 'He'd another reason, of course. More practical. He knew where Donray kept the cocaine before he passed it on. Adair wanted to get his hands on it before the police were even alerted to the fact that Donray was missing. Adair said he needed the money it would bring.'

'Why didn't the murderers from the *Eurydice* go for it?'

'Too risky for them once they knew Donray was suspect. They probably thought we'd be watching. We weren't. We hadn't got that far, neither had the Drugs Squad. We were never to know where he kept the stuff. But Adair knew all right. He got hold of it and hid it under his floorboards with his own little hoard.'

One question Kemp longed to ask. He did so, casually.

'Was Adair on his own when he found Donray?'

'Oh yes. Said he often went along that shore at night, it inspired his painting, the black and silver spray.'

That phrase was not the Inspector's, thought Kemp, it had come from the lips of the dying artist.

The Inspector went on with the story. Adair had indeed found Donray's hoard, there was enough left for Adair to think he could make some quick money to get away from the threats of the drugs smugglers. He went to Dr Sylvester. One thing Adair had made clear:

the good doctor had shown him the door. In a moment of anger, Adair had hit him, and in the same frenzy had struck out at the drugs cabinet.

He'd spent a wretched night in the open. The telephone threats were having their effect. He daren't go back to the Studio for they obviously knew where he lived, so he'd slept rough on a hillside between The Respite and Rocksea, hungry and desperate.

'But he kept on taking the tablets,' Kemp mused aloud, by now out on his own following Adair's footsteps and thinking of Mirabel's sleeping capsules, laced with cocaine, in the fugitive's pocket.

'You're probably right,' the Inspector agreed. 'If he had his own variety of drugs on him they must have given him Dutch courage enough – just like alcohol does – to do the daftest thing.'

For, whatever it was that livened his spirits, by the next morning Robin Adair had decided upon a positive course of action. He would go to the meeting place they'd told him on the telephone. He'd bargain with them: the cocaine for his guaranteed safety. Like Donray before him, he'd underestimated the foe. Both of them were little men caught up in something they thought they could handle. Adair had overweening conceit, imagined he could outwit them by trickery.

And the meeting place had been open enough: eleven in the morning at a quayside café in Padstow. They had listened, they had seemed amenable chaps but they would have to consult their principal. Would he board this luxury yacht with them and meet the Captain? So, the fly went willingly into the spider's web.

Once aboard, however, Adair was doomed.

'He took a terrible beating,' said Gudgeon, his anger

surfacing. 'What in God's name makes people act like beasts?'

'Money,' said Kemp. 'You've said it yourself often enough, there's far too much money in the drugs trade. One slip, the big men get nervous and out come the knives.'

'Damnable business,' the Inspector growled. Kemp could appreciate his feelings; he'd just watched a man die.

But it would be easier now for Gudgeon, going back to routine, pulling the threads of his case together. The south-western ports would be contacted for records of trips by the *Orfée* and the *Eurydice* wherever they'd touched land, shipping registers would be searched for ownership; higher up and further out the international agencies would be alerted and their computers too would click until somewhere – in Riviera villa or South American hacienda – the trail would end. Perhaps not this time. This time they might only catch the couriers, the deliverymen, the postmen, and they too scared to talk, but the example of their prison sentences might discourage the spreading poison – at least for a while.

The road led into Bodmin. Gudgeon, having finished telling the essence of Adair's statement, fell silent. Kemp stopped at the police station and the Inspector heaved himself from the car. He paused at the window.

'What was it you had in mind to ask Adair, Mr Kemp?'

'As he can't answer, the question has lost its meaning.'

Kemp drove off.

Chapter Twenty-four

Enough rumour had circulated in Rocksea by late afternoon that day to stir its inhabitants out of their normal tranqillity; even the bobbing boats in the harbour had a restless, expectant look.

It was warm enough for tea in the garden at the White House and Penelope steered Kemp firmly to a secluded corner, plying him with scones, Cornish cream and strawberry jam.

'I can't eat all this,' he protested.

'You can and you will. And while you're doing it you can tell me everything. At least from you I'll get the facts – the stories going around this place would make your hair curl.'

Kemp told her what had happened.

At the point of hearing about Adair's injuries and death, Penelope's face softened.

'Oh, the poor man,' she exclaimed. 'He was so much alive. For all his faults, there was that spark . . .'

'I know. He was like a shooting star . . . Black darkness and a silver streak.' He saw Penelope's sudden look. She knew he only said things like that when he was tired, or nervous.

He pulled himself together and went on to tell her of the statement the dying man had made, keeping it as official as Gudgeon would when it was filed. But Penelope was not deceived.

'He didn't mention Mrs Snape?'

Kemp was quiet for a moment.

'In the end Robin Adair did the right thing . . . or I think he did. I wasn't there so I can't be sure. Anyway, Gudgeon's got quite enough to go on without looking too deeply into Adair's little sideline. They've got the Frenchman. He was on the yacht when Adair was beaten up and he understands English. He must have heard all about how Donray was put to death . . .'

Penelope shivered. 'That was terrible. And what Adair did afterwards . . . Do you think Mirabel knew?'

She recognized the closed expression, the guard on his tongue; he wasn't going to answer that one.

'I too have news for you,' she said, 'about Mirabel.'

At least it brought back his wandering attention. He reacted sharply.

'Is she home yet?'

'No. Her aunt came here at lunch-time looking for you, Lennox. It seems her niece is being difficult again. She won't leave that place unless you go for her. You can imagine what Miss Trevanion thought about that!'

'I've had some difficulty following Miss Trevanion's line of thought, but this time I'm right on target,' Kemp said drily. He got to his feet, brushing crumbs from his lap.

'Now where are you going?'

'Why, to Greystones of course. If the lady of the manor wants my help, she shall have it.'

'Lennox?' Penelope looked up at him, her expression serious. 'What about Vincent Snape? Susan Trevanion says he's been out at The Respite all day. He's not going to take kindly to any interference from you.'

'If his wife refuses to go home until she's seen me, then he'll just have to put up with it, won't he?'

Penelope watched him striding across the lawn. This

was a new Lennox Kemp, but one she had always suspected was there, behind the laconic mannerisms, the deliberate obtuseness, and that lazy acceptance of the world as it was rather than what one might want it to be . . . But now he was not in an acceptance mood. Penelope sighed. This time Kemp had really been caught; his underlying romanticism had him by the throat. With cases he had solved in the past that romanticism had channelled itself into the search for justice on behalf of others, driven by his tenacity and a logical mind. Now it was thrusting him forward into an unequal struggle.

Sitting under the swaying tamarisk hedge which fluttered green shadows between herself and the sun, she weighed in her mind the confident power and influence of a man like Vincent Snape.

Lennox would be no match for him, and she was saddened by the thought.

Kemp drove Susan Trevanion up the winding valley road to The Respite. Neither had much to say to the other. She had not been surprised to see him at Greystones.

'I'll get my coat. The afternoons grow chilly once the sun's gone . . .' Weather seemed a safe enough topic. She followed him from the hall. She could not now complain of any lack of courtesy on his part; he was quietly polite, if abstracted, as though she no longer mattered, and that in itself was reassuring. In fact, Kemp was sorry for her. She looked her age today, for all that she turned in the doorway and issued a string of instructions to the nursemaid with her usual precision. But her feet stumbled on the pebbles of the drive, and she made no protest when Kemp took her arm and guided her. He relieved her of the small suitcase.

'They're Mirabel's clothes . . . What she asked me to bring.'

Once in the car she did not speak of her niece.

'Mr Kemp, I would like you to know that I have sent word for Tamsin Jago to return. Perhaps I was unfair to her . . . I should like to make amends.'

'That's kind of you, Miss Trevanion. She'll appreciate the apology. It doesn't do to undermine the confidence of the young, they need it so badly.'

She glanced at him quickly. Perhaps apology was too strong a word for her to swallow, perhaps she was surprised by his interest in the maid. At any rate, Tamsin seemed less of a pitfall as a subject of conversation than any other they might have at this juncture, so they spoke of her. Kemp said he hoped Mrs Marsden would advise the girl on the qualifications she would require to enter the nursing profession. Miss Trevanion even found herself confirming that Tamsin had talent, and was intelligent – an admission wrung from her by Kemp's persuasive talk. She began to re-think her previous estimation of him, too.

They drew up in front of The Respite, and he followed her through the porch. This time all the doors were open – as if the place were being given a thorough airing – and the uniformed receptionist at the desk rose instantly to her feet.

'Miss Trevanion, Dr Sylvester's expecting you – ' She eyed Kemp with interest, even amusement; by now the story of Mrs Snape's intransigence must have spread like wildfire – 'and Mr Kemp. I'll take you up.'

Susan Trevanion straightened her back. 'There's no need. I know the way to my niece's room.'

She went ahead of Kemp across the hall and up the wide staircase.

Dr Sylvester was standing in the top corridor. Kemp wondered how the other patients were faring while their doctor was so obviously hanging about doing nothing.

'How is she?' Miss Trevanion asked. Her voice trembled.

'I think you'll find a great change in Mrs Snape. I'd go so far as to say that she's almost completely recovered.'

'You go right in to her, Miss Trevanion,' said Kemp, handing her the case. 'I'd like a word with Dr Sylvester.'

Once alone, the two men eyed each other for a moment. If Kemp had thought Sylvester looked like a farmer, at the moment he was one whose main crop had failed. He gestured towards a side room and Kemp followed him in, closing the door.

'I meant what I said. She's all right.' The doctor was eager – and nervous.

'Has she been told about Adair?'

'I told her he'd been on the wrecked yacht . . . and that he was dead. I had to tell her. Everyone here has been talking about last night's disaster.'

'How did she take it?'

'She wasn't upset if that's what you mean. She seemed to accept it, it was almost as if she expected it. She's in a very strange mood. If it wasn't for this notion she has that she won't leave unless you're here, I'd say she was completely normal.'

'Must be quite upsetting for you,' remarked Kemp, smiling, 'you're not used to dealing with people who're normal.'

'You have to understand my position. My knowledge of Mrs Snape is of short duration only. All I had to go on was her previous medical history . . . and the state she was in when I saw her first.' Piers Sylvester was fighting a rearguard action, and he knew it.

'So you diagnosed her pretty swiftly as either an alcoholic or a manic depressive, and treated her accordingly. I'd hate to see you with a case of measles.'

'That's bloody unfair.' Sylvester gave up the struggle to retain any shreds of professional calm. 'You've no right to talk to me like that . . .'

'Forget it,' said Kemp wearily. 'What I want to know is, has she been harmed by any cocaine she might have swallowed in these capsules?'

The doctor was still seething under the insult, but an appeal to his judgement had to be answered.

'There's no damage been done,' he said sulkily, 'and cocaine isn't addictive in the ordinary sense unless the patient is foolish enough to go on taking it – which of course Mrs Snape didn't.'

'No thanks to you,' said Kemp grimly. He had his hand on the door knob, but the doctor seemed reluctant to let him go.

'Do you think the police are going to investigate why Adair took that bottle from the cabinet in my office? You see, I haven't told Mr Snape about it. He was anxious enough in view of his wife's condition. I didn't want to worry him further . . .'

'Of course you didn't. He's a very powerful man, Mr Snape. Word might just get back to that Foundation of yours. Speaking of that, can you answer me one thing? How come Mrs Snape was brought in here so quickly the night she collapsed?'

Sylvester showed surprise at the question.

'We'd known for some time to expect her as a patient. An inquiry had been made – in London, I understand – for a suitable hospital should Mrs Snape require medical attention while in Cornwall. The Respite was recommended, and I myself asked to take the case. So, naturally when Dr Griffin told me about her, I already had her notes . . . It's not at all an unusual request – many of our patients have their own London physicians – and I might add, we receive high praise for our treatments.'

'So, you came highly recommended, and without a Government Health warning?' Kemp sneered, then instantly regretted the gibe. Piers Sylvester had evidently obeyed Kemp's instructions to the letter and put Mirabel Snape back on her feet; he owed him more than cheap jokes.

'Look here,' he said, 'I don't think the police are going to bother with that smashed cabinet – they'll treat it as just another of Adair's tantrums. And if it's any comfort, he's admitted the assault on you, said he was angry because you refused to deal in cocaine. That ought to let you off the hook . . . And, now, it's high time I saw your patient.'

Chapter Twenty-five

The room was still overpowerfully rose-coloured though the last of the sunshine glimmered amber at the windows, catching Mirabel's long thin legs and turning them golden-brown. She was bending to fasten her sandals. Miss Trevanion was seated at the dressing-table fiddling nervously with the contents of the drawers. Vincent Snape was in the basket-chair, looking a sorely-tried man.

Mirabel stretched her arms above her head, and turned her eyes on Kemp.

'Hullo,' she said, 'I'm glad to see you.'

'And I, you. Are you ready and collectable?'

'Like a parcel,' she said. 'What do you think of the wrapping?'

The wrapping was a knitted suit much the same colour as her eyes, drooping uneasily along its seams as it showed up her loss of weight.

Kemp nodded, the corners of his mouth twitching.

She dropped her hands to her sides and twirled round once, as if testing her balance.

'You were a long time coming. I nearly gave you up.'

Kemp scrutinized her face; there was little colour yet beneath the faded tan but her eyes were bright and very clear.

He shrugged his shoulders. 'I had things to do.'

'To do with Robin's death?'

'Yes.'

'I was sorry. He brought me life, and now he's lost his.'

'I know.' For the second time he said it: 'He was a shooting star . . . But he only brought you a gleam of light. You already had life, and you still have it.'

'On another level?'

'A better one, I hope.'

'But will the level hold?'

'You might have to cling to the edges for a while, but, yes, it'll hold.'

It was as if there was no one else in the room. Indeed the others were being made to feel like spectators at a play they didn't understand. Dr Sylvester leant against the door, watching. Susan Trevanion's fingers were stilled, her eyes in the looking-glass in front of her flickering anxiously. Vincent Snape remained impassive, as though his steadying influence might prevent a further fall in shares.

'Whose car do you want to travel in?' asked Kemp, being practical. 'If you're ready?'

'She'll go in mine,' said Vincent, the wickerwork complaining as he got slowly to his feet, 'along with her aunt. If you've no objection.' Although the last words were addressed to Kemp they held only the suspicion of sarcasm.

Kemp raised his eyebrows at Mirabel.

'You mean I have a choice?' She made a pretty *moue* with her mouth, and gave her small croak of a laugh. 'Then I'll take Vince's offer. He's had a terrible day. Inaction doesn't suit him. Think of all those wasted hours when you might have been coining money, my dear . . .' The glance she tossed at her husband was one of amused tolerance.

'I have your things in the case, Mirabel.' It was a very subdued aunt who spoke as she snapped the locks.

Mirabel Snape walked over to the door, and Sylvester opened it for her. She held out her hand. 'But I must thank my doctor. Isn't that the custom? I'm overjoyed to be leaving your little grey home in the West, but I don't bear you any ill-will . . . I gave you a hard time.'

Piers took the outstretched hand. He was visibly disconcerted, his face crimson. 'It wasn't your fault . . . I think I misunderstood a lot of things . . .'

'Just don't put me in any of your books – not even as a footnote. We all make mistakes.'

The small, straggling procession walked along the empty corridor and down the stairs. Kemp followed them out through the porch to the waiting cars. The maroon Jaguar was showing its gleaming teeth at Kemp's workaday Ford.

Mirabel paused, and turned to him. 'Can I ask a favour of you, Lennox?'

'I'll do anything you want, Mirabel.'

'As a lawyer, you really ought to put strings on your promises . . .' She was laughing at him. 'But this would be a favour by someone else. Do you think your friend Mrs Marsden could come and stay with me at Greystones tonight? She is a nurse, and she's been kind to me before – or so I've been told. Wouldn't it be a good idea, Aunt Susan? After all, the woman Vincent has engaged for Simon must already have her hands full.'

Whether either Miss Trevanion or Vincent Snape thought it a good idea – and the latter's scowl showed he didn't think much of it – there was no spoken objection to Mirabel's plan. Her face was stubbornly set, her eyes were fixed on Kemp's and no longer laughing.

'I'm sure Penelope would be glad to be of any help she can,' he was beginning to say, when she interrupted him.

'Thank you. I'll expect her after dinner.' She must have realized how peremptory she sounded, for her voice faltered and suddenly she was no longer so sure of herself. 'Dr Sylvester says I have to rest, at least for a day or two, and I know Vincent is anxious to get back to Town.'

Kemp came to a quick decision.

'Don't worry. I'm certain Penelope will come – if that's all right with you, Miss Trevanion?' He felt it only courtesy to ask; Mirabel seemed to have the reins between her teeth.

'I too would be pleased if Mrs Marsden could come,' Susan said firmly, 'though it would be an imposition . . . She's on holiday.'

Kemp was conscious of Vincent Snape's eyes upon him as he murmured that their holiday was in any case almost at an end.

The two ladies were soon settled in the car. Vincent Snape closed the passenger doors, and walked round to the driver's side where Kemp was standing.

'Well, thank you, Lennox, for all your assistance with my wife,' he said heartily – or as if it came from the heart. 'You seem to have exerted a considerable amount of influence on her,' he went on, his tone changing. 'Unstable women do have the oddest fancies when it comes to picking up men – just look at the last one Mirabel went to bed with . . .'

He got in and closed the door, not with a slam but with a quietly-satisfied crunch, leaving Kemp with that kick in the stomach. It had been a vicious blow, well-aimed and directed with absolute accuracy where it would hurt most.

Penelope had never seen Kemp so angry. In fact she had rarely known him to be angry at all. Of course it must have happened at some time in the course of his work. And yet, when she had talked to his colleagues or the staff at Gillorns they had always said the same thing: he might get frustrated by delays in the legal system, annoyed at prevaricating clients, irritated by nit-picking clerks at the Probate Office, or openly rebellious under the strictures of some unworthy magistrate, but showing real anger? Never, they said. As his secretary, Elvira, put it: 'He just seems to remove his mind to another place. You expect an explosion but it never comes. Never against anybody personally . . .'

Yet here he was striding up and down their bedroom – she couldn't possibly let him loose downstairs in this state – exploding with furious, uncontrollable rage against one person.

'He planned it. He bloody well planned the whole thing. Right from the beginning. What is the beginning? How long's it been going on?' Kemp was talking to himself, shouting to himself, anger half-throttling the words.

'You're not making sense, Lennox. How long's what been going on?'

'How long does it take in the City to plan a takeover? No . . . that's not it . . .' He raked through his hair with distracted fingers. 'How long does it take to destroy a company? Months, years? All you need is money, and flair – and knowledge. And you can buy the knowledge. That ruthless bastard, he even bought the knowledge . . .'

'For God's sake, sit down, and calm yourself. What's this about Snape planning something? For it's Vincent you're talking about, isn't it? But you've got nothing to do with companies in the City – you haven't even bought British Telecom shares . . . You're a complete innocent in Vincent Snape's field . . .'

Kemp flung himself into a chair.

'As he was in mine. And I gave it to him on a plate. But it must have been happening before that. All he wanted was confirmation. He said he had areas of ignorance – he wanted them filled in . . .'

His anger could not be contained. It was causing him to stammer incoherently. That worried Penelope; words had always come so easily to Kemp, he made his living by the correct use of words, the accuracy of their place in a document, their careful hidden strength in cross-examination; now they were spluttering out, a mish-mash, making neither sense nor reason.

She ran downstairs, asked for a tray of coffee, glasses and some brandy. She'd have to treat him like a hysterical patient.

It was the hour before dinner, but she managed to draw Phyllis to one side. 'Lennox has had a bad day. I don't know what's the matter with him. Over-tired, I expect.'

She took the tray upstairs.

He was still in the same chair, but now seemed to have got his wits together. He looked at her gloomily.

'I suppose you think I'm mad?'

She poured out coffee and brandy, watched him drink.

'Now, tell me. Take it easily, step by step so that a moron like me can understand the detection process.'

He gave her the ghost of a wry smile.

'I'll try.'

He was silent for a long while, then he began to speak.

'There is a pattern,' he said, 'but only in the little things. Vincent Snape's interest in divorce. I put it down to him playing around, wanting to know how he stood in the event of being found out. That wasn't it. What he was looking at were the custody cases, and there have been a lot of these recently. A change in the judicial view . . . Not so automatic nowadays that young children should stay with the mother . . . The rights of the child, the well-being of the child, particularly where there's an upright father wealthy enough to provide the best upbringing . . . Snape's obsession with his son, the way he spoke about Simon, not about his wife . . . He wanted rid of his wife, but he wanted to keep his son . . .'

'Oh, Lennox, you can't be sure of that.'

'I've got no proof. I've got proof of nothing. But, well, you said take it step by step. Snape was careful to tell me the marriage was happy, then he hinted, ever so gently, that his wife was perhaps not the perfect mother. Little remarks like she'd ignored an appointment with the child's doctor, just a whisper that she was careless, left the child too much with other people. Even his secretary was in on it – quite unwittingly. She was bound to have absorbed her employer's view.'

'It's all much too vague.' Penelope could not help but think that it was Kemp who was obsessed.

'Then there was the engagement of the nursemaid,

Brenda Arbuthnot. That wasn't done on the spur of the moment. She'd already been interviewed in London. It was anticipated she'd be needed. And the ground-work had been laid for Mirabel to be taken to The Respite Hospital.'

'But surely both of these arrangements might be done by anyone who had an unstable wife, and Mrs Snape's history shows her to be that.'

Kemp glared at her.

'How the devil do we know? What proof have we that she was ever as bad as everyone makes out?'

'Her aunt?'

'Her aunt be damned! I've already got that lady well taped. She went along with the plan – I'm not saying she knew the whole of it – for reasons of her own. Money, I suppose. Snape would promise to look after her if she turned a blind eye to what was going on.'

'I can't believe it of Miss Trevanion,' Penelope faltered.

'There's a knavish quality in all of us, dear Pen, when it comes to our own ends, and under the cashmere and pearls, Aunt Susan's no exception.'

Penelope was silent as she struggled with impli-cations she was reluctant to admit. Finally, she said with some trepidation: 'Are you saying that Adair was part of this plan – as you keep calling it?'

Kemp nodded.

'The king-pin. It all turned on Robin Adair playing his part. And I think he played it too well. Like many an amateur actor, he went over the top.'

Penelope thought for a moment.

'But Mirabel only met Adair when she came to Cornwall. There was no connection . . .'

'Between him and Snape? Oh, but there was. Snape

lied to me about that, when there was no need to lie. He could easily have told me he had one of Adair's pictures in his office, that he'd once been generous to a struggling artist. It would have been in his nature to tell me, showing himself in a good light as a benefactor . . . So, why did he lie? That was one thing set me wondering. Then other things began to fall into place.'

'I can't believe any of this.' Penelope's mind was confused. She wanted to believe if only to assure herself that Lennox Kemp hadn't altogether lost his mind, but the starkness of the truth – if there were truth in it – horrified her. She needed time to think. She went over to the dressing-table and began brushing her hair.

'We should be going down to dinner soon,' she said tonelessly. 'I don't think I can be of any more help to you. I can't see it the way you do.' What she meant was that Kemp was being towed wildly along by the force of his own desire, and she pitied him for it. She tried to explain: 'You're trying to say that Mirabel is the victim of some plot concocted by her husband in order to get rid of her . . . Why didn't he simply kill her, if he's as bad as you make out?' It was said with a bite of derision.

'Because that's not how sensible businessmen operate.' Kemp's temper had improved now that there was the clash of argument. 'Leave murder to the hoodlums in the drugs traffic . . . there are other ways to snare a rabbit without actually killing it. And, Penny dear – ' he got up and took her arm – 'you can help me. One last favour . . .'

He told her of Mirabel Snape's request.

Penelope was quick, her thought already halfway to the point.

'Does she feel she's in danger, even at Greystones? Is that why she wants me there?'

'I honestly don't know. She took me completely by surprise when she asked for you. Of course there could be a perfectly simple explanation. She must still be physically weak, she doesn't want to put too much burden on her aunt . . . No, I don't think she's in danger.'

'I'll go,' said Penelope, smiling a little, 'for one reason only. I'm curious. Feminine curiosity, Lennox, not your kind. I rather took to Vincent Snape but I find his wife a bit of a mystery, and anyway I did see her in rather unfortunate circumstances. If anything you've said is true, then I want to know why her husband should go to such lengths to make her out as something you think she's not. There, I told you I'm no good at words . . .'

'You're good, Penny, that's all that matters. And thank you.'

Chapter Twenty-six

It was a long night for Kemp who hated enforced idleness while a case was reaching its dénouement somewhere else. Not that he had any case, in the professional sense, nor even a client in the light of Susan Trevanion's gracious turn-around over Tamsin.

As the White House was in a lull, the fortnight at an end, new visitors prepared for but not yet arrived, the Morrises had joined them for dinner so that little could be said of the Snapes. Phyl did not seem surprised at Penelope's impending visit to Greystones. Penelope had insisted on first telephoning Miss Trevanion. 'As far as I'm concerned,' she said, 'she is still the mistress of the house and the proper formalities should be observed.'

She had returned from the phone, mollified and rather pleased with herself; Susan had warmly upheld the invitation. 'It would do Mirabel the world of good to have a sensible person like yourself as her companion on her first night home – particularly as Mr Snape has had to return to London.'

After Penelope had gone, Kemp watched the financial news; there had been no catastrophic downward plunge on the markets, nothing there to send an eminent stockbroker scampering back to the centre of things . . .

Kemp regretted his going. He would have liked a last fight – if only to hit back while his anger was still fresh.

Instead, he went for a walk. He avoided the estuary, though he knew the search for Donray's body in those bleak sands could not be done in the dark. He remembered that remark of Mirabel's: 'It's all spoiled. Even my own beach . . .'

Now he knew why.

But there were other unanswered questions which had nothing to do with the ill-fated smugglers, and too much to do with his own future.

He took a grassy track inland between high hedges starred with dog rose, until he could no longer hear the noise of the sea. He sat down on a rough stone wall and tried to make his mind function rationally.

He had to look closely, and without self-deceit, into his own motives, and face the fact that the evidence he had against Vincent Snape was thin enough for the wind to blow away . . . All he had were the two pictures, and that possibly demented outburst of Adair's to Dr Sylvester about being 'the tool of the Medici . . .'

Kemp had looked again at the painting he'd bought from Adair, and summoned to his memory the glimpse he'd had of the other in Snape's office. Was it simply because of his certainty that the two paintings were by the same hand that he had phoned his old Agency in Walthamstow and asked them to run a discreet check on Vincent Snape? He hadn't told Penelope about that . . . At the time it had seemed mere curiosity but he knew now there had been more to it than that. He had already met Mirabel Snape . . .

And when the report had come back negative, Vincent Snape both in his business dealings and his personal life, irreproachable, hadn't he been disappointed?

And is it not true, Mr Kemp (Defending Counsel

purred in his ear), that when you made that call you hoped to find some gossip, some breath of scandal that would discredit my client?

Silent acquiescence.

And when my client was found to be upright and honest in business, and innocent of any extra-marital affair, a good husband and a worthy father, did you not then, and with malice, fabricate this hotch-potch of lies you now have the audacity to bring before the Court?

Pause for tacit assent.

And do you therefore admit that you have brought this disgraceful action (Counsel's voice raised in thunder) for one reason only, and that is you are in love with my client's wife?

Sensation in Court; case thrown out, with costs against you, Mr Kemp.

He walked slowly back to the hotel, had a drink with Bob at the bar, and then climbed the stairs to bed. He felt utterly weary, but could not sleep.

He was glad to see the first rays of the pale morning sun. It shone from a pearly sky, the weather uncertain yet whether it would laugh or cry.

He took his time about going down to breakfast. Eventually he ate alone, scanning the day's papers but unaware of anything they contained. Afterwards he set about doing his packing. There was little joy for him in any of these activities.

From his window he saw Penelope hurrying up the drive, and in a few minutes she was with him. Her face was troubled.

'Sit down,' she said. 'I have a lot to tell you.'

They drew up chairs beside the casement, hers a little turned away.

'I've been wrong,' Penelope said. 'Perhaps I should have known sooner. I did see something, and ignored it . . .'

'Is Mirabel all right?'

'Yes . . . but she had to tell me. She had to tell another woman. She couldn't tell you. And she'd already tried to tell others but nobody would believe her. I should have guessed . . . because I've seen it before. Mirabel has been what they call a battered wife. No, don't.' She put a hand out to stop his sudden movement. 'You mustn't be angry. There's been enough of that already. You just have to try and understand.'

'How long has it been going on?' Kemp managed to get the words out from tight lips.

'Since their honeymoon. It was a terrible shock . . . but she tried to come to terms with it. They loved each other very much, and she thought at first it was the violence of his feelings for her. She was inexperienced in such things. And it was intermittent. When it happened, he felt guilty afterwards, said it would never happen again.' Penelope sighed. 'But of course it did, time and time again.'

'Surely she could get help? Her doctor?'

'She tried. But, you see, most people don't imagine it can happen in nice middle-class families. A beating-up on pay night when the man gets back from the pub . . . That's the usual view, isn't it?'

'Not any more,' said Kemp, 'I've met cases . . .'

'Yes, we both have, Lennox, in our work. But remember that Mirabel Snape had no such experience. She did try to tell her own GP but Vincent found out and there was the most dreadful row. He swore he'd never hit her again . . . that everything would be all right. For a time it was, but it seemed to her that it was something he couldn't control. He's a very repressed man. He had a strict upbringing, and even before the marriage he'd never loosened up, as it were. I think his impulses were as much of a shock to him . . .'

Kemp tried to think objectively about Vincent Snape, the solid personable figure, the boyish charm and the quick mind, the upright man of business who could not be maligned. Whose secret was safe, wedlocked . . .

'Why on earth didn't she complain? Leave him?'

'You don't understand women, Lennox. When I've come across patients like this, there's that degree of shame, the indignity of letting yourself be knocked about . . . Anyway, she became pregnant with Simon. And Vincent changed. He wanted that child so much. Mirabel was safe the whole nine months, and she thought now they had their son things would get better.

'But they didn't?'

Penelope shook her head.

'It was then she stood her ground. The first time he struck her after Simon was born she told him she would divorce him for cruelty. Vincent was very clever then, I think. He's been playing a cat-and-mouse game with her over these last two years. She won't talk about it. Somehow he managed to frighten her, said she'd let it go on too long, no one would believe her story. And she'd got so depressed – I think myself it was his attitude did that . . . All his affection went to his son, with Mirabel he became cold and distant. That was what finished her off . . . and brought her down here.'

'But Vincent Snape couldn't afford to have her talk

to anyone about their married life. Now he'd got something to fight for. He wanted that boy.'

'You were right, Lennox . . . even to the plan.'

'You didn't tell her?'

'Of course not. She's a woman, and still half in love with her husband. I couldn't.'

'So, what happens now?'

'She wants to see you, Lennox.'

That was all Kemp wanted to hear.

Chapter Twenty-seven

She was playing with Simon in and out of the little shrubbery at the end of the drive. It looked an absurd game of darting to and fro making clucking noises, but whatever it was it had the child shrieking with laughter. He finally rolled over in a heap on the grass, and she scooped him up. She saw Kemp.

The two pairs of eyes of the same startling sea-blue were turned on him.

'You've met Mr Kemp before. Say hullo . . .'

'Hullooo.' Simon wriggled down and ran off across the lawn, hooting as he went.

'Birds,' she said, 'he's into birds. Future ornithologist, do you think?'

'The future's a long way off.'

They stood looking at each other. Her face sobered. 'Perhaps we ought to go inside. We've things to talk about – not in the open air, somehow.'

She called her son. 'Game's over for now. Come on.'

He needed persuasion; to children games must last for ever, time being not something they reckon with.

Brenda Arbuthnot was in the kitchen. She looked different, less starchy. There was no sign of Miss Trevanion.

'Aunt Susan's having a morning in bed. Against her principles, but she had to give in. She's really exhausted.'

'I'll see to Master Simon, Mrs Snape. Shall I bring in coffee?'

'That would be nice – but please, none of that flim-flam with the silver tray. Mugs will do.'

Miss Arbuthnot smiled faintly as she took Simon firmly by the hand. 'Simon wash dishes?' he said anxiously.

'Yes, you can help at the sink but no putting your nice engine in the water this time.'

The kitchen door closed and Kemp followed Mirabel into the sitting-room.

There was greyish light from the wide windows, the pure colour of the morning sea and sky.

Mirabel sat on the sofa and Kemp took a chair beside her. She looked paler now, the flush that had come into her cheeks while she ran about with Simon had faded.

'I thought you were supposed to rest?'

She dismissed the suggestion impatiently. 'That was only an excuse. I'm fit as a flea. But I had to get your Penelope here. Is she your Penelope any longer? Vincent said something about you not being engaged?'

'We're not. This holiday was meant to be a sort of decision time. She decided.'

'I'm glad it was she . . . I don't know why but I'm glad it was Penelope who . . .'

'Who turned me down?'

'Yes. It puts you on my level.' There was a pause. Mirabel was gazing out of the window. 'She told you what we talked about last night?'

'Yes.'

'It was such a hard thing to do. I've tried before . . . tried to tell people, but it was no good. Like punching pillows, I couldn't leave a mark. No one wanted to hear. Oh, they were sympathetic enough but I could feel their disbelief, hear them say afterwards . . . there must be something wrong with that poor Mrs Snape. I found their sympathy worse than their not believing.'

'When it began again after Simon was born you threatened to divorce Vincent?'

'I was at the end of my tether. I simply couldn't take it in that it was going to start all over again. I thought it was finished, that we could be happy . . . Instead it was worse than before because I knew Vincent had stopped loving me . . .'

There was a knock at the door, and Miss Arbuthnot brought in mugs of coffee on a wooden tray. She gave Mirabel a nod, almost of complicity. 'I don't know what Miss Trevanion would say,' she remarked as she went out.

'She's not a bad sort,' Mirabel remarked, 'but I don't really need her. I can look after Simon perfectly well myself. It was Vince who insisted I should have other people for him because I'd got so depressed, and all the doctors prescribed were pills and more pills. The only way I could bump myself out of it was to drink . . . It was an escape. And not only from depression.'

Kemp was careful not to interrupt. He sipped his coffee and listened.

'When I had been drinking, Vincent wouldn't touch me. Oh, he called me everything, said I was disgusting . . . but he would never hit me. So it became a kind of protection.'

'Why didn't you leave him, Mirabel?'

She sighed. 'I suppose I'm an optimist at heart. I always hoped the bad times would go away. And for a long time I still loved him. When I did get absolutely desperate I just said I needed a holiday, and I came down here. I think I realized then that I'd come to the end.'

'And your husband knew it too?'

She grew restless. 'Can I have a cigarette, Lennox?'

He lit it for her, and she leaned back, one hand twisting the collar of her jumper. 'He'd beaten me a few days before I left. I screamed at him then, told him I'd take him to Court, let all the world know . . . I yelled stupid things at him. I shouldn't have . . .'

'Why not?'

'Think of his position, his own family, his partners . . . I know now how dangerous to him I must have sounded.' She sensed Kemp's anger, and leapt in before he could speak. 'You don't understand! Vincent isn't a monster. He can't help what he does. He told me once – oh, quite early on – that it was my frail look, my thin bones . . . I don't know. Perhaps if I'd been a muscular tennis-playing girl he wouldn't have. A psychiatrist might understand it, but of course with Vince that was out of the question. For him, at any rate. Then he began to suggest there was something wrong with me – depression shouldn't last that long. I began to realize that the doctors he was sending me to at the Northminster Foundation – I wanted to tell you that when Dr Sylvester mentioned it, I knew the name; Vincent's firm deals with their investments – anyway, these doctors there weren't ordinary practitioners, they were all specialists in mental health. They began to talk about how sometimes very depressed patients had fancies about being persecuted and attacked.'

'And you never suspected?'

'That Vincent was behind it?' She responded quickly to his look of surprise. 'Oh, don't worry. Your Penelope didn't tell me, but she knew, didn't she? I could see it in her eyes, and all the things she didn't actually say.'

'So, you know?'

'Yes, I know now for sure. Perhaps the suspicion had been there weeks ago but I couldn't bear to think of it . . . Those pills I'd been taking – and I suppose that nasty little creep Dr Griffin was well bribed – they kept me from thinking. Everything faded from my mind, all the past was gone, there was no future, I was living in the present. And that meant having a jolly good time while I was still alive. That's where Robin came in – right on cue.'

She stubbed her cigarette out with a shaking hand.

'And you know the reason for this plan of your husband's?'

'Funny you should call it a plan. But that's just how Vincent works. He's told me so often about his business deals: prepare, plan, then pounce.' She gulped. 'I never thought I'd be the rabbit . . . And I gave him the chance to finish it. That awful night when I saw that head buried in the sand, I did think I'd gone mad. And it was worse afterwards when I knew it had been real, and Robin had . . . That sent me overboard. This little bunny was doomed. Vincent could either have me put away for good as a hopeless alcoholic or divorce me for adultery with a degenerate drugs-taker who was plying me with the stuff . . . And Vincent, either way, would get custody of Simon.' She shut her eyes, and squeezed at the lids with her fingers.

Kemp restrained the impulse to touch her.

After a moment, he said gently: 'And what happens now?'

She dropped her hands. Her eyes were brilliant.

'There will be a divorce – but on my terms.'

'Mirabel, how can you be so sure of that?'

'Vincent has no choice.'

Kemp considered the situation, and shook his head.

'You know your husband. He has tremendous power, and he has his pride. He'll simply deny everything. We have no proof of this plan of his . . .'

He was astonished by the sound of her laughter; she clapped her hands. 'Oh, I'm so glad you said "we", Lennox.' Then she became serious. 'Haven't you wondered why Vincent has gone back to London, why he has given up the fight?'

'I knew he'd gone back to London, but I don't know why he should give up . . .'

'Because I told him yesterday evening that I had evidence of all that he had tried to do.'

'What evidence?'

'Some mail was waiting for me here at Greystones when I got back from the hospital. No one had bothered to look at it. There was a letter from Robin Adair. He wrote it in a café in Padstow. Penelope told me how he had to meet those men in that café on the quay. I know the place. We'd been there together.' She gazed out at the cool grey line of sea just visible beyond the garden hedge. 'There's a postbox beside it . . .'

Kemp drew in his breath. 'What did the letter say?'

'How sorry he was . . . And a lot of other things. I think he really was sorry. He took my bottle of pills away from The Respite – he couldn't bear the thought of me taking any more. He wanted to make amends. He knew things looked black for him but he hoped he'd get away. France, he said. Poor, poor Robin . . .'

'And he mentioned Vincent?'

'Oh yes. He'd met Vincent years ago in London when he was just out of Art College. He was poor but very ambitious, and he was looking for a patron in the City. Vincent bought one of his paintings and got him some commissions. I suppose to Vince he was simply another investment. But Robin liked the easy life and he was already on drugs. He came to Cornwall, and Vince kept in touch, sent him money from time to time. Robin always needed money for the drugs. Vincent promised him a windfall if Robin would do a little job for him.'

'Like having a flirtation with his wife, and getting her on to the drug habit?'

'Something like that. It must have seemed easy money to Robin, chatting up the little wife . . . playing the gallant lover.' For the first time there was real bitterness in her voice. 'And Robin could be very sweet . . .'

'And Vincent knows you have this letter?'

'Better than that. I gave it to him quite casually before dinner last night while both Aunt Susan and the good Miss Arbuthnot were in the room. I said it was a note from an old friend which he might be interested in reading, and could I please have it back. I kept my hand out for it. With those two witnesses looking on he didn't have any option. It quite put him off his dinner. When we were alone we came to an agreement. I know Vincent, he's a man of his word, that agreement will stick.'

'He will let you have the divorce?'

'After a year's separation. No recriminations on either side.'

'You're letting him off lightly . . .'

'And he knows it. I agreed there should be joint custody of Simon. Did I do right?'

'Yes. He loves the boy. To ask for anything else would have been cruel. You're very magnanimous – but then I suppose one should be in victory.'

'And poor Aunt Susan will get that annuity he promised her for her cooperation in his scheme. How easy it is to pin labels on people . . . Elderly aunts must be kindly and well-disposed, whereas they're human beings with ordinary feelings – like a spot of avarice and an instinct for self-preservation. I see her differently now . . . But I'm going to stay here at Greystones with her and bring Simon up in this place that I loved as a child.'

Kemp got up and walked over to the window. As he looked out the sun struck silver across the water.

He had meant to say so many things to her, but now he hesitated.

In the brisk new tone she used when speaking of Vincent, in the lucidity she brought to her fresh, unsentimental view of Susan Trevanion, he sensed a change as if traumatic experience had laid bare a steely strength, the essential bedrock that earthquake could not shift. He was not certain that the change augured well for him whose feelings had been so inextricably mingled with pity for her weakness . . .

'I'm glad for you, Mirabel. You've come through this very well.' Even to his ears the words sounded stilted, artificial, a mannered expression giving away nothing of deeper emotions.

'I owe you, Lennox,' she said softly, coming up close to him so that he turned. 'I couldn't have done it without you . . .'

Now he could look straight into those astonishing blue-green eyes, and as they met his he saw the shadow in them as though a scudding cloud had rippled the surface of the sea.

Instinct told him what was in her mind; she'd been damaged, she would take months to recover, perhaps years. She understood the frailties in her own nature, only time would allow her to build defences against them. Her future lay in that rebuilding, her future and the future of her son.

Kemp could see no place in that future for himself; the timing was all wrong. Perhaps it was only in the romantic land of legend that the hero invariably won the lady.

Modern myths were made of stronger stuff.

Fontana Paperbacks: Fiction

Fontana is a leading paperback publisher of fiction. Below are some recent titles.

- ☐ JUSTICE Ian St James £4.50
- ☐ FIRST STRIKE Douglas Terman £3.99
- ☐ NOW AND THEN, AMEN Jon Cleary £3.50
- ☐ THE SHEIKH AND THE DUSTBIN
  George MacDonald Fraser £2.95
- ☐ FLASHMAN AT THE CHARGE
  George MacDonald Fraser £3.50
- ☐ BLACK WIDOW Bart Davis £3.50
- ☐ PAPER DOLL Jim Shephard £2.95
- ☐ TRAPP AND WORLD WAR III Brian Callison £2.95
- ☐ THE LAZARUS FILE Stuart Prebble £2.95

You can buy Fontana paperbacks at your local bookshop or newsagent. Or you can order them from Fontana Paperbacks, Cash Sales Department, Box 29, Douglas, Isle of Man. Please send a cheque, postal or money order (not currency) worth the purchase price plus 22p per book for postage (maximum postage required is £3.00 for orders within the UK).

NAME (Block letters)_____

ADDRESS_____

_____